Picki

M000211502

Kimberly M. Miller

This is a work of fiction. Names, characters, places, and incidents either are the product of the author's imagination or are used fictitiously, and any resemblance to actual persons living or dead, business establishments, events, or locales, is entirely coincidental.

Picking Daisy
COPYRIGHT 2017 by Picking Daisy

Contact Information: titleadmin@pelicanbookgroup.com

Scripture quotations, unless otherwise indicated are taken from the King James translation, public domain.

Cover Art by *Nicola Martinez*

Prism is a division of Pelican Ventures, LLC
www.pelicanbookgroup.com PO Box 1738 *Aztec, NM * 87410

The Triangle prism logo is a trademark of Pelican Ventures, LLC

Publishing History
Prism Edition, 2017
Electronic Edition ISBN 978-1-943104-97-0
Paperback Edition ISBN 978-1-943104-98-7
Published in the United States of America

Dedication

For Christopher, Molly, and Anna. Because of you, I know what love is.

You were old enough to know better
But young enough to care
Tired of waiting
Ashamed of faking
A love he didn't share

Forever isn't so long
It's where you'll find me
Waiting
For the one you were supposed to be

Waiting for you
Waiting for me
To turn around and realize the things
You couldn't see
Waiting for someone to say
It really didn't end
Someone more than just a friend

I didn't know
You'd ever go
Instead of waking up to be free
No more dreams, relieved from schemes
Left with what you made of me

No more waiting for forever
No more waiting on me

"…for the Lord seeth not as man seeth; for man looketh on the outward appearance, but the Lord looketh on the heart."
~1 Samuel 16:7

1

After nearly two years, Daisy Parker was finally awake.

Maybe it was the way spring suddenly appeared to shake the cold, gray skies back to swirls of blue dotted with white puffy clouds. It was the end of a long winter. Flower buds now waited to burst forth in striking colors and the spiky grass would soon need to be cut.

And today the birds sang just for Daisy, their music a challenge—an inspiration.

Spring was awake and, just like Daisy, it was ready to play.

She smiled as she tried to ignore the way the melting snow left trails of dirty tears down the once-sparkling window pane. There would be time to deal with the fallout of a bitter winter and its impending hours of clean-up. She shouldn't think about anything but the work that waited for her in the next room, the kind that would help pay bills.

And yet it was easy to shove aside the thought of hours in front of a computer. She wanted to open windows, go outside, sing… Yes, she wanted to sing.

Daisy went to the piano, remembering how her father's long fingers danced across the same keys eight years before. His absence was still painful. But he would be proud of her even if she still wasn't sure what she was supposed to do with her life. She'd been stuck for so long that getting moving again seemed impossible.

She reached her hands out and started to play. She should get her coffee and go to work, but the draw of the music was too strong to ignore.

Slowly, she found the rhythm again, hoping to release some of the jumbled emotions that confused her. As usual, the music hurt like a stab wound, yet it was a healing balm to her soul. It was a tune she bore the weight of each day.

She closed her eyes as the melody built to a crescendo, fulfilling a promise it made from the start. It was nearly perfect. She had almost conquered her fear of playing the whole song when a door slammed, shattering her reverie.

"Daisy?" Nick Patterson's voice jarred her back to reality. She stopped abruptly, grimacing, her fingers hitting the keys harder than she'd planned as the ballad, once again, came to a jolting and inconclusive end. Like so many other things in her life.

It didn't matter that Nick was barely past seventy years old. His deep voice filled every inch of Daisy's small home. She only hoped the music escaped his notice or she'd be forced to explain herself all over again.

Or worse, he'd try to talk her into leaving the house.

Daisy awkwardly lifted her hands from the keys

and set them in her lap, almost as if she'd been caught breaking the law. But she wouldn't try to hide anything from Nick. He wouldn't judge her despite his strong opinions on everything from her relationships to career choice.

"I brought doughnuts—peanut butter." Nick appeared in the doorway, grinning broadly as he held up the box in his calloused hands. His eyes sparkled under the brim of his worn baseball cap, which bore the name of a team that could no longer be read.

Nick was kind and funny and often brought Daisy groceries or fixed whatever was broken in her house. Sometimes she wished she were about twenty years older so she might seriously consider marrying the man. As it was, she settled for thinking of him as the father she'd lost.

"Mmm..." she slowly placed the fall over the keys and pushed her wheelchair back. She grabbed her lip gloss and methodically put some on, to let him know his arrival was more important than the music.

Daisy nervously ran her hand over the smooth, blonde hair that hung above her shoulders in a style that was easy to maintain yet not terribly risky. It suited her better than the way she'd worn her hair for so many years, down the middle of her back and curled so as to draw attention, something she now avoided at all costs.

"You're looking gorgeous today, princess. Prince Charming stop by yet?" Nick asked with a wide grin. Daisy loved that he complimented her when he sensed she was down, which unfortunately was more often than ever lately.

"Not yet."

Nick's gray-blue eyes twinkled. "Play me

something?"

Daisy smiled and lifted the fall. While she wouldn't play *that* song for anyone, she was happy to play him anything else. She lifted the fall and fixed her hands on the keys, drew a deep breath and closed her eyes as she started playing a slow and beautiful melody.

When she finished, she gazed over at Nick. He put the doughnuts on the end table and then leaned in the doorway, his arms crossed over his chest. He smiled.

"Now that's something else," he whispered in approval. "How 'bout the other one?"

Daisy cleared her throat. "Did you say you brought doughnuts?"

Nick nodded. "I did."

Daisy moved toward the kitchen where the coffee waited. She was nothing without her coffee.

Nick followed silently. Although a man of few words, his presence in her life was sometimes what made her get up in the morning. After the accident, he'd sat by her bed in the hospital for so long that when she woke he'd grown a full, silvery beard.

"Coffee?" she asked as she got herself a mug. Nick nodded and went to the refrigerator for the cream. He handed it to her.

"You're too good to me, honey," he said as she prepared his mug of coffee. "Any chance you'll consider marrying me? I'd make an amazing husband."

Daisy laughed. "Are you really flirting with me again, Mr. Patterson?"

Nick chuckled wryly as he sipped his coffee. His deep green eyes betrayed his thoughts, however, and Daisy averted her gaze lest she be forced to deal with them. She cleared her throat awkwardly as she fixed her own mug.

"Got a pretty good visiting pastor this week—and the ladies auxiliary is doing a luncheon after the service. Those women can cook like nobody's business...want to join me? We can even call it a first date."

Daisy's heart nearly stopped beating. And it wasn't because he acted as if he would date her given the chance. They both knew that was the only thing not to be taken seriously.

"Nick." She tried again, avoiding his eyes as she did her best to yank her hair back into a clip. For the last two years, Daisy's church attendance was a familiar argument. But Nick refused to understand it wasn't that she didn't want to go, it was more that she couldn't go. Perhaps he felt she and her problems—or was it her excuses?—were a nuisance he no longer wanted to bother with. She hung her head shamefully, wanting to erase all that haunted her and forced her to hide in her home.

Nick silently sipped his coffee, but Daisy could tell he was working on his next angle. He rarely pressed her, but it was clear he wasn't going to let this go easily. It didn't matter that there were no words to change her mind. And for as much as she'd been praying, the resounding silence from above made her fear there were no answers.

Or maybe God was annoyed with her constant requests.

"Robby's going back on tour again," he said. "I'd like to finally introduce you."

Daisy nearly spit her coffee across the room. This unexpected turn in the conversation blindsided her.

Creative didn't begin to describe this tactic. This was war.

"What is with you today?" she snapped. She finally looked at Nick and saw he was clearly amused, even as he tried to hide his face behind his coffee mug, sipping slowly at the rich brew.

"What?" he finally asked. "Can't a man dream?"

Daisy busied herself with last night's supper dishes, putting them into the dishwasher in an effort to show she didn't care for the conversation. She reminded herself to breathe.

"You've been trying this for years," she muttered. "I'm not interested. I doubt he is either."

"You might be surprised," Nick said and Daisy turned to him. She nodded. It was better to let Nick think he was winning. And he did mean well. He was just misguided.

Carefully, she finished cleaning up as Nick leaned against her low counter, his long legs crossed at the ankles in front of him.

"I think he's still afraid to talk to me. But I trust his brother. Warren says he's different this time." Nick drank deeply from his mug, finishing his coffee. He put the mug into the dishwasher as he continued speaking. "Since you play that piano like it's your religion, it seemed right you two form a professional relationship."

Daisy swallowed hard. "If I tell you I'll think about it, will you drop the subject?"

Nick smiled. "Two things Robby loves—beautiful women and music. He'd be defenseless against you…"

Daisy blushed, reminding herself to bake Nick a pie for all the flattery he was dishing out.

"I'll leave the doughnuts." Nick pushed away

from the counter. "I got some work I want to get to in the barn today."

"Oh no, you don't!" Daisy hustled after him. "What about Steve? He said he'd help you after work, but that's not until six o'clock. Why don't you wait?" Although he was in his early seventies, Nick still lived as if he was twenty. He fixed everything from rooftops to sidewalks with the agility of a much younger man.

Nick waved his hand at her. "I'm cleaning out some hay and replacing a few boards. You act like I'm an old man."

With a sigh, Daisy put her coffee down and moved toward the door. "I'm coming with you," she said. "Let me grab my computer."

2

Robby Grant rose swiftly to the surface of the pool, his long, choppy hair slicked back against his scalp. Spring and summer meant the start of tour season. He loved it—especially now that he was sober enough to enjoy it. While it might still be a bit cool for swimming in the early May morning air of New York, he didn't care. He was finally alive again and he wanted to try everything. He was born again.

As he clung to the edge of the pool, Robby kept one slightly interested eye on the flat screen television near the back door. The entertainment network was reviewing the day's news, little of which was of any interest to him—that is until his picture appeared over one of the host's shoulders. Excited, he lifted himself easily from the heated water and reached for a thick towel.

He regarded the pictures flashing on the screen. He'd made such a transformation over the last few months that he barely recognized himself as the man in those shots. Although he'd always been described as a heartbreaker, Robby knew that at nearly forty years old he was getting over his appearance—or at least he was trying. His hair, though still wild, was consistently clean for a change, his teeth were fixed after a fight that knocked out a few, his skin was healthy and his muscles were finally strong. The pictures were a reminder of how far he'd come from the glassy-eyed, strung out days that were part of his past. And he intended to keep it that way.

Since Robby got home from rehab, he'd been shuffled from studio to studio, rehearsals to autograph signings and back again. The attention filled that long-empty need for love, but some little part of his heart remained vacant, and he understood why. All that he'd learned in rehab haunted him. If he was capable of the real change his life needed, it would be harder than all the times he'd spent detoxing put together.

As Robby rubbed his arms dry, he stopped for a moment to consider the tattoos covering them. He shook his head. It wasn't that he regretted everything about them but some of them seemed juvenile now. And yet they were a testament to all he was before rehab and all he was choosing to be now. He smiled as he continued toweling off.

"The lead singer of the mega-successful rock group For Granted was released from rehab recently after spending more than six months getting clean. Robby Grant's agent, Lily Horton, indicated that Grant was ready to set off on the band's tour in support of their new album, *Noise*, in a few weeks."

"That's right, Jake," the other host said. "It's been a full two years since we've heard anything out of these guys, so I guess time will tell whether this effort is going to produce as many hits as their previous album, *Traction*."

Robby rubbed the towel over his head. They'd know soon enough that he, at least, was different and there was nothing to stop him from getting back on stage again. While he couldn't speak for his band or their behavior, Robby was confident his new songs were better than all of his old stuff. That he'd written them before going into rehab and recorded most of them back then as well was of little consequence. His band was frustrated by the wait, but all of the men were on board with the direction the band was taking and seemed to believe Robby was back and better than ever.

"Hey Robb-ie!" the deep voice surprised Robby so that he nearly dropped the towel as he turned to face the stone walkway. The members of his band came forward as a unit, almost mechanical in their gait. Robby went back to rubbing his head dry as they approached. They were an odd lot to be sure, but he trusted his friends—after all, most of the group had been together since high school and until recently, little had changed in any of the men.

"You're nuts! It's freezing," Reggie Harris said as he flopped on a lounge chair near the pool. His jeans were ripped and dirty, as usual, and his eyes were covered by a pair of dark sunglasses meant to hide the fallout from the previous night's partying. Robby raised a silent eyebrow as Reggie wasted no time pulling a flask from his pocket. Apparently, the party was not yet over.

Robby considered telling his friend the guy needed help, but he didn't have the confidence yet to make a stand. Although he was trying, it was still too soon. Reggie was more adamant about his ability to party than Robby ever was—and that's what worried the lead singer. There would be no telling his friend to go to rehab until… Robby let the thought fall away, not yet ready to deal with where it might lead.

"Nice interview with Seacrest," Mike Walker said as he sat. He nudged Reggie who took a longer drink in defiance. Always the peacemaker, Mike would say nothing to clear the air. Despite his shaggy, multicolored hair and wild whiskers, Mike was a teddy bear. Even at his lowest point, Robby still hadn't managed to get his friend's mood to falter.

"Yeah, figured it couldn't hurt with the tour starting in a few weeks. Besides, my phone's been ringing like crazy. I can't tell everyone no." Robby tossed the towel aside. Dave Shaffer sighed as he sat with the other men. Although the band was named for Robby, and he was its lead singer, Dave and Reggie often consorted to make decisions for them all. It had been one of the many factors that led Robby to the bottle and sometimes instigated epic fights, but in rehab, Robby learned he needed to speak his mind and not retreat inside himself, even if it made someone angry.

Robby's counselor asked him numerous times if he shouldn't consider a solo career or a start with a new band, but he wouldn't listen. How could he desert his friends? Besides, change was hard for him to come by given what he'd already put himself through. At least with his friends—there was solace in a familiar enemy.

As Robby pushed thoughts of the future aside, he noticed his band exchange quick glances before Dave plunged ahead with a topic that clearly was being considered for some time.

"Actually, that's what we came to talk to you about," he said. The tone of his voice caught Robby's attention and he glanced at each of his friends who skillfully avoided his eyes. "Where do you get off saying that we aren't supporting you?"

Robby turned to him, shocked. "What? I...I didn't say that."

Reggie belched loudly. "It's the top story. Check

your phone."

"As if the media ever knows what's really going on." Robby threw his towel at Reggie, who didn't seem to care when it landed on his head. He slowly took it off and tossed it aside.

"We saw the interview," Mike said. "You said this tour would be different since you'd been to rehab and the rest of us still partied."

Robby's stomach clenched. It was quickly becoming clear that the transformations he'd made in rehab had become obstacles that would change the dynamic of the band altogether.

He glanced at the men who regarded him coolly. He desperately searched for words, trying to figure out how to explain his physical and spiritual awakening. Even though it had been a few months, there were still times it seemed his head was spinning.

Robby thought back, trying to remember when he'd first gotten to rehab. In minutes, it had seemed he was aware of little beyond the peaceful surroundings where he meditated quietly, wrote, or met with counselors and other patients to learn how to deal with the problems he'd so long ignored. The world as he knew it was gone, and restoring himself and his health were what remained. And this time was different. This one changed everything, because rather than delivering Robby to his "doctors" or even the police to take care of him, his brother selected the latest facility himself, based on its religious distinction as well as its success rate for addiction rehabilitation. While Robby never bought into the faith that seemed as important to Warren as oxygen, something about the way the counselors explained things finally made sense. He continued to struggle with how to make it work in his life. But now at least there was something he believed in for the first time, and he was certain it wouldn't let him down. Regardless of his band's opinions, he wasn't giving up on trying to become a better man.

Calmly, Robby gestured toward Reggie. "What about him? He drinks more than I ever did…"

"Reggie isn't the point," Dave said as he paced the outer edge of the pool. "You aren't better than us, Robby…but ever since you've been back, you don't even hang with us anymore. You don't…swear…you don't drink…all you do is judge us for who we've always been. How is the tour going to work like that? We're already sick of you."

"The feeling's mutual," Robby muttered, trying to remember what his counselors had said about dealing with stress. He came up empty. "Not one of you came to visit me in rehab—or even called for that matter—except to ask when the songs would be done so we could go on another stupid tour."

Reggie belched as he stood. "Don't call this tour stupid or I'll…"

Robby laughed wryly. "You aren't even sober enough to finish that thought."

"This isn't why we came." Mike stepped between the men, his shoulders serving as a barrier from the fight that was brewing.

"Well, what did you come for?" Robby asked. "And you better not say a word about those songs because they're solid."

The final cuts of the new tracks pleased Robby. Sure, it was more of the same thing he'd always done, but if something wasn't broken, and so much of his life already was, he didn't foresee changing anything musically. The songs would win awards, go to number one, and make Robby even more money. He sighed. His agent was still on his case to do something with the money he already made. In rehab, Robby finally understood what she meant. In making more money than he could ever spend, he'd avoided his real needs—to be loved for who he was as a human being, and he finally understood he also had a drive to make someone proud of him. How to go about that, however, was still a mystery. He was certain he'd never been told he'd done something right and there was a distinct need inside him to discover that place of peace. While he wasn't sure those songs were the ticket, music was his life, and it seemed the only place for him to start looking for peace.

"The songs are fine," Dave said, sounding bored. "What's not fine is your holier-than-thou attitude."

Reggie belched loudly and tossed his empty flask aside. "We replaced you," he said simply. "What do you think about that?" He laughed to himself.

Dave's blue eyes went steely as he glared. Clearly, that was not how the news was supposed to be delivered.

"That's not funny," Robby said, his heart skipping a beat. But even as he looked at his friends—men he had made incredible, award-winning music with for over twenty years, he knew it was true. The ground seemed to sway beneath him.

Mike paced again. "It's nothing personal, man. We can't wait anymore, and we can't take the chance that this time is going to be different. I don't know anyone that's been to rehab as much as you. Why don't you just admit you're a drunk and get on with it?"

Reggie laughed. "Alcoholism is a fine religion. I practice it myself."

Robby stared at them, his mouth hanging open as he digested the most horrible words he'd ever heard. "Being an alcoholic is nothing to be proud of. And I'm different now!" He threw his hands out at his sides. "Look at me!" Robby's brain went into overdrive as he attempted to think of how he could convince them his words were true. But even as he paddled through his thoughts, he was aware the ship had already sunk.

They'd canned him.

Dave slowly stood and went to stand beside Mike, looking every bit of his forty-five years old. "No hard feelings."

Reggie laughed again as he stood and stumbled feebly to Robby. He pushed him. "Yeah there's hard feelings—personal ones. We are done with you and we're keeping the songs and your name and there ain't a thing you can do about it. The lawyers said so…"

Robby looked from one man to the other, the truth slowly sinking in. His own band was getting rid of him. It didn't seem possible.

Reality hurt, which was why he avoided it for so many years. He couldn't remember a time when his family, his band, and his life hadn't been a big mess. Immediately Robby longed for the comfortable fog he'd shaken off in rehab. Surely there was alcohol somewhere in the house that would…

No. He tried to focus. There were other things he could do to handle this.

He'd call his counselor, his brother, his uncle Nick…his agent. He shuddered. There wasn't a person left who would want to hear it. Why couldn't he grow up and handle things himself? More importantly, he wondered why life couldn't leave him alone already.

Reggie pushed him again. "Aren't you going to

say anything?" The shove brought Robby back to the moment. There was no more restraint in him. Reggie always knew how to push his buttons, even the paparazzi was aware of the animosity between the men. Many an article had been written about their fights, and most included pictures too.

Robby grabbed a handful of the bassist's shirt to pull him close, so the men were chest to chest. Since he was several inches taller, he looked down his nose to meet Reggie's eyes. "For Granted is nothing without me!" He snarled before shoving him. The smaller man fell into a lounge chair where he tried to catch his breath as he glared at Robby. There was a time when, despite his smaller size, Reggie might easily have overpowered Robby, who was often too stoned or drunk to fight back. But now, the jealousy over what Robby had become flared in Reggie's eyes.

"Take it easy. We don't have a choice..." Dave interrupted. The diplomacy in his voice turned Robby's stomach as he continued. "It's best for the band."

Robby spun around to glare at his friend, though he wasn't sure he could still call him that. For years, the band had played low-paying gigs, sleeping in tiny apartments—often on the floor—just so they could stay together. To think they would get rid of Robby like an overworked set of snow tires was a blow to his ego. And in the face of his too-recent recovery, it told Robby how little they thought of him.

"You always have a choice!" Robby ran his fingers through his hair as he searched for words. "This doesn't make any sense—I write your songs and sing them. Are you insane?"

Reggie laughed. "Yep. But we're doing it anyway.

Bye, Robby." He stood and came at Robby, this time surprising him. The men fought hard, years of pent-up frustration coming to the surface. They knocked over chairs and a table before Mike and Dave pulled them apart.

"Enough!" Mike shouted as he struggled to restrain Reggie. "Dang it, Rob, you always do this! It's more than the addictions, it's...we're tired of the drama."

Robby gaped at him as wrestled with Dave, trying to get free. "I spent the better part of a year in rehab— do you think I did that for myself? It was for the band—everything I do is for..." Robby grabbed a towel to wipe the blood from his nose. "Get out of here...all of you!" he said. "See if you make it without me."

Mike shoved Reggie toward the walkway that led away from the patio.

"Hey, no hard feelings, man," Dave said. Reggie snorted and Dave gave him a shove forward until they all disappeared and the gate swung closed loudly behind them.

Robby stared after them for a long time before he flopped into a chair, his head dropping into his hands. They'd been through plenty of arguments before, but this was different. They weren't coming back. He glanced at his cell phone innocently lying near an overturned chair. He doubted there was anyone left to call who would be able to help him. His agent would want to make a plan right away to get him back on the road and keep the momentum of his recent return to the spotlight going, but Robby couldn't do it now. He didn't have a band behind him and that changed everything.

Now what?

Robby was in his early teens when he started down the path to alcoholism. He was defiant of all his parents stood for, and especially his father who was never around. But even with all the trouble he got in, his father steered clear of him, leaving the discipline to Robby's mother who preferred to be her son's friend instead. One sweet glance at his mother, a bit of a smile, and maybe an excuse blaming someone else, and Robby knew he could get away with anything.

When he was eighteen, the family had all but given up on Robby, while his brother, Warren, accepted the responsibility of continually rescuing him from whatever scrape he'd gotten into. Back then it usually involved being drunk at a party or getting a bit too intimate with some angry man's daughter, but the future was clear from that time on. When their parents divorced that same year, Robby's band was doing well and he was living on his own, playing small clubs. The group was offered a recording contract and with a lot of touring and hard work they found success that seemed to just keep coming in larger waves with each album they produced. There seemed no end to the party.

Robby's magnetic personality drew people in and his fan base grew. He accepted the support of his dearest fans and celebrities—most of whom were in the same boat he was—drunk on popularity and fame among other drugs of choice, yet Robby forgot his brother, who was stationed in Europe with the Army. Warren took after their father, Martin, while Robby was much more like his mother, Jackie. Martin was a military man through and through. He lived for his job and his country and never seemed reachable to his children, or his wife, as it turned out.

Jackie, on the other hand, was a free spirit. She designed clothes and eventually found a niche in the athletic wear industry. By that time, she'd decided her boys were grown and didn't need her. She ran off to Paris with her assistant, Grace, and a new boyfriend who was almost twenty years her junior. The silence between Robby and his parents had now stretched on for close to ten years.

It's funny how time passes so quickly when you focus on yourself and little else.

Robby partied, drank, smoked, and committed more sins than he could name. He nearly lost touch with Warren, who insisted, to Robby's dismay, that they touch base—in person if at all possible—at least two or three times a year. Despite being in the military and in constant danger, the older Grant brother was intent on keeping Robby out of trouble. While Robby absorbed the emotional drama of the family, Warren managed to transcend it all and grew into what his younger brother felt was a perfect man.

Robby hoped one day he could be called a man. Only now did he see he'd lived his whole life as a child. It was time to grow up.

Robby wiped his forearm across his face, which was still bleeding from the fight. His mouth, his body, his hands, his mind longed to find the alcohol he'd kept as a safety net. It was the good stuff. His stomach churned as he thought of it, but he was too confused to commit to standing and getting it.

He'd gotten sober for his career, but now what reason was there to stay that way?

3

An hour later, Daisy was working on her computer quietly while Nick stood in the barn loft, tossing bales of hay to the ground. They spoke occasionally but mostly enjoyed not being alone, a fate dreaded by both. Daisy tried not to stew over their earlier conversation, instead choosing to focus on the work before her. She needed to finish the article so she could get paid and hopefully appease someone to whom she was in debt. There were so many it was getting difficult to keep track of it all and her bank account was, as had become typical, dreadfully low. Daisy was always careful with money, which made her situation unsettling. She feared there was no out, short of being evicted and after that...well, she couldn't follow the thought to its certain end. Where would a lonely woman in a wheelchair end up? The options weren't at all tempting.

"Bill collector called me this morning." Nick's voice startled Daisy so that it took a moment for his words to register. When they did, the nausea that often plagued her was aroused and resettled itself in its familiar spot in the pit of her stomach. Rather than say anything, she put on some lip gloss and continued working.

"I'll help you," he said gently. "How much you need?"

Daisy gulped. She needed more than she cared to

admit. She felt him watching her, expecting an answer. She was ashamed that her problems were becoming Nick's too. He'd been so good to her already. Where did bill collectors get off calling him?

"I'm fine," she lied. "I'm sorry, Nick. You don't need to..."

He sighed heavily and Daisy finally forced herself to glance up at him. It was clear how much he cared for her and wanted to help. She didn't want to offend him, but she couldn't accept his help. She wasn't raised that way. Daisy had to make her own way in the world—sink or swim. When her mother left, that's what her father had said. It became his mantra. They didn't need her grandmother to come and help raise her, and a babysitter was a luxury Douglas Parker couldn't afford. Daisy's dad insisted he handle things himself. Sure, sometimes it was difficult, but they grew closer because of it and she'd quickly learned the benefits of hard work and dedication. She wasn't going to sit by and let someone take care of her now. It wasn't her way.

"Move in with me. I've got plenty of room." It appeared he'd been thinking about this for some time. Her heart nearly melted at his kindness.

"And despite my flirting, you can rest assured that I'm making the offer as a gentleman..." Daisy tried to ignore the twinkle in his eyes. She shook her head.

"You wouldn't be able to control yourself if I were around all the time, handsome," she said, teasing, but quickly growing serious. "I appreciate it, but I can't move in with you."

Nick met her eyes. He seemed to understand.

"You can be too prideful, you know. Admitting you need help and accepting when it's offered doesn't make you weak."

Daisy gulped and nodded. He was right, but she wasn't sure what to say.

"Yeah," she finally whispered. "Thank you."

Nick went back to work, his eyes intent on the chores that rejuvenated him. It seemed there was no end to the lessons she was supposed to have learned and yet still was unable to accept. Today it was pride—and before it was vanity, anger, and even contentment. It was wrong, but she was growing tired of all the lessons God seemed to want her to learn. When would she get it so she could find peace? Most people had lives that were, well, boring, and Daisy's just seemed to throw one curveball after another in her direction.

"Sadie got you a date for Jennifer's wedding," Nick said as he went back to work. Daisy groaned, shaking her head as she turned her attention back to her computer where she saved her article. He was in rare form. It crossed her mind that maybe her friends should spend some time finding Nick a girlfriend instead of focusing on her.

Daisy laughed at the thought of having a date. Quickly schooling her features, she looked down at her work and was shocked when Nick tossed a heavy bale of hay in her direction. It landed at her feet with a loud *thud* that made her jump. Nick pointed at her, his expression serious.

"We aren't all like him."

Daisy's shoulders slumped. She didn't want to think about Alec, and talking about him was out of the question. Already she'd wasted too much of her life on him. "But too many of you are," she mumbled, ashamed. She drew a deep breath and smiled up at him. "Sadie hasn't mentioned a date…" she stopped herself, unable to continue the lie. Meeting someone was foolish and she wouldn't lie about her feelings on the subject. Besides, what man wanted a defective woman? Daisy wasn't one to pity herself, but she was realistic. There were few men who'd relish the idea of taking on a handicapped wife and those who did certainly weren't going to show up at her door.

Nick wiped his forearm across his sweaty brow. The day was extraordinarily warm, and dressed as he was in jeans and a long-sleeved shirt, Daisy guessed he was probably uncomfortable.

"You weren't afraid of anything when I met you."

She met his eyes and forced a smile. "We aren't talking about relationships anymore, are we?"

Nick grinned and gave a slight shrug. "Give my nephew a chance..."

Daisy sighed heavily. What would it hurt to humor the old man? "Maybe." She was no less the person she'd been before the accident. So her legs refused to work? The roller coaster of emotions she'd gotten used to recently was now on an upswing and she was glad for it. Daisy forced her heart to clutch this new hope in order to stuff it down inside her soul as a lifeline.

Nick smiled, bowing to her. Before Daisy could reply, one of the brittle boards in the barn loft that he was standing on snapped loudly, causing him to hurtle to the floor. He landed with a hard smack that shook the wheels of Daisy's chair.

Daisy froze in shock. It felt like it lasted for hours.

"Nick!" she shrieked, struggling to lift the weight of her useless legs to a nearby hay bale where it would be easier for her to get to him. He lay, still breathing, but unconscious. Daisy grabbed her backpack and dug until she came up with her cell phone. She quickly dialed as she touched Nick's cheeks.

"Don't you dare leave me too," she whispered. "Please..."

~*~

The ambulance arrived in minutes and Daisy was relieved when her friend Steve Englehart jumped out and ran into the barn.

Daisy met Steve shortly after her friend Jennifer claimed she'd found "the man she would grow old with" at work. They visited Daisy after their first date—when she was still in the hospital. She recognized that Steve was a good man when he didn't flinch at seeing her with a partially-shaved head, helpless to do anything for herself. She'd liked him instantly.

"Daisy, what happened?" Steve asked as he began checking Nick over. Shock held Daisy in silence, unable to tell him. She attempted to form the words, her desperation increasing with each syllable. She stared at the place where Steve's dark hair slipped over the collar of his shirt. He leaned across Nick as he searched for a pulse. Daisy swallowed and choked back tears. Steve didn't even glance at her.

"I need you to be calm," he said evenly. "Tell me what you can."

She tried her best to explain but somehow the explanation didn't come out in the right order and she feared she was confusing Steve more than helping him. She was so happy he was there when she was unable to help Nick herself. She burst into practically uncontrollable tears of relief as Nick began to come around.

Steve seemed to understand and motioned to his partner to take over. He lifted Daisy carefully back into her wheelchair and squatted in front of her to give her a hug. She sniffed, embarrassed, as he reached out to wipe her tears away. Even as he did so, Daisy was relieved. Her friend was marrying a wonderful man.

"It's just a broken leg," Steve said softly, his deep brown eyes warm with compassion. "His heart's strong and he's breathing fine. At his age, he'll take quite a while to heal, and I imagine he'll be bruised and sore but he's going to be OK."

Daisy nodded, sniffing again. "I told him to wait until you got off work but he..."

Steve laughed wryly as he helped get Nick on a stretcher. "He doesn't like to wait..."

As she regained some control over her emotions, Daisy shoved her cell phone into her backpack.

"We can let you ride with us. I can bring you home after my shift," Steve said. "It's no problem." Daisy raised an eyebrow as he skillfully avoided her eyes while he worked. She understood his real meaning, and she realized that he knew it too, though neither of them said a word.

Daisy shook her head, nervously wringing her hands. While she may have barely begun to entertain Nick's idea of taking her to church, Daisy's faltering confidence was now at its lowest. "I can't..." she whispered. "Jennifer can call me, though."

Steve reluctantly nodded as a paramedic wheeled Nick toward them. Daisy looked up at the old man and bit her lip as his eyes slowly opened. She wondered if how she felt was anything close to how he hurt when she was the one in pain.

"Nick..." her voice caught in her throat as she tried

to think of what she should say to him. She cursed her wheelchair. Nick nodded as she touched his hand. Daisy blinked back tears as the paramedic took him from the barn and began loading the stretcher into the ambulance.

"I'll walk you back home..." Steve said. "If you're sure you don't want to come with us..." Daisy shook her head and pushed her wheelchair toward the barn door. Steve followed.

Daisy wasn't sure she'd ever felt more alone.

4

Robby was still on the patio alternately convincing himself to get a drink, and then not to get one, when a car door slammed on the other side of the house. Already he was getting goose bumps from sitting outside in the crisp spring air without a shirt on, but going inside was too much effort. It had been nearly two hours since the band left him, beaten and alone. Robby was certain he should call someone, but saying the words out loud seemed more than he could manage. It wasn't fair he was struggling this soon after rehab.

"I've been calling you all day," a deep voice said as the gate banged shut.

Robby's stomach sank as he raised his head to find his brother entering the backyard. This day was never going to end.

Warren's buzz cut was the same, his muscles bigger. His T-shirt was stretched so tight across his broad chest that Robby wondered how he'd gotten the thing on in the first place. The man towered over Robby, all solid muscle and discipline—things Robby respected but himself would never be.

Warren inspected Robby for a moment before sitting in a chair nearby. "So what is it now?" he asked with an overly dramatic sigh. "Drug deal gone wrong or did you steal some poor schmuck's wife? Or wait. Don't tell me. Your stylist can't take you until *next week.*"

Robby stood and paced, his mind too full to handle whatever his heroic, patriotic, Bible-beating brother thought of him. Warren was everything a parent wanted in a son. He'd been to Iraq three times and returned a decorated war hero. His dedication to the military was too firm for him to retire and at forty-three years old he was likely to head back into the thick of things as soon as he was allowed.

Robby, on the other hand, was enough to be one of the main catalysts for his parents' split. He'd broken every rule ever given him. He was tattooed, pierced, and had been arrested a time or two, more if you count all the times he was picked up and left in a cell to sober up. But his talent and charisma were enough to make most people forgive him. It finally caught up with him a year ago, when he was found passed out in an alley. Although he'd overdosed before, nothing came close to that moment.

Physically and emotionally he'd barely made it, and yet here he was—a survivor booted from the very thing that gave his life purpose. The depth of his despair was endless. The last thing he needed was Warren to remind him what a failure he was.

Warren waited. Robby paced for several moments before he finally spoke.

"That eye is going to swell shut without some ice."

"It's fine."

Warren never took anything Robby did seriously. He'd lost count of the number of times his brother told him to get a real job or do something that mattered.

"Right." Warren stood. "Listen, Uncle Nick's neighbor called. He fell from the loft in the barn and broke his leg this morning—the neighbor said she'd call me when he was out of surgery." He released a deep breath. "You're going to need to get out there and take care of him. I don't want him in a nursing home. It would kill his pride to be laid-up and surrounded by all those old people."

"He is old," Robby muttered.

"Dare you to tell him that."

Despite the connection Robby and his uncle once shared, Warren's words barely registered as he reached for the door that led into his kitchen. He waved his hand. "Jazz can handle it," he said absently. Robby's bodyguard Jazz Kenton was even larger than Warren and skilled at everything from organizing to defending and protecting Robby. From drug dealers to angry spouses, the man ran defense over the fifteen years he'd been with the band. As was often the case, Robby usually asked more than he should of the poor man.

Warren stared at him, his dark eyes glittering coldly. "You are the most self-absorbed jerk I've ever met in my entire life."

Robby stopped, his hand still on the door as he turned around. "Why don't you go take care of him? I'm getting back on the road! It might be my last chance!"

Warren went to Robby and glowered down at him. At six foot two, Robby wasn't small, but his brother was just enough taller—in both size and honor—that Robby was certain he'd never measure up.

Warren punched Robby in the chest with one finger to remind him who was in charge. "I have to go to Iraq. And you will go to Pennsylvania or I'll make you wish you..."

"Come on..." Robby backed away from him, rolling his eyes. It didn't scare him that his brother was capable of hurting him. Robby couldn't feel any worse.

So what if he was going back to Iraq? He practically lived there anyway. He'd earned so many medals for honor and courage Robby wondered if it was even possible to count that high. He'd stopped trying to live up to the man his brother was, certain he would continue to be a failure no matter how successful. Robby's stomach turned. He'd soon be tapping into his reserves.

"My band dumped me after I spent six months in rehab. You think anything you do to me is going to be worse?"

Warren shoved Robby to the ground, the shock and force combining to knock the wind out of him. "You want to find out?" he asked, the words dripping with sarcasm. He straddled the younger man, years of experience and training coupled with frustration at Robby's lack of concern working together to pin him there. Warren hadn't yet given half of what Robby deserved and still he seemed to be struggling to restrain himself.

"What happened to 'I'm different' and 'going to be a better man'?" Warren didn't wait for an answer as Robby gasped for breath. "Mom didn't do you any favors giving in to you all the time." He grunted. "All she did was make you into a self-absorbed idiot." He gave Robby one last shove and stood.

Robby was getting off easy and yet he continued egging his brother on. He gasped for breath and rolled onto his side before he spoke. "Dad...didn't do you any favors making you into a militant moron." He stood and shoved past Warren. He went inside without a backward glance, the door banging closed behind him. The fight in him was nearly gone and the realization was settling in that he was alone and needed to make a new career plan. The thought was overwhelming. Navigating life was something other people did. Robby made music.

Warren slowly followed him inside, pulling the door closed behind him.

Robby yanked open the freezer door and dug a chunk of ice free to hold against his tender and stinging eye. He wasn't going to be ready for any photo ops soon—that was for sure. Stupid Reggie. Robby fumed, wishing Warren would go home so he could drink it all away.

Rehab was worthless.

"You ought to try living by the preaching you throw at me all the time," Robby mumbled as his cheek and eye began to go numb. Warren paced the kitchen, flexing his fingers open and closed as if trying to convince himself not to kill his younger brother.

"Don't start." Warren's voice held a note of warning. His priorities had always been God, country, family—in that order. This outward view of life was foreign to Robby, who preferred looking out for himself so he didn't get hurt. "I was trying to help you understand what you were missing. There are things you need..."

After Warren claimed Robby from the police, the singer went to rehab and was forced to deal with the things that caused him to rely on drugs and alcohol rather than people. It was an ugly time. The party was over and the work to find sobriety remained. Numerous times Robby nearly gave up and let himself die, but Warren refused him. As much as Robby wanted to hate his brother, he couldn't. The man did for him what no one else would—he loved him unconditionally even though Robby feared, deep down, he was unlovable.

During rehab, Robby realized that outside of God, a force he wasn't entirely sure of, Warren was one of the very few trustworthy people in his life, and more intense still, the only man besides Uncle Nick worth emulating.

Their father sent a letter telling Robby he was a waste and their mother called a few times, weeping, but offering little in the way of support. She was too swamped with work in Paris to get away, though she insisted Robby would be fine and even offered to spring him from rehab if he wanted. She thought Warren was too hard on his little brother.

Robby stopped taking her calls when his counselors said it was impeding his progress. Even the woman who'd claimed to be madly in love with him dropped him after he'd been gone a month. Apparently, she and her husband worked things out. Robby was glad for it. He'd always wondered if she was an attention-hog and that was his answer. When he no longer held the title "sexiest man alive" and stopped being the life of the party, no one wanted him except Warren, Jazz, and his agent, Lily.

It didn't bother Robby that Nick didn't visit him in rehab. His uncle sent letters to him consistently, but Robby didn't have the nerve to read them. His mother's brother held strong opinions on the direction his life was going and Robby lacked the stability to deal with it. He'd disappointed the two people in his life that mattered to him. He'd walked all over Nick and Warren for years and he needed rehab to work through the guilt of that, along with so many other things.

Warren brought Robby a Bible and religious books, and he'd begged him to go to the church services offered at the clinic. To quiet him, Robby made a few appearances and flipped through the books and the Bible, but it only served to drag him down. The hope it gave Warren was foreign to Robby. Besides, if God were real, and Robby wasn't yet convinced that He was, Robby was sure He'd want nothing to do with him. Robby was too messed up and made too many mistakes to be of any use to a holy being.

Robby laughed at his brother's presumption. "Right," he said. "I get it. I owe you for all the amazing things you've done for me like introducing me to God, and picking me up out of that gutter so you can remind me about it every day for the rest of my life." Robby wanted to be honest but he refused to lean on Warren. He itched to get a drink, trying desperately to focus on his annoying do-gooder brother instead. He needed to release his anger on his band, not Warren.

"Go win the war, desert storm," Robby said, his voice dripping with irritation. "I'll handle Nick."

Warren stared at him incredulously, the hurt in his eyes clear. Robby wished he hadn't seen it. His stomach rolled again.

"You don't owe me anything, Rob. Don't you get it? I did what brothers are supposed to do—not because I have to, but because you're my flesh and blood." Warren shook his head. "You ought to try it sometime, you know? Help someone since it's the right thing to do, not to get anything out of it. If that's all you get out of the 'preaching' I'll be happy." It was clear Warren was irritated and disappointed that so little of the rehabilitation center's Christian atmosphere had rubbed off on Robby.

"I help plenty of people." Robby didn't want to defend his actions, mainly because he couldn't. Warren was right. He never bothered to help anyone but himself. But there was no guilt for it either. Hadn't he earned it all? His house, cars, guitars, and clothes were all paid in full and there was still plenty left for other frivolities. Robby worked hard to overcome the parents he was born with, not to mention his addictions and hang-ups. Was it wrong he now wanted to enjoy the material things?

To be fair, though, Robby did toss money at several charities occasionally—and he'd allowed some to use his image or name to promote their causes. It might not have been much, but it hardly seemed fair for Warren to think he was entirely selfish.

Warren rolled his eyes. "Right. Well, pardon me for forgetting you occasionally help people you don't know and have never even spoken to and with money you won't miss. It's no hardship for you...and it isn't what I'm talking about. Forget it..." Warren sat on a tall stool near the kitchen counter.

Robby tried to look pathetic in an effort to win some sympathy, but Warren ignored him, taking in the large, immaculate kitchen. Other than Robby's cook, no one ever ventured into the room to do anything but talk or nose around for snacks. The whole mansion, set on three hundred acres of rolling New York hills, was a lonely waste of space. Though it was decorated beautifully according to Robby's persnickety desires, he wasn't much for being there alone since he became sober. It seemed to him that the walls echoed with his every step and the floor was too cold on his bare feet. He wondered why he'd ever built it.

"Hey, I'm sorry about your luck," Warren said,

still glancing around the room. "But those people you call friends aren't anything but..."

"All right—I get it," Robby said, cutting him off. He was allowed to be angry with his band, but he didn't want Warren cursing them. When they came back around that would be awkward. Robby tossed the ice across the room where it landed with a thud in the sink. "I said Jazz can take care of it. Shoot, Warren, you don't trust me at all, do you? I've been sober for six months."

Warren laughed wryly. "In all my life I've never heard anything funnier!" He met Robby's eyes and shook his head in disbelief. "No, I don't trust you. Why should I?" He stood, still shaking his head. "Forget it. I'll call the doctor and tell her when Uncle Nick's ready he can go to a nursing home until he's good enough to be on his own at home. Then I'll have a nurse come in to check on him. I'll take care of it. Like always. You just...go do whatever you think is more important. *Like always*."

Warren walked out of the kitchen and through the living room. He headed down the long hallway toward the main entrance as Robby followed and wondered why he was unable to speak. He hated that his brother thought so little of him. But what could he do? Now that he was without a band, there was a lot of work ahead. He had to call his agent, get another band together, and write at least a handful of new songs. How could he do all of that from Pennsylvania? The overwhelming burden rested heavily on his shoulders.

Warren stopped, his large back reminding Robby that his brother had taken on a lot over the years. He'd been a man, the kind that Robby wanted to be now that he was sober and alive again. Sure, things were bad now, but maybe given a little time...

Robby cleared his throat as Warren opened the door. He turned to Robby and waited, expectantly.

"I'll do it. I'll go," Robby said quickly.

Warren drew a deep breath, doubt covering his face. "You can't make a promise like that—especially where Uncle Nick is concerned, and then..."

"I'm not. I won't." Robby glanced around quickly at the gold and platinum records that covered the walls of the hallway and foyer. What was it all for anyway? Robby suddenly thought that maybe getting away from New York was a good idea. Maybe the farm would give him a better place to think. At home, the press would hound him so that leaving the safety of his fortress would be a chore.

"I'm not the family embarrassment that you think I am. I'll go and...take care of Nick. I'll stay as long as it takes. I won't let you down."

As if a prayer might convince him, Warren put his head back and closed his eyes for a moment before responding,. His squared, defiant stance softened. "If you screw this up, I've got nothing left to hold me back." His eyes piercing into Robby's. "We will not be family anymore, you hear me? I'm not sure how much more of this crap I can handle."

Robby swallowed the lump that formed in his throat. It was plain, direct, and unlike anything spoken before between them. This was Robby's chance. He nodded slowly.

Warren's lips were drawn in a thin line. "I'll be checking up on you. Daily if possible. Even one slip-up and your head will spin."

And with that, he was gone.

What did I do? Robby wondered.

5

By the time Robby finished packing he'd also located the bottles of vodka and whiskey he'd stashed in the back of his closet. As sick as it made him to open the first one, the pull was strong and he was too empty to fight it.

With the first drink, he swallowed guilt. With the second, he swallowed the self-hate that was his constant companion for years.

From there, it was an easy slide, swallowing everything from anger to injustice.

He might have talked to Warren, or called his counselor, or even Jazz, but somehow admitting that he was doing the same thing again was too much. What was all the rehab for anyway? He could handle this. It was just one time after a terrible day. Surely they would all understand that his world had been taken from him and he needed the comfort. And even as he drank, he swore this was the end. After all, it was the last of it. This was the emergency fund and it was being quickly spent.

Robby threw two heavy suitcases down the long staircase and returned to his bedroom for his beloved guitar. He closed the expensive case, grabbed a set of drumsticks, and stuffed them into his pocket. It would take several hours to get to Nick's place and he was going alone. Sadly, he was getting used to going solo, and for an egotistical man like Robby, it was suffocating. He needed people to tell him how amazing he was, to show him love. He didn't get that from Warren and he doubted he would from Uncle Nick either. One of their worst conversations consisted of Nick telling him to grow up and be a man when Robby was in the news for yet another embarrassing display at an awards show. After that, Robby avoided calling for some time, until his counselor encouraged him to make amends with those he'd wronged.

While Nick did accept his apology without question or comment, Robby felt humiliated and ashamed. Nick had never been anything but good to him and Robby treated him with complete disregard. The man deserved more respect, and yet Robby struggled to give it to him.

Nick wrote him many times after that, but Robby never seemed able to read the letters, still ashamed of his childish behavior.

As Robby trudged down the staircase and headed outside to load his truck, he realized Nick was right. He'd never been a man and he wasn't sure at this point in his life whether he grasped how. He was already thirty-eight years old and still living alone. No wife, no kids, and now he was without a career. He'd left a message for his agent that the band dumped him and she needed to get him some work, but he feared even Lily was finished trying to corral him and solve his problems.

How did a man who'd never been a man, become one? Robby threw back a long drink of whiskey and sighed as the warm liquid seared a smooth path down his chest and into his stomach. The familiar action gave him peace and at the same time shamed him. He slipped into the truck slowly, his head hanging. At least no one would see his fall. And maybe by the time he got to Nick, he'd be thinking straight again.

And with that, he started his truck and slowly drove away, hoping he was doing the right thing.

~*~

Dinner time came and went with Daisy barely eating any of the stew she'd left simmering in the crock pot to share with Nick. Eating was too difficult when her mind was in overdrive. Could she have protected her friend? Talked him out of going up there?

Daisy knew this line of thinking was futile, but she followed it anyway.

Jennifer called from the hospital to say Nick was stable. The surgery to set and cast his leg went well, and he was likely to be awake before the day's end. Again, her friend begged her to come to the hospital but Daisy resisted. She had no interest in getting into a car ever again. Surely Jennifer understood that.

Besides, they had plans to have a Marx Brothers' movie marathon that night. Even though her heart told her to crawl into bed, it would be good for Daisy to spend time with her friends and try to think about something other than the day's events.

Daisy headed for the kitchen and began making chocolate chip cookies. Her friends were capable of polishing off an entire double batch in one movie night and Daisy wanted to be ready. As she worked, Daisy decided that she'd wait until seven o'clock before calling the hospital to talk to Nick. In a feeble attempt at distraction, she turned on the small television in the corner of the kitchen to the entertainment news station. It was a weak form of company and she scarcely paid attention to what was on until a voice said, "And Robby Grant is in the news again..."

Daisy's head lifted and she stared at the television while her hand grabbed for the remote to turn up the volume. She found it strange that twice in one day she'd heard the man's name when in the last few years she'd had no interest in him. Regardless, whatever he was up to now would be of interest to Nick. Daisy left the cookie dough for a moment and moved closer to the television.

A dated picture of Robby appeared over the host's shoulder as she spoke. The shot had been taken at an awards show that ended with Robby's arrest after a brawl with some of the members of his band. She recalled Nick shook his head when the reporters called him. He told them, as he always did, that he wouldn't comment on his nephew's shenanigans.

"For Granted was expected to begin their summer tour in a few weeks but stated through a rep that Grant has left the band to, and I quote, explore other creative outlets, end quote," the host said. "This is interesting since a few days ago the band held a press conference to announce Robby was out of rehab and doing well. Surely the band is reeling at the news of Robby's exit."

Daisy turned the volume back down as she shook her head, wondering what Nick would think. The man had barely spoken to his nephew over the last few years even though he sent letters to Robby almost weekly. She decided she'd keep the news to herself until her friend was able to handle it. Right now, he had enough on his plate since he was going to be in a wheelchair for a few weeks. Nick would hate sitting still for so long.

Daisy went back to the cookies, certain they would

still be warm from the oven when her friends arrived. She was thinking about what Nick said, wondering if she could ask Sadie about a date for Jennifer's wedding. Trouble was she didn't know if she had the courage to get into a car to go. She drew a deep breath remembering a time when she wasn't afraid of anything. It seemed so long ago.

You can do this, Daisy. She was sure if she said she wanted to go for a drive that very night her friends would take her anywhere she pleased. The question was whether or not she could actually get into the car and not be overtaken by anxiety.

Her heart raced even as she considered it.

As Daisy finished taking the first batch of cookies from the oven, headlights flashed in the window. A quick glance at the clock told her it was too early for her friends, which made her suspicions rise. A wrong turn would mean the driver would be gone before she arrived at the door, but this vehicle was parked already and Daisy saw that the driver appeared to be taking a drink. Curious, she shoved another tray of cookies into the oven, set the timer, and headed for the door. The large, black truck wasn't familiar. A shiver of nervous anxiety passed through her.

As she slowly went across the driveway to where the driver parked, partially hidden beside the garage, Daisy clasped the gun Nick gave her months ago. He'd been concerned about her being alone, so he trained her to use it. She was a good shot and not afraid, though her stomach flopped when she saw the size of the man inside the truck.

Rather than make her presence known, Daisy chose to hide behind a large bush and wait for his next move. After a brief moment and another swig, he emerged from the truck, stumbling a bit over his own feet. Then he slammed the door and tripped his way to the front porch.

As he moved, Daisy sized him up. He was well over six feet tall with a lanky but healthy build despite his obvious inebriation. The color of his shaggy hair was a mystery, and his face was well hidden in the shadows. His jeans, T-shirt, and jacket were the kind of perfectly worn chic that Daisy never understood. She had a closet full of old clothes she'd managed to wear out herself and for much less money.

Daisy clasped her phone, ready to dial 9-1-1 at a moment's notice. Curious, she continued spying as the man tried to open the door. He proceeded to beat on it as if he expected someone inside to answer.

"Nick!" he shouted. "I'm here! Let me in!" He hit the door repeatedly before dropping in a defeated slump on the porch swing, his head falling into his hands. Daisy couldn't waste any more time.

"Who are you?" she asked, slowly raising the gun at him. In the dim porch light, the man stared at her and stood, lifting his arms over his head.

"Easy, lady. I have to get in...there," he said, his speech slurred. Daisy didn't doubt he thought he needed to get into the house, and that was the last place he was getting if she had anything to say about it. She kept her weapon aimed confidently with one hand as she lifted her cell phone with the other.

"Please..." he begged again, seeming to sober with the word. He gulped as he stared at the gun, not at her. "I'll give you an autograph if you don't shoot."

What a strange plea. Daisy lowered her arm slightly. She could barely see him in the lighting.

"This is my Uncle Nick's place. I'm supposed to

take care of him," he said, stepping to the edge of the porch, his hands still raised. Daisy squinted, trying to make sense of the man before her. He vaguely resembled Robby, but he was thicker, and judging by the bruising and dried blood on his face, he'd barely made it through one heck of a day. Could it be Robby's brother? She lowered the gun and set it on her lap as she moved still closer. No, this was Robby Grant himself. Well, probably.

The handsome, mischievous man she'd seen so many times on television, the internet, and in magazines may have been in there somewhere, but it was going to take some serious scrubbing and hair product to find him. Her heart lurched.

He needed her.

She imagined her father commenting on all the strays she'd taken in over the years. She pushed the thought away, certain that compassion wasn't a detrimental quality.

"Daisy Parker," she said softly, assessing him. "I live next door. I'm keeping an eye on the place while Nick's in the hospital..." When Robby didn't say anything, she continued. "You look horrible. Can I help you? Are you all right?"

Robby ran his fingers through his hair. He was uncomfortable and she was glad of it. Maybe he wouldn't do anything stupid—at least she hoped that was what it meant. She would keep the gun on her lap for now. Daisy didn't trust her judgment of people anymore.

"Horrible?" he asked, disappointed. "Baby, I was the sexiest man alive two years ago." His voice dripped with the confidence Daisy would expect a rock star to possess. She groaned inwardly and stopped being afraid of him the moment he gave her the smile that must have made every woman on the planet melt. But Daisy wasn't just any woman. She stuffed her gun back into her bag and turned toward her house, deciding an ill-tempered cat held more trouble than he did.

"You're not getting in there until Nick says it's OK," she said over her shoulder. "So why don't you move your truck out of the way—by the barn—and come to my place so you can get cleaned up...and sobered up...before you go to the hospital."

With that, Daisy went back to her house.

6

Robby had been in his share of weird situations, but he'd never before had a woman in a wheelchair pull a gun on him. Correction. A gorgeous woman in a wheelchair. He wished his mind was less fuzzy to fully appreciate the magnitude of it all. Surely there was a song there. But maybe that would be too country for his fans.

The singer rubbed his spinning head and wondered if he drank more than he remembered. She was stunning, and she didn't seem to be at all impressed that he was standing there. He even tried his smile—the one that worked every time. The sexiest-man-alive smile had failed him? It hardly seemed possible.

What a strange, fascinating woman. He wished he could recall her name.

As he went back to his truck to move it where she instructed, Robby wondered who she was. He loved women, especially complicated ones, and it appeared she was as good as a thousand-piece jigsaw puzzle. He smiled as he grabbed his bags and headed to her house. He would prove to Warren he was an adult, and if he needed to go through this woman at least it would be fun.

But as he stepped onto her porch, nausea set in. The alcohol had been out of his system long enough that what he drank earlier in the day wasn't sitting well in his otherwise empty stomach. His brain accepted the familiar fog of inebriation but his body resisted. He cleared his throat and tried to ignore it. As he let himself into the kitchen, he dropped his bags near the door as if he owned the house.

The woman moved easily about the kitchen. Robby noted that she was even more beautiful in the light than she'd been in the dim driveway. With short, blonde hair and sparkling blue eyes, she was everything he might have taken straight to bed less than a year ago. But not now. Warren expected better of him, and he wanted to prove he was up to the challenge. While he could never compete with his perfect brother, he needed to try and improve his ways nonetheless. With a silent vow to behave, he tried to decide what that meant.

She removed a batch of cookies from the oven and shoved another one in to bake before turning to him.

"Cookie?" she asked, holding out a tray of fresh cookies to him. Despite the delicious, warm smell, his stomach rolled and he shook his head, praying he didn't throw up. She smiled and went back to work as Robby wondered if she didn't know exactly what she was doing. It was clear she was in control and not about to let him into Nick's house until she'd spoken to the man himself. If she told him Robby showed up drunk, Nick would send him home and Warren might just kill him. Not to mention that the press would have a field day and he'd never get a new band. Inwardly, Robby groaned.

She poured a mug of coffee, crossed the room, and thrust it at him. Before he considered refusing, she was already gone and he held a steaming mug. He took a drink, the coffee swirling a warm path to his stomach, as he wondered again if this woman was more to Nick than a neighbor.

Robby's attention was caught on the small television in the corner of the kitchen when his picture appeared on the screen and the host said, "It appears For Granted has already replaced lead singer Robby Grant with former Bad Blood lead singer Chase Slater. Slater..."

Before the woman continued, Robby angrily set down the mug of coffee and punched a nearby cabinet. The noise made the blonde before him jump in her chair.

"They can't replace me!" Robby spat. Almost without thinking, he reached into his pocket, pulled out a small flask, and drank from it. But even hindered by a wheelchair, the woman moved to his side faster than he anticipated. She grabbed the flask and dumped it down the sink before he could protest.

She was a streak of lighting. He would need to be more alert if he was going to do battle with her and win.

"You shouldn't be drinking if you're right out of rehab," she said, a hint of compassion in her voice.

Robby stared at her, his shoulders slumping as he realized he was slipping back into habits he'd sworn off only a short time ago. He'd already disappointed a complete stranger. What was next?

"I was..." he said softly. "Six months...until today." He pointed at the television. "Try to understand..."

The woman nodded, yet didn't turn from him as he'd expected. Instead, she gave him a once-over and he wondered how bad the damage was, wishing he'd bothered to glance in a mirror or tried to clean himself up after the fight. He guessed his hair was disheveled and his face a mess, but the only thing she showed was compassion. Something about him broke her heart and that made him angry. He didn't want her pity, and yet he vaguely recalled a scripture somewhere in the forced rehab lessons about showing hospitality to strangers. Maybe more of that church stuff broke through to his mind than he'd thought.

Was she an angel? Robby didn't know but for some reason, she was certainly tender toward him.

With a deep and heavy sigh, she pulled out a chair and took him by the arm, urging him into it. Her touch was surprisingly strong and reassuring in the sea of pain Robby was quickly giving himself over to. He let her pull him back to the world he'd so gingerly placed his feet in only months before. A wave of relief washed over him. It wouldn't end here.

"All right, tiger. Sit still," she said.

Robby did as he was told, though his head was beginning to pound. He waited as she went to the sink and found a clean washcloth she doused with water. She returned to him to wash his face gently. The woman worked efficiently, with no hint she was treating him any differently than she would anyone else who appeared on her doorstep in such a predicament. Clearly, his status as a multimillionaire celebrity was of little consequence.

As much as he wanted to be repulsed by his current situation, Robby liked that she was touching him. He was sure a woman had never been this kind to him without wanting something. He tried not to let her affect him. Suddenly, Robby was ashamed. His once-solid reputation was uncertain. Who was he now?

"Ouch!" he exclaimed as she dabbed the cut over his eye. "Easy..." He glared, but she only met his eyes with compassion.

"Sorry." Her tone was genuine as her soft hand lingered a moment too long on his cheek. She cleared her throat and returned to the sink for another towel, band aids, and a bucket she brought back with her as she again went to work. Robby was overcome by another wave of nausea, but before he said a word the woman thrust the bucket into his lap. She even held his hair out of his face as he threw up several times. It clearly wasn't the first time she'd taken care of someone like him.

She set the bucket aside and resumed her work, putting a band-aid on his cheek.

"I can't believe you made it here alive," the blonde said softly as she finished. "The bathroom is through there. Why don't you go take a shower and start over?" She punctuated the offer by gently squeezing his arm. Robby nodded and stood slowly. The peace that settled over him with that touch meant nothing.

He grabbed his things and headed toward the bathroom, unsure what to say. This woman showed him more kindness than he deserved. He held a strange hope that he'd come to the right place for healing to begin.

~*~

Daisy finished taking the last batch of cookies from the oven and piling them on a platter as Robby emerged from the bathroom in clean clothes, his hair still damp. At another time in her life, she might have said he was handsome, despite the bruising on his face. Right now, she needed to see Robby as a man—a person with a soul. It was so much easier for her emotionally than recognizing him as a handsome and somewhat dangerous singer who might just share her deep love of music.

"Uh, my agent can write you a check for helping me out and for...you know, keeping all of this quiet," Robby said as if he were sealing a business deal. "I just don't need this kind of press right now. You know?"

Daisy's heart sank. Was that really his life? A series of rewards and bribes? She forced a smile.

"I don't want your money," she said honestly. "You needed help..." Maybe it was too long since she'd been around people. Having this strange man in her home made her uncomfortable. "Was Nick expecting you?" she asked. "You should call. He might be worried."

Robby sat slowly at the small kitchen table and shook his head. "Only my brother knows where I am...and it would probably be better if you didn't mention our introduction to him or Nick. The family has opinions about me and...sadly most of them are accurate."

Daisy smiled. She knew what Nick thought of his nephew. She regarded Robby for a moment before speaking. He squirmed as she looked him over, realizing she was beginning to sense the person she once was coming back into the room in time to handle this.

You'll be fine, Daisy. He's only a man.

"Do you want to eat? There are some leftovers from the dinner Nick and I..." Daisy paused to clear her throat. "Um, the dinner we were supposed to...we usually eat together on Thursdays." She was babbling, but somehow she kept going, fearing she'd dissolve into a puddle over her own tough day. So much for the old Daisy. That woman would be entertaining Robby and getting him to laugh. As it was, he just stared at her as if she was crazy.

Robby shook his head, looking uncomfortable. "No. Thanks, though." He paused to smile at her. "So, you and Nick, huh?"

Daisy poured a cup of coffee and took a sip. She waited a long time before answering. He certainly wasn't the man she'd seen on television. That rock star was arrogant, strung-out, and…dare she admit it? He was beautiful. But this guy didn't have the same confidence at all.

"Yes, of course, I'm getting it on with your seventy-year-old uncle. Dinner is our cover," Daisy said sarcastically as headlights flashed in the window. Her stomach dropped and she made a quick assessment of the room fearfully before focusing on the hallway and finally back on Robby's amused face.

"My friends are here. They'll die if you're…I really can't deal with that on top of everything else…"

He nodded and stood quickly. "I'll, uh, make myself scarce," he said, snatching a few cookies from the platter. He pointed at her with a grin as he slowly walked toward the hallway. "Good one about Nick, by the way."

Daisy wished she didn't like that he enjoyed her joke, or that the twinkle in his eye reminded her so much of his uncle. Robby did resemble him, though Daisy wondered why she'd never before noticed. But there wasn't time to dwell on it either. Robby went into her bedroom and closed the door. She wanted to scream. She did not want him in there, but she had no choice, as her friends would be inside any second.

The bucket!

Daisy grabbed it and set it in her lap and tried her best to appear nauseated as the door opened and Jennifer and Sadie entered carrying several bags of groceries each.

"Hey, Daze. How's it going?" Sadie asked, her curly ponytail bobbing as she tossed two full bags onto the counter, barely giving Daisy a glance as she did. Daisy hoped the eggs she'd told them to bring weren't in that bag.

Sadie was the charismatic, boisterous, fun one in their trio. She owned a trendy coffee shop in their small town that often hosted musical acts or art shows. She brought Daisy coffee almost daily, helping to feed the addiction her friend enjoyed so much. Sadie liked to keep things light and was a significant force in getting Daisy to accept her situation and move on, though of course there was still a long way to go.

Jennifer, on the other hand, was the reasonable, safe one in the group. As a physical therapist, she worked with Daisy to get her to be as mobile as possible after the accident. Daisy could sometimes move her legs a bit, thanks to her friend. Unfortunately, it was unpredictable and not strong and probably never would be, but the glimmer of hope gave Daisy some solace.

"You OK, honey?" Jennifer asked as she unloaded a bag and put the food into the refrigerator. She yanked a hair clip from her bag and tugged her thick straight hair back out of her eyes.

"I...I got sick..." Daisy said. "Maybe you guys better go. It's a stomach bug or something."

Sadie stopped putting groceries away and turned to her, concerned. "Hey...Nick's accident wasn't your fault. A board snapped. He shouldn't have been up there without someone to help. He said so himself."

Jennifer smiled reassuringly. "He's going to be fine. I checked on him before I left the hospital today. He's worried about you. You want us to take you over there? Might do you good to see him."

Daisy shook her head as the women exchanged a glance, her earlier promise forgotten in the melee of Robby's arrival.

"Suit yourself, but I do think the Marx Brothers will make you happy," Sadie said as she dug through a bag. She yanked a lip gloss out and tossed it in Daisy's direction. "New one for you."

Daisy caught and opened it immediately. She slathered lip gloss on all the time but especially when she was nervous. And in that moment, her nerves were humming, knowing Robby Grant was steps away in her bedroom. The crazy thought almost made her laugh out loud except for the fact that her friends were there. She only hoped they didn't notice her strange behavior. The juicy scandal might make Sadie happy, and she'd think Daisy should kiss him, while Jennifer would wring her hands anxiously and call Steve to defend Daisy's honor.

It was the way they'd always been. But now she wondered how she fit into their circle. When they'd met in high school, she'd been the funny one—making a joke out of anything. But that wasn't her anymore. Now, Daisy rarely made jokes and laughed only occasionally. She didn't like it, and it was time for a change.

Well, maybe when Robby left.

Or after Jennifer's wedding.

"Did Nick tell you I think I found you a date for the wedding? He's really sweet, Daisy." Sadie smiled hopefully. "He comes into the coffee shop every day before work. He's a mechanic at..." her voice trailed off.

Daisy turned away, shaking her head. "Maybe," she whispered.

"Humph," Jennifer released a deep breath as she rooted around in the refrigerator, putting things in their proper places. "And why not?" she asked, irritated. "It's not like a man will show up here for you. You're a few cats away from trouble."

"I'm allergic to cats...and men," Daisy muttered and forced herself to be interested in washing the cookie sheets. Neither of her friends would believe there actually was another man in the next room. While he didn't exactly come to find Daisy, she was what he'd gotten—like it or not.

"You are not allergic to cats or men." Sadie went to her and leaned against the low counter, folding her arms over her chest. "And we want you to be happy."

Daisy forced a smile. "I am. What would I do without you guys?" Her friends seemed appeased, but the matter of the man in the next room remained. Daisy clung to her resolve and smiled while still trying to look weak.

"I really think I may be sick. Can you guys come back tomorrow? I'm going to go to bed and sleep this queasiness off." The words came out in a rush. Daisy wondered if they would believe her.

Jennifer finished putting the last of the groceries away and tossed the sacks in the garbage. She raised an eyebrow. Sadie merely shrugged.

"All right..." she said. "Do you still want to do the centerpieces for the wedding? We were going to go get the supplies tomorrow morning. We can stop in afterward and check on you."

"And I'll bring you some coffee," Sadie chimed. Daisy smiled and nodded.

"Oh!" Jennifer exclaimed. "So, For Granted broke up. Can you believe it? I didn't have the heart to tell Nick yet. Figured today was rough enough."

Daisy feigned surprise. "Oh? Hmm...that's weird."

"Yeah. Poor Robby. Seems like that guy's had it bad for a while," Sadie said.

Jennifer rolled her eyes. "Right. Must be so hard to be wealthy, get anything you want and then squander it away on drugs and alcohol. I'm pretty sure his band put up with enough and decided to get out while they still had careers left," she said as she headed for the door. She stopped and turned to Daisy. "Take care of yourself, OK? We'll be over in the morning. And call if you need anything." Jennifer grabbed the bucket and took it with her. Sadie glanced over her shoulder.

"Go crawl into bed and watch the Marx Brothers. I guarantee Groucho will cheer you up."

Daisy smiled, reminded of her friends' love for her. "Thanks," she said. "And...thanks for finding me a date. I was thinking today that it might be time for me to get out and go for a drive. Can...can we maybe talk about that...soon?"

Sadie turned and stared at her, the door Jennifer was holding smacking her in the rear end as she stopped, shocked.

"Did you say...?" Sadie let the sentence remain unspoken.

Daisy forced herself to nod. "I...I'm thinking about it," she said. "But, maybe." Jennifer and Sadie nodded as one, smiling as they did.

"Right. Maybe," Jennifer said. "Call if you need

anything."

Daisy watched as they left, not believing she'd even brought it up. Was it possible she go on a date with someone she'd never met? Was she crazy? She released a deep breath as she grabbed the remote to put on the movies. She needed a few minutes to process what she'd done.

Before long, Daisy quickly became so engrossed in her thoughts that as she watched the movie and cleaned up the kitchen she completely forgot Robby was still in her bedroom.

7

Robby took in the very pink and frilly bedroom with a grin. He'd been in his share of women's bedrooms, but hers was priceless. It was decorated like she was still a teenager rather than a grown woman. The walls were painted a deep dusty rose, the flowered curtains hung to the floor, swirled and ruffled. This girl was something else. He dropped his big body onto her silky comforter and put his feet up as he ate the cookies he'd taken from the kitchen. He groaned. She was a good cook. He'd need to be careful or he'd gain too much weight if he stuck around very long.

The woman's voice was barely audible as she talked to her friends in the next room. Robby quickly grew bored eavesdropping. If the conversation didn't involve him, he wasn't interested. His ringing telephone was a nice distraction.

"Grant," he said, fingering the smooth comforter.

"Robby, I talked to Lil. She said you're going solo. I think I got the perfect project for you." Ron McAllister was a music producer Robby and the band worked with before. He mostly produced music for movies, but Robby wasn't about to be picky.

"Yeah?" Robby lay back and stared up at the ceiling. It was cracked and the paint was peeling. Figures. He was far away from the posh hotels and mansions he was used to sleeping in but this place truly needed work. He wondered for a moment how stiff and lumpy the guest bed would be at his uncle's house.

It had been ages since Robby spent any time in a real home like this one. It reminded him of his childhood which was about as middle class as it came. His own brother still lived in a tiny apartment on a military base even though Robby offered numerous times to get him a big house of his own. When had he become conceited? He didn't deserve any of his success, and yet he didn't know how to think any differently about his lot.

"So I need a love song for some movie this new director is making," McAllister continued. "Word is the thing is going to be epic so it's a great opportunity for you."

Robby's stomach clenched. "I don't do ballads."

"It's not a negotiation. You either want to write it or you don't."

The man had a point. Robby sighed heavily, hating himself. He was ill-equipped to write a ballad. The only person he'd ever loved was himself and he was sure that wasn't what his producer or the filmmaker was after. And to come out as a solo artist with a love song might be career suicide. He'd written rock anthems, drinking songs, songs about women, and even break-up songs, but there wasn't a love song in his entire music history, and there was a reason. Against his will, he found himself asking, "When do you want it?"

"The sooner the better. Two or three weeks would be perfect but I might be able to get them to hold off longer. There are other musicians who are interested..."

Two weeks!? Was he crazy? Robby didn't write under pressure. He wondered if this woman kept alcohol around or if he'd need to...no. Not this close to Nick. He'd figure out what Robby was up to before he even took one drink. The man was possessed with superpowers.

Robby sat up slowly and put his feet on the floor., noticing a notebook on the nightstand. He lifted it and began flipping through as he pressed the phone between his ear and shoulder. "Sure, fine. I'll write whatever you want." The tone in his voice revealed he would prefer anything to this. "Send me the details so I'm not way off."

"I'd hate to pressure you." McAllister sounded happy. The producer was probably trying to see if Robby was really sober. And screwing this up wasn't an option.

The days when life clicked easily had faded into Robby's memories. Maybe that was another reason he'd started drinking. Making it in the music industry required no small amount of effort on his part. Writing and composing the music, battling with a band that favored fighting over playing gigs, and desperately trying to get his family to pay attention to anything he did, worked together to consume him. The family only acknowledged him when he messed up. By the time he was fifteen, he'd met more walls in his childhood home at the hands of his father than most kids did over their lives.

Robby stopped flipping the pages of the notebook as his eyes landed on what appeared to be a poem. And it was good—better than anything he'd ever written. He grinned broadly. This little lady was sure full of surprises.

"I'll be in touch." Robby tossed his phone aside and re-read the words.

The answer was right here.

Robby hopped off the bed and went to the door, listening. Those women were still in the kitchen. He didn't even bother to wonder how long they'd talk. He might be waiting a long time—after all, it wasn't like the blonde was going anywhere. He really wished he could remember her name.

Robby paced the small room before his eyes rested on a laptop on the desk nearby. He set the notebook down on the end of the bed and sat, touching the mouse so that the screen came to life. For a moment he wondered what he was seeing, but soon realized it was the woman's bank account. A part of him was aware of the ethical dilemma. He shouldn't look, but the small numbers registered in his mind before he could close the page.

"Whoa..." Robby forgot the last time his own account was that low. Or had it ever been that bad? Even when he was struggling, his mom, Nick or Warren saw to his needs. He'd get Lily to write his guardian angel a check for all she'd done to help him. He smiled. Warren would be proud since he'd be doing something useful with his money for someone he'd actually met.

Maybe all of that preaching was getting through to him after all. He was thinking of someone besides himself and it felt good.

He minimized the screen and opened his e-mail where he began composing a message to his agent. He needed a band. Immediately.

~*~

Nearly twenty minutes after Sadie and Jennifer

left, Daisy was caught up in the Marx Brothers instead of cleaning the kitchen as she'd been intending. She paid only some attention to the screen, wondering about the man Sadie found to be her date to Jennifer's wedding. After all, her friends wouldn't set her up with anyone they felt didn't deserve her. She hoped he had a good sense of humor and liked to eat, because if she was going to go anywhere with him, she meant to have a good time.

You'd need to stop being afraid to leave the house, she reminded herself, glancing at the window. And would she need strong medication to get into a car? That would be embarrassing.

"Did you write these?" Robby's voice shattered Daisy's daydream and for the second time since he'd arrived, she jumped in her seat, her heart racing.

"Oh, my goodness!" she shrieked. Quickly regaining control, she cleared her throat. "I forgot you were here," she muttered and went to the sink where she tried to appear busy with the cookie trays, ignoring that he seemed to fill her house with his presence. What was she supposed to do with him now? She dreaded calling Nick and she didn't think Robby was to be trusted alone either, which meant she was stuck with him until she came up with a plan. At the moment she had none.

Robby grinned. He clearly was used to making women fall all over themselves to be near him. And it was obvious to Daisy he thought he'd charm her into whatever he wanted. She swallowed her smile at his naiveté. She was too strong-willed to fall for this foolishness.

Well, at least she was now.

"Did you write these?" he asked again. Daisy

didn't want to but she glanced at him. He was holding up her journal. She'd never shown it to anyone. The book held her precious dreams—the words she shielded from the world, the ones she hesitated to even write for fear they'd be real.

And she'd stupidly left it out on her nightstand.

Daisy's heart stopped for a moment, and she moved quickly across the room where she grabbed it out of his hands and tucked it under her leg, her face warm with embarrassment. She hoped he hadn't read it but she understood it was already too late.

"I do not appreciate you rooting in my things," she muttered.

"I was locked in that room for like an hour. What was I supposed to do, try on your panties?" he asked coolly, sitting at the table.

"That would be less invasive." Daisy wrestled a cookie sheet from the drying rack and moved to put it away. "You were in my room for twenty minutes. I didn't say you needed to hide forever. My friends weren't going to...besides, I didn't invite you here in the first place."

Robby shook his head as he grabbed three cookies from the plate and tossed them down. He smiled. "Yes, you did, Angel."

Daisy glanced across the room to find Robby grinning flirtatiously at her. He glanced at the television and then back to Daisy, his eyebrows raised. "I like Animal Crackers myself," he said. "'Girls that are tall and short and slim and stout and blonde and brunette. That's just the kind of girl I crave.'"

He was going to drive her insane.

"You like the Marx Brothers?" she asked incredulously. Robby was not what she expected—if she'd been expecting him at all.

He nodded, his eyes back on the television. "Lots of time on the road...and Uncle Nick always made me and Warren watch movies with him when we came for the summer."

Daisy tried to mask her surprise. "Duck Soup is better than Animal Crackers," she said, annoyed. She did not want to make friends with him or Nick would insist she talk to him about a career. Already Robby was getting too close for her comfort.

He smiled at her and gestured toward the journal again. "Sing that for me?"

Daisy scoffed at him. "I think you should help me tidy up," she said.

"What?"

"You know, clean up...that thing I'd guess other people do for you. Bring me your mug and put it in the dishwasher," she said.

Robby stood slowly, seemingly appalled that she'd ask him to do anything so menial. He brought the mug to her and held it out. But Daisy refused to take it, pointing toward the dishwasher. Robby stared at it as if he'd never used one. Daisy sighed again and opened it for him. She pulled out the rack, and he clumsily set his mug inside. As she started to close the door, he grabbed her hand and she gasped, too shocked to move. His eyes challenged her to argue.

"You did write it, didn't you?" he asked huskily. "Those are your songs." Daisy forgot her name when he looked at her like that, with his big, sparkling green eyes.

A man shouldn't have lashes that long.

Daisy's mind remained blank.

Robby grinned. "Thought so..." he said, releasing

her hand as he stood to his full height. He leaned against the counter and gazed down at her, his legs crossed in front of him in a way that was reminiscent of his uncle. "Are they lyrics or poems? Not that it matters but I'd love to buy the whole thing. It's decent stuff. Really good. Name your price."

Daisy gawked at him but moved quickly away. Who did he think he was?

"Come on, I'm good for it. And I need new material."

"No."

"No?"

Robby was silent for so long that Daisy finally turned to take a peek at him. He seemed to be wrestling with himself as he leaned against the counter, staring at her.

"Are they poems or lyrics?" he asked.

"Lyrics mostly," she admitted against her better judgment. What did he really care? He wasn't serious. Now that he was laid-up, Nick probably called him from the hospital and told him to check on her. Inwardly Daisy was comforted by this thought. Her good friend did think enough of her to worry how she'd fare in his absence.

Robby stood a little straighter at her affirmation. She glanced at him again and a broad smile swept across his face. "You mean to tell me I landed in the home of a songwriter?" He laughed, victorious—over what Daisy wasn't sure. "There is a God and He does not hate me." He walked slowly to the other side of the room where he fell into a delighted lump on one of her kitchen chairs, drinking in his good fortune.

Daisy cleared her throat and shook her head again. "Of course there's a God and He doesn't hate people.

He created them!" She paused. "I am not a songwriter. I write press releases and content for websites, a news piece occasionally. I play a little piano but I don't…sing. Not anymore."

Robby laughed, making Daisy instantly angry. "Liar. You write music and we…will work together on something." Daisy tried to ignore him but was certain he would stare at her until she spoke.

She caved. "No. I've got a life. There are other things I need to do…"

Robby laughed. "Your bank account tells a different story. You need, what, about twenty grand? I'd gladly pay you that, maybe more for *Waiting* alone," he said.

Daisy turned to him fully before she spoke, her heart in her throat.

She seethed at his audacity. How dare he insinuate that she needed his help? When he threw around numbers like that it showed how disconnected he was from reality. And her reality was a bank account that had dipped to less than fifty dollars. She was already frightened and didn't need him reminding her how low her life had fallen.

She remembered Nick's words about pride. Against her will, Daisy wondered aloud, "You'd pay me twenty thousand dollars…" her voice trailed off as her courage failed. She all but tore the phone from its place on the counter and started dialing. "I'm calling Nick."

Robby was at her side in an instant. He yanked the phone from her and turned it off. "Sing. Come on." As he loomed over her, Daisy wished she weren't aware of how good he smelled, fresh from the shower, or that his arm brushed hers.

But as quickly as those thoughts sailed through her mind, Daisy cursed her wheelchair, reaching for the phone that Robby held out of her grasp. Clearly, he was angry too. His face grew redder with each second. Would he hit her?

"Since it's all over the news, I'll bet you know I've been in rehab six times. Impressive, huh? Six?! And this last one was nothing to sneeze at. I lost my girlfriend, my friends, and even most of my family. Now, my career is shot until I come up with something...and I am not about to stop until I get back on that stage again. If I can't control anything else in my life, at least I can try to take back what's left of my career. But I'm on a timeline. And you will help me."

The rage in his eyes should have scared her, but Daisy refused to be intimidated. Her ex-boyfriend was worse. She just wished she could knee Robby in a place that would jerk him back to reality. She managed to glare instead. "Maybe you should take a deep breath and come up with a plan that doesn't include me."

She crossed her arms over her chest and stared at Robby defiantly, trying to ignore that he truly was a very handsome man with a commanding presence. The clarity in his eyes and the muscles in his arms both surprised and unsettled her. A scrawny, weak, and strung-out Robby she'd have expected and could have handled. This man was unexpectedly healthy, yet he was also angry, hurt, and alone. She saw it in his eyes. And she realized what was happening.

"I'm stuck..." Robby said weakly. "This is exactly what I need..."

Oh, no, Lord, Daisy pleaded silently. *I can't even help myself. How am I supposed to help him?* And yet no answer came. But even in the silence, Daisy understood.

Although she'd technically lived on her own for years, Daisy was never really on her own. She'd only survived everything she'd been through thanks to relying so heavily on God. And He'd given her more help than she deserved in the form of her friends. In isolating herself, Daisy realized she could try to squeak by on her own, forget God, or pushing her relationship with Him to the side as she worried about her next set of bills or why she wasn't finding enough work. Now, the truth was upon her, and like it or not there was real work to do in the form of helping Robby.

She wished God would pick someone else. Robby was as annoying as a tiny splinter in the palm of her hand, and she wanted him out immediately.

"My friend has a café where you might perform." The offer was lame, and Daisy did not intend to connect Robby with one of her dearest friends.

"A café?" The singer's mouth hung open as he gaped at her. His teeth were perfect. Why wouldn't they be? She would feel better if she could find in him some sort of gaping imperfection. Other than being a recovering alcoholic, there appeared to be nothing to pick apart.

"Are you kidding me?" he continued. "I play stadiums, not cafés!" A huge vein popped out of his neck and she feared she'd pushed too far. A café was probably a terrible insult to someone of his status. She managed to shove that thought away. Even if he was angry, Daisy didn't think he was that kind of man, which was why she let herself continue to push him further. Maybe then he'd leave for good.

She wanted to stop, but she needed to keep going so he'd go away.

Daisy...
Sorry, Lord.

Her apology was flat and wrong, but her heart and her mind wanted nothing to do with helping Robby Grant.

"Listen, I'm sorry you have problems but guess what? We all do—that's life—and you are not one of mine. The songs aren't for sale—especially *Waiting* — so I'd appreciate it if you'd forget about that book. Now give me the phone."

Like a child, Robby placed the phone on top of the refrigerator and crossed his arms. "Nope. I don't get what I want, you don't get what you want." Robby considered her for a long time, his eyes presenting a challenge. He shook his head and she wondered if that was the end of his fight. Some tough guy.

"Fine." He reached for the phone. "Why don't you call Nick and tell him we're on our way? Wonder what he'll think about all of this."

Daisy stared at him as he held the phone out to her. He was now one step ahead of her and he wasn't even aware. Still, she thought about telling Nick that Robby was there and let him deal with his inconsiderate nephew. If Nick knew Robby had shown up drunk...

"I am not going anywhere with you..." she muttered as she reached for the phone. Once again, Robby yanked it away from her, irritated.

"Really? There are millions of women who'd do any number of things for a ride in my truck."

Daisy rolled her eyes. "Well, call one of them!"

Robby placed the phone back on top of the refrigerator with an irritated sigh. "Your friends said Nick was asking for you. Don't you care?"

His words cut Daisy to the core. She glared. "Nick means more to me than you'll...never mind. It's too complicated to bother explaining."

Robby grinned again before slowly stepping toward her. He placed one hand on either of her shoulders so that he was nose-to-nose with her. He smelled heavily of expensive, masculine cologne that made her dizzy. Daisy's chest constricted, and she reminded herself she needed to breathe. He wasn't going to kiss her. Not that she'd mind...but surely even Robby had his standards.

But it had been such a long, long time since anyone had even hinted at kissing her.

Robby continued smiling and gently brushed the hair back from her face. "Come on. Let's go for a visit. I have a feeling he'd be happy to see you," he whispered. "You'll be home in time for Duck Soup. And Uncle Nick will love that I'm so thoughtful I brought his good friend."

Quickly, Daisy gathered her wits and managed to push his hand away, knocking him off balance as he tried to stand.

"Don't you ever touch me again," she said, moving away from him. Incredulous, Robby regained control and resumed his original stance, his eyes blazing.

"You have no idea who you're dealing with."

Daisy laughed, pointing to her backpack. "You don't either. Thanks to your uncle I'm a darned good shot."

Angrily, Robby reached for her and lifted her from the wheelchair, surprising them both as he held her close.

"I don't play games...Rose. We're going to see

Nick... and before this night is through I bet you'll beg me to take your songs."

As Robby started for the door, alternately kicking the wheelchair in front of him as he went, Daisy was beginning to come to her senses.

"My name is Daisy!" she shouted feebly. "Put me down!" She beat against his solid chest but to no avail. They were outside in the cool night air before she even thought to scream.

It didn't matter. There was no one to hear.

As Robby carried Daisy across the driveway, he leaned close to her hair and inhaled, his wild hair brushing against her cheek. "Man...you smell amazing," he groaned.

At any other moment, the compliment would have meant something, but Daisy was too overcome by fear. With each step away from the house, her body reacted violently, culminating in trembling so severe her teeth were chattering.

Robby didn't seem to notice as he set her in the cab of the truck. It was parked in the shadows and she realized with desperation that she didn't even grab her cell phone, which lay useless in her wheelchair. Her friends wouldn't know what was happening and there was no way to plead for help. She was completely at Robby's mercy. Nick would not be happy, and Daisy was going to enjoy every minute of him ripping his nephew's head off. But that didn't solve the immediate problem. She was not in control anymore.

Robby slammed the door and turned quickly to retrieve Daisy's wheelchair, which he easily collapsed and placed in the back of the truck bed.

She was in his truck and he intended to drive to the hospital with her in the passenger's seat. Daisy's mind jumped from disbelief to anger to hysteria.

The night of the accident was as calm as this one, the stars decorating the satiny sky with diamonds, not unlike the one she'd once worn on her finger.

Bile rose in her throat as she remembered. She was supposed to be safe.

Oh, please, Lord, she begged.

Without thinking, Daisy threw open the door and stared below. She was trapped. There was no getting out and going home, which was only a few yards away. If she leaned forward she would fall onto her face, probably knocking out all of her teeth in the process. Without someone's help, she was at the mercy of this madman who intended to force her to go with him to the hospital whether she wanted to or not.

Daisy's insides raged. Before she realized it, she was retching on the ground below, her dinner all over the pavement. Robby's sympathetic gaze only made her feel worse. She didn't want his pity.

Although his mouth remained closed, his eyes asked a million questions while she gasped for breath. She hated to be pitied. It was a look that was sadly familiar, and she didn't need to guess what he was thinking.

But to her surprise, he said, "I'm not going to hurt you. I promise." He tried nudging the door but Daisy kept her hand on it, her strength at its end. Again, Robby nudged it until it was closed and Daisy, at a loss for what else to do, waited until he walked around the truck and got into the driver's seat.

"I...I can't do this," she said weakly, reminding herself to breathe as her lungs resisted. Robby glanced at her, though it appeared he didn't see her as he lit a cigarette and cracked his window. He said nothing as he started the truck.

"You don't understand," she pleaded. "I haven't been in a car for over a year...or maybe it's two..." She desperately grabbed at his arm as she spoke. Robby gently removed her fingers and sighed as he backed out of the narrow driveway, a large tree branch scraping Daisy's window with a hair-raising screech. She jumped, her chest numb with the effort of breathing.

"Well you're in luck, baby, because this is a truck," he said.

To Daisy's horror, he took a drag on his cigarette as the truck lurched forward, taking her away from the safety of her home.

8

When they arrived at the hospital less than twenty minutes later, Daisy started to calm down as far as the trip went, but her anger toward Robby intensified. What kind of person would toss a woman he'd never met into his truck and drive off with her—and against her vehement protests? A conceited, overbearing, selfish jerk would do such a thing and once Daisy got everything straight in her mind she intended to tell him what she thought of him. Never mind that it wasn't at all what God wanted her to do. She'd deal with that later when she was alone. Robby made it impossible for her to think straight. Being reasonable was going to take time.

At the moment, though, she sat rigidly in her seat, waiting as Robby got her wheelchair out of the back, set it up, and slowly opened her door, his face remorseful.

He squashed his cigarette on the ground. They were eye to eye for the first time, which only made Daisy squirm.

She did her best to hang onto the anger that burned in her chest, but in order to do that she swore silently that she wouldn't look into his eyes again. They unsettled her. She turned her body away from him as he awkwardly cleared his throat.

"Hey. I'm sorry about tossing you in here and...well, everything..." he began sincerely. "I'm not really myself today…"

Daisy kept her eyes forward as she responded to him, hoping Nick would take care of his disrespectful, pain-in-the-backside nephew when he learned all the man had done to her. "I get it. You're a clueless pretty boy," she snapped. "Your apology means nothing." For a writer, she sometimes struggled with eloquence. She gritted her teeth, knowing she would have to apologize for her words. She cleared her throat, but the words would not come out.

Finally, she managed to turn her eyes in Robby's direction. She was incensed to discover he was smiling, the slight dimple in his chin catching her notice.

"I'm a pretty boy?" he asked, leaning against the truck. "Someone should teach you to cuss properly. I probably know some people who could help you."

Daisy folded her arms over her chest and turned back to the windshield. She prayed he didn't hear her heart drumming. "Let's get one thing straight, Mr. Grant," she said, her face warm with rage. "I've been nothing but kind to you. But I can't trust you, and I'd like it very much if you'd leave me alone." Even as she spoke, she was convicted of her venomous thoughts. Although Robby reminded her of Alec, taking her anger out on him would be fruitless, not to mention foolish.

Stop before this gets out of hand. Daisy realized she was already out of control.

"OK…" he muttered. "If that's what you want…but you better do Nick the courtesy of visiting him since you're here." He pulled her from the truck and dropped her into her wheelchair carelessly. He slammed the door, locked it, and was halfway into the hospital before Daisy realized he was leaving her. Did the man really pack that much nerve that he felt it was reasonable to treat a handicapped person this way? Her anger was palpable as she made her way into the hospital, trailing slowly after him.

She wordlessly boarded the elevator behind him and he pushed the button, his back to her. She didn't care.

Good riddance.

It had been so long since Daisy went anywhere that even the familiar hospital was strangely new. As the elevator doors clicked open with a cheerful "Ding!" she realized two things—she survived the truck ride and Nick might have a heart attack at the sight of them. She said a quick prayer that the surprise wouldn't be too much.

Robby stepped out of the elevator while Daisy glared at his back for her own satisfaction. It didn't work. The longer she clung to the rage, the more immature she felt.

She followed him up the hallway until he paused and slowly opened a door. He held it for Daisy, but she glared at him and pushed him out of the way, choosing to struggle with it herself. He shrugged and waited.

Nick was lying with his leg up in a cast, suspended partway above the bed. Several machines near the head of his bed beeped at random moments, reminding Daisy of her own hospital stay. Even the sterile, serene smell of the place took her back to the time when Nick and her friends kept constant vigil at her side. She remained close to the doorway, holding the door as if afraid to enter, lest the moment become too real. Robby glanced at her but said nothing as he stuffed his hands in his pockets and leaned against the wall, nodding for her to enter.

Daisy gulped.

Nick appeared to be asleep, despite the television being tuned to one of his favorite game shows. Robby cleared his throat and sat softly in the chair beside the bed, obviously ignoring Daisy's presence altogether.

"Hey…" Robby tapped his tennis shoe against the bed frame. "Uncle Nick."

Nick's eyes opened slowly and he stared at Robby as if unable to take in the sight. Daisy saw him struggling to make sense of his wayward nephew's presence. He rubbed his head and then his eyes before turning his attention to her, his eyebrows knitting together. He looked from Robby to Daisy and back again—his mouth open in shock.

"Hey, Nick." Daisy approached his bed and reached for his hand. "How are you?" He was a tough old man. It would take more than a fall from the barn loft to really hurt him. Her heart filled with relief as she realized he would recover.

"I wanted to call...but..." Daisy glanced at Robby and back at Nick's face. "Um, there wasn't time. I'm so sorry about today."

Nick finally seemed to process his visitors and cleared his throat calmly, waving his hand at her as if to dismiss all the worry she'd worked on throughout the day.

"Eh, wasn't your fault," he said. "If I waited for Steve to come it wouldn't have happened." Nick turned back to Robby, confused. "How did you end up with him?" Leave it to Nick to not only take it all in stride but to get right to the elephant wearing ripped jeans in the chair beside the bed.

Daisy refused to turn her eyes to Robby, afraid she'd forgive him, or worse, be reminded of her earlier compassion. "I'm still trying to figure that out," she grumbled. Robby rolled his eyes while Nick shook his head as he took in his nephew's appearance.

"Robert River Grant," he said. "You look terrible." Daisy embraced the strange pleasure Robby's grimace brought her. The bruises on his face darkened some and the cut near his eye was still puffy. Despite Daisy's nursing, he was going to be bruised for days. She realized suddenly that he never bothered to say what happened to him and she didn't ask. Some hospitality she'd shown.

"Warren said you were on tour," Nick continued.

Robby shrugged. "I would be, soon, but...well, I came to help." He stood and paced the room as they waited for him to continue. He glanced at Daisy, the irritation plain as he jerked his thumb in her direction. "But she wouldn't let me into your house without asking you first. So, here we are." He peeked out through the blinds, clearly uncomfortable. Daisy noticed he stayed quiet about the state of his arrival. She wasn't about to bring it up either, but not for Robby's sake. She simply thought Nick needed to stay calm.

The old man grinned. "She's no dummy."

Robby's cell phone rang. He peeked at it and stuffed it back into his pocket.

"They said I'm going to be in here a few more days—maybe a week even," Nick said, grimacing as he tried to adjust himself to a more comfortable position. "Apparently, I did a number on myself. You plan to stay a while?"

Robby shrugged, surveying the parking lot below as he did. "As long as you need me, I guess."

Nick kept his eyes on Robby and lifted a coffee

cup from the tray beside his bed. He took a drink as he thought for a moment and nodded in Daisy's direction.

"Good. Stay at Daisy's house until I get out."

Daisy grimaced. "What? There's no reason he can't go to your place. I'd be happy to feed him if that's what you're worried about." The words tumbled out faster than she was able to think. But whatever it took to change Nick's mind was fine with her. She did not want Robby Grant staying in her home. She wasn't entirely sure either of them would live through it.

"He's in trouble."

"But that's not my...I mean, I shouldn't have to..." Daisy met Nick's eyes and understood that no matter the level of her protest, she had to give in. But having Robby stay in her guest room was beyond the pale. Maybe she could stick him in the barn.

Before that thought could take root, Daisy's conscience caught her attention. Whether she liked Robby or not he was a man in need of help. And after all Nick did for her, the least that was required of her would be to let his nephew sleep in her guest room.

"I wouldn't be in trouble anymore if you got her to sing that song for me," Robby muttered, playing with the window blinds.

Nick met Daisy's eyes before she turned away. "Well. How did that happen?" Now he was intrigued. Stupid Robby. "Eh, never mind," he continued. "Let him help you. Do it. For me..." Nick whispered. But Daisy shook her head.

Robby turned from the window and angled his body toward Daisy. "Yeah. For Nick, Daisy..." It was the first time he said her name and it struck Daisy that she liked it.

She hated herself.

"I won't do it for anyone." *There. Take that!* She only wished the defiant words made her stronger. She was still so weak.

"What did you do to her?" Nick asked with a grimace. "She's usually the sweetest girl in the world."

Robby shrugged. "Dr. Jekyll and Ms. Hyde…"

Nick grunted. "Fine," he relented with a heavy sigh. "But let him stay with you. He's a mess. No telling what trouble he'll find if he's left to his own devices." Daisy glanced at Robby, who rolled his eyes and turned back to the window. Although he was older than she was, he acted like a spoiled child. She was not a fan of children.

Daisy sighed heavily. "Fine, Nick. I'll…he can stay."

Nick smiled and nodded. "Good. Now, get him out of here and don't bring him back. It will be chaos if anyone finds out he left New York or California or the gutter, or wherever he spends most of his time."

Daisy nodded and slowly started for the door, Robby reluctantly following her. Nick cleared his throat to get their attention. Robby turned.

"Keep your hands to yourself. I won't be responsible what I do otherwise. She's a lady, treat her like it."

Robby rolled his eyes and saluted Nick before following Daisy out of the room. She pressed the elevator button and they went inside together.

Robby glanced at her. "I'm not staying with you," he said firmly.

Daisy shrugged. "I don't care what you do," she snapped.

"Fine."

Daisy said nothing as the elevator doors opened

and Robby rushed out of them and to the parking lot. She trailed behind him, dreading that to get into that truck he was going to touch her again. It was hard to be independent and angry when she needed him to lift her into his ridiculously high truck.

Robby opened the door and reached down so he could take her in his arms and raise her up to the seat. Daisy hated that she'd been rude to him, but protecting herself from more hurt was the only thing she knew to do.

Robby might take that song and record it and she'd listen to it on the radio for the rest of her life. Was it worth it? She hoped that someday soon she'd be over everything. To hear that song forever was too much.

Daisy should apologize, but as Robby set her down and slammed the door all she managed was to watch him collapse her chair and return it to the bed. He hopped into the driver's seat and lit another cigarette as his cell phone rang. He touched the screen to turn on the speaker before starting the truck. Daisy did her best to ignore him.

"Yeah." He set the phone on the bench seat between them.

"You there, little brother?"

"Just left the hospital. Nick's fine," Robby said as he steered out of the parking lot and drove in the wrong direction. Daisy opened her mouth to stop him but thought better of it. What did she care if he got lost? She still knew how to get back home from anywhere in the county.

Warren snorted. "Really?" he asked.

Robby glanced at Daisy with a grin, gesturing at the phone as he exhaled smoke. "Trust me. I'm being helpful," he said. "I'll call you later. I'm busy."

Daisy rolled her eyes. *Busy getting lost.*

"Right. I'm cautiously optimistic about you."

"Wouldn't dream of asking for more, desert storm." Robby hung up the phone and tossed his cigarette out the window. Daisy focused on the passing world outside her window.

"No one trusts me," he muttered.

"Ever given anyone a reason to?" Daisy asked, annoyed.

Although Robby seemed as though he tried to mask it, he looked wounded. Daisy sighed heavily and resumed looking out the window. She used to be good with people.

"You went the wrong way out of the hospital," she said. "Turn around and take me home so I can forget this whole horrible day happened."

When Robby didn't respond, and in fact kept driving in the same direction, Daisy wondered if he was listening to her at all. She glanced at him to repeat herself but before she spoke she found him smiling. It irritated her more.

"What?" she demanded.

"Horrible? How on earth can you say this day was horrible?" he asked. "I got dumped and landed in two fights, I was nearly shot, we both threw up, you were manhandled by an unemployed but—dare I say— devastatingly handsome rock star...I'm not sure what more you want out of a day." Against her inner turmoil, Daisy found herself smiling, which something she rarely did anymore. It seemed the old, frisky and fun Daisy had disappeared years ago.

But now, here she was riding in Robby Grant's truck—smiling at him. It was almost ridiculous. He was an international celebrity, on the cover of every magazine, the sexiest man alive. And she was...Daisy sobered for a moment. Who was she? At one time, she'd believed she was an attractive woman who danced circles around anyone and sang like an angel. But now? Daisy wasn't so sure. Maybe that woman was still inside her. What would it hurt to flirt a bit with him? She could have fun. It certainly wouldn't go anywhere given the circumstances.

A peace settled over Daisy at these thoughts and she grinned back at him but remained silent. Robby's smile brightened at her response, his teeth glistening in the lights around them.

"A party. I came here for a party," he said in a Marx Brothers impression. "And what happened? Nothing. Not even ice cream."

Daisy wondered if he'd gone crazy.

"Are you up for some ice cream, Harpo?" he asked.

Daisy shrugged. She was out of the house for the first time in a year. Why should she rush home?

9

Robby pulled into the all-night drive-through restaurant reminiscing about his teen years. Like now, no one knew where he was or who he was with—the only difference being that back then it didn't matter to anyone—and neither did Robby.

He knew he'd pushed Daisy's buttons and he didn't care. She fascinated him. That she didn't seem to like him only made it worse. She was a challenge, which hadn't happened in so long he'd forgotten a woman could have that effect on him. The whole thing fed into his rebellious nature. And it was never far from his mind that a hit song waited for him in her home. If he and Nick worked on her together, maybe they'd convince her that Robby was the man to get her out of whatever sad state she was currently in.

"Well?" Robby asked as he opened the window to place their order.

Daisy thought. "Um, a coffee milkshake."

He nodded and leaned out the window. "Yeah—one large coffee milkshake, one large vanilla milkshake, French fries and an order of onion rings please."

As the woman told them to drive through, Robby glanced at Daisy who grinned widely at him. He sighed heavily, rolling his eyes. "Speak, Harpo," he said as he dug into his pocket for his wallet. Most women wouldn't shut up, but he was stuck with one who barely said a word. She watched and listened more than she spoke. He glanced at her while he pulled out some money and drove to the next window. She merely shook her head and kept smiling.

"Come on..."

Her big blue eyes sparkled. "I'm surprised you're a vanilla guy. You seem a bit more...interesting than that."

Robby smiled as he passed the money to the clerk, who instantly recognized him. He turned on his charm and winked at her before turning back to Daisy.

"Really? And what should I get?"

"Banana split, orange dreamsicle...not vanilla..." she said it with a disdain that surprised him. Apparently, there was a human being inside the shell.

Robby met her eyes and smiled. She was a beautiful woman. And he saw already that she was too good for him. She was a lady, and in the past Robby discovered a female of that caliber was out of his league. He tried once to date a doctor who'd patched him up after a fight, leaving him with five stitches on his back. She was a lady who'd all but laughed when he showed his interest. She didn't need his drama or his lifestyle—he doubted Daisy did either. He only seemed to snare women who loved his bad-boy image. Funny that this one didn't seem to want that at all. She was much more interested in the person inside than the carefully-crafted facade.

"Sorry, baby. I'm Vanilla," he said as he drove to the next window. The realization that she was after his soul and not his body was unsettling. His body meant little to him, but his mind and heart were something else. He'd never let anyone that close. He no longer knew if he was capable of it.

Daisy waited until he got their drinks and passed hers over. He handed her a bag of food but carefully avoided her eyes. He drove to a secluded parking space but he said nothing, suddenly having too much to think about. He sipped his milkshake as she drew a deep breath, which made him turn his attention back to her.

"Well...thanks, Vanilla, for getting me out of the house," she said softly, as if the words were difficult. She focused on her hands, almost afraid of his being there beside her. It seemed they were both holding back.

"Nick's been after me for the last year but I...guess I've been too scared," she continued. Something inside Robby told him she desperately needed to be taken care of. For a moment, he forgot about the song and considered that she had more value than her ability to write a hit.

You have your own problems, you don't need hers too.. But Warren's challenge continued to resonate in the back of his mind. What would his brother do? How would a real man speak to this woman? She seemed so fragile.

Robby cleared his throat. "I didn't exactly give you a choice. I'm surprised Nick didn't do that himself."

Daisy chuckled and finally raised her eyes to meet his. "I think if he were younger, that might have been an option." Robby laughed and they considered each other for a long moment, saying nothing. He held out the French fries to her and she took a few as a handsome older gentleman approached the truck on Robby's side.

Robby sighed, glancing at the man who clearly wanted to talk to him, but he spoke to Daisy first. "This guy is a thorn in my backside," he muttered.

He put down the window but continued looking forward, away from the man. "What?" Robby sounded bored, even to himself. He'd battled this gossip columnist so many times it was as if Mac Robinson were Robby's nemesis, intent on finding out everything about the rock star and his life no matter the cost. That he'd managed to find him in some Pennsylvanian hole didn't surprise Robby at all. Mac was relentless.

"Who's the lovely lady?" Mac asked, eyeing Daisy through the cracked window. "And what are you doing here?"

"Don't I have a restraining order against you?" Robby calmly popped another fry into his mouth. He glanced at Daisy who observed the exchange. She sipped her milkshake quietly and Robby said a silent prayer of thanks that she really was like Harpo Marx. Hopefully, she stayed out of the way too as run-ins with Mac were usually ugly.

Mac once staked out an area outside Robby's hotel room to break the story of Robby and his married girlfriend. Since Robby was in it for the fun and not to hurt anyone the incident enraged him. The husband would have killed Robby if it wasn't for Jazz. That now he was sitting in his truck drinking milkshakes with a handicapped woman wasn't exactly news anyway, though he was sure Mac was going to try and make it into something.

For some reason, the public's thirst for information was insatiable. Did Robby sleep on his left or his right side? What was he allergic to? Chocolate or vanilla? Paper or plastic? Blonde or brunette? Boxers or briefs? It gave him a headache. Just because he made music for a living didn't mean his whole life should be fodder for public consumption, and yet it was. When he was drunk it didn't matter much to him, but now he understood it wasn't healthy, and he made a promise not to do it anymore. He needed to protect the parts of himself that were private. In order to do that, he still had to understand who he was.

"How did you find me?" Robby asked, not bothering to mask his irritation. "I just got here for goodness' sake."

Mac smiled, toying with the camera around his neck. "You're my job security, Robby. There's always a story," he said. "Tracking you since you got out of rehab. You've been keeping clean." Robby snorted and tossed the bag of food to Daisy who caught it and set it on her lap. Robby winked at her. He was satisfied when she blushed.

She had feelings after all, and he hadn't lost his touch. Well, not yet anyway.

Mac took it all in. "Finding you in this truck wasn't hard—and the band of loudmouths you call friends made it easier too," he said. "The rest of the paparazzi are on their way."

Mac leaned against the truck. "Five minutes is all I need."

Robby whistled between his teeth. "For what?" He paused. "OK...how much to forget you saw me? There isn't a story here." It was a weak offer. Mac would sell his own soul for the right story or picture.

"You aren't rich enough." Mac changed his position to get a better view of Daisy. Despite her evasion, he caught her eye and smiled. "Hey, honey. Robby's latest conquest?"

Daisy glanced at Robby who barely masked his

shock before recovering. He placed one finger under her chin and steadily held her gaze. Now more than ever he was putting his trust in a stranger and it scared him.

Daisy visibly gulped but maintained eye contact. He made her nervous. He hoped that would be enough to keep her quiet, at least for now.

He leaned close and nearly touched her ear with his lips. "Don't say a word," he whispered. She nodded slowly and relief swept over Robby as he sat back in his seat, still holding her gaze with his own. Her eyes said she was scared, but she could be trusted. And his uncle seemed completely taken with her, which made Robby even more confident.

Mac continued grinning as he stared at the two of them.

"You can read the story before it goes to print. Anything you don't like I take out." Mac leaned against the truck. Robby hated when anyone touched his truck. The man was trying to make him angry.

"All I want is the story. What happened with the band, why you're here, who this pretty little thing is...that's all. You tell me, I go away. Simple as pie." Mac offered a shrug. "I'm no genius, but if those guys got rid of you and saw how quickly you rebounded with this girl, they'd insist on finding out what else you're up to. If it were me, I'd be fine putting pictures of her out there. Fans will love it." Mac winked. His words had thrown Robby off his game.

He glanced at Daisy, fully aware that she was gorgeous and underneath all of her opinions she seemed pretty likable. But Robby also knew he was going to be stuck with her, and vice versa, for longer than he wanted, thanks to the fact that his own uncle didn't trust him. He might as well make the most of it.

In a flash, he was the old Robby again. He forgot about his promise to Warren and his intentions to be a better man. A plan formed quickly in his mind to get his fame and his career back, and without thinking of the consequences, he plunged ahead telling himself that both he and Daisy would benefit. He took a long drink of his milkshake and glanced at Mac with a nod.

"You caught me. Happy?" he asked, a tinge of annoyance in his voice. "Now leave us alone."

"Happy? Oh, yeah. Very." Mac jotted notes in a small notebook. "How 'bout a picture?" Robby lowered the window, grabbed the camera from around Mac's neck and tossed it across the parking lot. It shattered into a million pieces. Mac looked like he was going to crawl through the window and wring Robby's neck.

"What do you think you're doing!?" he demanded. "You'll pay for that!"

Robby laughed and started the truck.

"Send the bill to my agent," he yelled and sped away.

~*~

Daisy stared at Robby, unable to believe what she'd heard. Had he really told a reporter that she was his girlfriend? She glared at his profile as he gunned the engine, making another wrong turn. He was smiling as he lit a cigarette. The nerve of this man both angered and shocked her. Surely, he wouldn't let the world believe they were in a relationship. The progress they'd made in the last hour was gone.

"It's brilliant!" he muttered with a glance in

Daisy's direction.

He really was too handsome for his own good. She cursed his eyes again as she folded her arms over her chest and frowned.

"What? For crying out loud, Harpo, this might be easier if you speak."

Daisy seethed. Why did he insist on calling her that? She didn't think it necessary to waste her breath on useless words to a man that refused to listen when she spoke. It didn't mean she didn't know how to talk. She spoke when it mattered. And boy, did she have something to say now.

"I have no intention of making this easy for you. Not that you care about my feelings or thoughts of course," she said feebly. What she wanted to say shouldn't come from a lady's mouth. Ever.

"Try me..."

Daisy rolled her eyes. "Well first you'd get lost in a shoebox since you made another wrong turn," she snapped. "And second, you're insane if you think anyone is going to believe for even one second that *you* would be dating *me*."

Robby exhaled and glanced at his ringing phone. He silenced it and tossed his cigarette out the window before slowly turning around. "You've got to understand..." he began. "This is really going to mess with all of them."

"All of who?" Daisy noticed he didn't even deny her words. Her heart sank. Even if it was a lie, she longed for him to say he'd be thrilled to date her.

But Robby wasn't even having the same conversation.

"Everyone. The band will think I don't need them and the fans...well, everyone loves a good love story.

It's perfect," he said.

Yeah. It's perfect for you.

Her teeth hurt from clenching them, and she had to force her hands to relax when she noticed her nails digging into her palms. The man was one bundle short of a load.

As was the case so often, Daisy was being carried away by someone else's desires for her life and she was powerless to stop it. Her silence ensured it. But who was this guy to her anyway? Sure, he was Nick's nephew, but that wasn't her problem. Nick would understand her tossing him out on his ear and making him go to a hotel, or better yet, home, after what he'd done.

But something deep down told her not to do that, at least not yet. As her thoughts waged a war inside her, she was unprepared for Robby to take her hand, lift it to his lips and gently kiss her fingers.

He was playing her.

She hated herself for enjoying it. But it had been so very long since anyone had touched her…

Robby pulled the truck into a deserted parking lot and set the brake. His eyes searched her face.

Just a man in need.

"Things should be easier for you. Let me help," he said, the words a sincere promise she wanted to believe. His voice was gentle, caressing her ear, silken and sensual. "I mean, in exchange for the help with my career. I'm…not a bad person. I've got to have my life back." Robby drew a deep breath. "Will you help me? I can't do this without you." The sincere pleading in his voice was unsettling. He was a human being.

She refused to turn his way. If she did she'd be powerless to say what she really thought. "No one would believe it," she whispered.

"Come on, Harpo," Robby pleaded. "You'd lose your house to save your pride? We'll do this while I'm here helping Nick...that's what? Two weeks or so? Max?" Robby leaned across the seat so that his lips were near her ear as he spoke in a whisper.

"Come on. I'm hot, I'm rich, I'm an excellent kisser..." he paused when she squirmed as if he were ready to seal the deal. He dropped his voice low so it came out husky and tempting against her ear. "I'm even better at...other things."

Daisy's head spun and they were nose-to-nose. Even Alec hadn't done this to her. She was certain her physical response to his offer was nothing to be proud of. Her father's face popped into her mind and she forcefully pushed Robby back to his own side of the truck. Her father was a man of God, respectful and kind, but also driven by the rules of the Bible. Daisy had been raised better than to fall into Robby's lustful trap.

"I don't want your money," she stammered, brushing Robby's touch from her arms in an effort to make the tingling sensations stop. "And I definitely do not want your body!"

"Humph...you'd be the first," he grunted, seeming to forget himself.

"Not everyone is like that."

"Right, so when you realized who I was, why did you help me?"

It wasn't difficult for Daisy to give an honest answer. "I was nice to you even before I put it together." She looked at her lap, feeling silly and uncultured, but forging ahead anyway. "I did it because I...it's what I was supposed to do. When someone needs help, you help them. It's basic Sunday School."

Robby smiled. "Well, I will be forever grateful to you and all of your Sunday school teachers..." He kissed her hand and she was suddenly aware he'd never let it go in the first place. Daisy yanked herself away and scowled at him.

Robby grinned. "We can break up in a few weeks. Happens all the time. No big deal and you'll be free to go on with your life, never again thinking of the way you slummed with me."

"If that's how lightly you take relationships it is a bigger deal than you think," she said.

Daisy longed to take him to Nick's house and forget about him, but unfortunately, Robby's uncle had more than one bottle of alcohol, and if the singer was left alone she didn't know what would happen. She'd never forgive herself, and she doubted Nick would either, if he hurt himself or slipped back into his old habits. Making Robby go away was out of the question, but that didn't mean she'd be forced to agree to this. She hadn't liked babysitting when she was younger and she didn't want to babysit a grown man now. But most of all, she didn't want to pretend with her fragile, empty heart that she was in love with him.

Trusting herself seemed impossible. If she was pretending, she might become unable to recognize the difference between fact and fiction. That was her problem with Alec too. Her stomach turned.

"Say the word and you got twenty grand to bail you out," Robby continued. "Even more if you throw in the ballad."

"No," Daisy said adamantly. "Forget about the song!"

Robby groaned. "Why?" He was whining like a child. Daisy wondered when was the last time anyone denied him anything.

She glanced out her window as he started the truck and drove for a few minutes. He stopped at a red light. She looked back at him. Robby reached for her hand again but she pulled away.

"I told you before to stop touching me!"

Robby took a drink of his milkshake. "I promise to be really nice," he said. "And hey, the little charade could spice up whatever boring life you've been leading up till now. I mean—you've been stuck in that house for a year and I got you out. Imagine what more we'd accomplish if you do this."

Humph. That's exactly the problem.

"You aren't selling me," she said, though she already was thinking that twenty thousand dollars was a lot of money for about two weeks' worth of work.

"We'd get our pictures taken, go out to some nice restaurants...it wouldn't be bad," Robby pleaded. "You'll be famous." He said this as if fame fixed all of life's problems. Then again, for him, it would, or so it seemed. What did he know of Daisy's life? Fame meant her life would be splashed across the newspapers, tabloid magazines, and the internet. She wondered briefly how that would affect her business. Although having her debts forgiven might lighten the heavy worry she'd been living with for so long.

"Twenty thousand?" she asked, slowly raising her eyes to meet Robby's. She wondered for a brief moment if she'd gone crazy. He smiled, nodding.

"And the song?" His voice rose with hope.

"No." She extended her hand and he shook it firmly.

"You drive a hard bargain," he said with a smile. Against her good judgment, she'd made a deal. Days ago it would have seemed crazy, and yet Daisy smiled genuinely back at him, accepting the peace that settled over her as she did.

10

Robby and Daisy fell into amicable conversation and even enjoyed several belly laughs as they drove around late into the night. Robby forgot the last time he had such good and easy fun. He wasn't trying to impress Daisy and there was nothing for him to prove since he wasn't trying to sleep with her or date her. She was so astounded to be out of the house that she stared at everything and hardly seemed interested in him much of the time. It was good to talk to someone who didn't want something from him, but instead just enjoyed his company.

But you want something from her, a voice inside Robby urged. Irritated, he pushed it aside. Was it wrong to like the lyrics she'd written? He hardly thought so. He figured that it wouldn't take him long to talk her into giving them over. In the meantime, he'd work on the music and put it all together. Surely if she listened to the song when it was produced she'd stop fighting him.

Robby pulled into Daisy's driveway after one o'clock in the morning. He parked the truck in her garage as she instructed.

"I doubt anyone would come here searching for you but if that reporter already figured it out..." she stifled a yawn. Robby nodded, noting that his own fatigue was setting in as well. He helped her inside and Daisy showed him the guest room before going to her own bedroom. As she closed the door behind her, she paused and said, "Good night, Robby. Thanks."

"Yeah," his voice cracked as he stared at her bedroom door. He wanted to thank her too, but he didn't. Had anyone ever been so kind to him without motive? Daisy had done that—despite her instincts telling her different. It was difficult to swallow. He made a mental note to give her an extra five thousand after this whole thing was all over—lyrics or not.

~*~

Hours later, Robby awoke to a woman's voice screaming and weeping.

It's a dream, he thought until it started again. He was awake enough to know it wasn't in his head. Where was he? For a brief moment, it seemed his drinking had led him into yet another unbelievable situation. The curtains were frilly and green, the walls a light purple illuminated by a small nightlight that was shaped like a flower at the other side of the room.

Robby shook his head. He was sober.

And the screaming wouldn't stop.

Robby tried to block out the noise with a soft pillow but it seemed to grow more desperate the longer he waited.

Irritated, he threw off the covers and stood, wearing only a pair of boxer shorts. With a sigh, he ran his fingers through his hair and walked to the door as it dawned on him where he was. He tiptoed across the hall and listened to the mayhem.

"No!" she squealed. "Stop!"

Robby opened the door and found her thrashing about, her covers tossed aside.

He kicked the edge of the bed in annoyance. "Wake up, you're having a nightmare."

But Daisy's fighting only grew worse. "No!" she shouted again. "Stop! Please!"

Robby yawned as he sat beside her on the bed, trying to blink his eyes enough times that he remembered he was human. It wasn't working.

"Hey..." he said, gently nudging her. "Wake up."

But she was somewhere else, the nightmare holding her hostage. Robby fixed the covers and crawled into bed next to her, wrapping her in his arms to still her.

"Shhh..." he whispered, his own fatigue almost claiming him. He yawned and started singing, "Sweet little flower...perfect and right. How did you end up in my messed up life, oh Daisy..." Robby continued singing for a moment, relishing Daisy's small, frightened body against him. She settled quickly and melted into him as he held her. Complete contentment washed over him. He helped her—just because. It was so simple it frightened him. The old Robby would have screamed and told her to shut up because she was ruining his sleep. Or worse, he would have been passed out, too drunk to even hear her cries.

Finally, it seemed he did something right—and for someone who desperately needed it. Robby smiled and sang some more.

He meant to stay only for a few minutes, but the fatigue finally overtook him and he fell asleep while holding Daisy against him.

~*~

Daisy awoke the next morning more refreshed

than she'd been in a long time. Most mornings she was exhausted, as if she'd spent the whole night fighting a war. She didn't think she had nightmares, or at least she didn't remember them, but she struggled to get to sleep and once she was sleeping, to stay that way. Rest eluded her—she was always awake and thinking. But that morning she was warm and fulfilled and it made no sense.

And better still, instead of nightmares, Daisy was dreaming. Someone was kissing her neck, which seemed impossible since there hadn't ever been a man in her bed.

Boy, was she lonely.

What a delicious, amazing dream. She let herself fade into the embrace until a voice rang out.

"Daisy! Where are you? It's nearly noon."

Daisy woke with a start, realizing she wasn't in bed alone. Robby's arms were wrapped around her, his strong, long legs tangled in her dead ones.

"Hey!" she whispered, trying to push away from him. "What are you doing? I thought we were clear on the…touching."

Robby stirred slightly and Daisy gaped at him to find he was grinning, one eye opened and looking at her. "You didn't mind a minute ago…or all night for that matter, Angel."

Daisy groaned. "Shut up and stay put," she demanded, tossing a blanket over him so that he was hidden. There was no time to think. She ignored his comment but was ashamed of herself nonetheless. She'd never invited a man to her bed, and now that one was there, she couldn't remember if anything happened. That wasn't saying much for Robby or the skills he'd bragged about the night before.

Daisy wondered how she was going to get out of this.

The door opened and Jennifer and Sadie stood there, worried.

"Are you OK?" Sadie asked, holding up a cup of coffee. "It's late. We called a bunch of times..."

Daisy forced a fake yawn as she nodded. "I'm sorry. It was a rough night," she said, trying to sound pathetic. Her sleeping problems were familiar to them all. "Give me a few minutes and I'll get dressed."

Jennifer regarded the mound of blankets curiously. "Maybe you need sleeping pills."

"I'm fine!" Daisy said a little too loudly as Robby tickled her side. She grabbed his hand and held it firmly. He giggled, but to Daisy's relief, the women missed it.

Sadie stepped back a moment, now considering the mound of blankets. Robby's toes were poking out, but just barely. Sadie touched the blanket pile with one finger, which brought a muffled giggle. She jumped back, shocked.

"Daisy!" she squealed. "Who is that?"

Daisy feigned horror. "What? No one!" she tried to look sick. "I'm still not feeling well. Maybe you guys should go..."

Sadie reached over and yanked the covers away, the light exposing Robby.

He squinted, grinning at Daisy. "Sorry, baby," he said. "I'm ticklish."

Daisy rolled her eyes in irritation. He would turn this into a disaster.

"I thought you were Vanilla," she muttered. What was she doing sleeping with Nick's nephew? It was obscene. It didn't matter that nothing actually happened, Daisy's nightgown slid a bit higher than it should have, exposing much of her legs, and Robby was wearing only a pair of shorts—revealing his bare torso, which Daisy noted was nearly covered in tattoos.

Sadie and Jennifer continued to stare at them. Finally, Sadie pointed. "You're...you're..." she stopped and grinned as she turned her attention to her friend. "Daisy...you got some 'splainin' to do."

Daisy made a face. She was clueless what he was doing in her bed. Would she regret anything? Had he taken her agreement to go along with the charade as permission to do what he wanted with her? Her head was spinning and showed no sign of stopping.

For his part, Robby yawned rather calmly and lazily as he ran his fingers through his hair. Clearly, this situation was of no consequence to him.

Did he insist on being so perfect first thing in the morning? Daisy was sure her hair was sticking up in all directions and her breath could rival that of a dragon.

"You were in here screaming and thrashing last night and it woke me up," Robby explained as he threw his arm around Daisy's shoulders. "So I came in to check it out but you calmed down when I sang to you. I guess I fell asleep too." He said it so simply that it all seemed quite rational.

Sadie sighed dreamily, but Daisy feared she'd be sick. He was not helping and he was not going to be able to stay with her any longer. The deal was off.

Jennifer smacked Sadie, who winced. "OK, so what is he doing here?" she asked. After only a short pause, she continued, annoyed. "Well?"

Daisy flinched as Robby casually used the arm that was around her shoulders to pull her closer against him. "I'm the new pool boy," he announced with a grin.

Daisy pushed him away. "I told you not to touch me!" She turned back to her friends. "He showed up last night...we went to visit Nick. He asked if Robby could stay until he's out of the hospital." She threw a glance in Robby's direction. "But I'm quite sure he thought you'd stay in the guest room."

Jennifer stared at Daisy, her mouth hanging open. Sadie poked her, though she too appeared shocked.

Here it comes...

"You left the house?" Sadie asked softly. "Like...left the house in a car?"

Daisy nodded awkwardly. "He tossed me into his truck, against my will."

Sadie chuckled and Jennifer nudged her. "You rode in a car...and now he's staying with you?" She shook her head. "Wait till I tell Steve."

"But it's not..." Daisy started.

Robby cleared his throat and tossed his arm around Daisy's shoulders again. She really wished he'd stop doing that. "Uh, we're not exactly telling a lot of people I'm here. You feel me?" he paused. "For Nick's sake. Of course."

The women nodded as Daisy tried to shrug him off again. He grinned at her but refused to move. Instead, he leaned closer to her, nuzzling her neck with his nose and lips.

"Knock it off..." Daisy groaned, pushing at him.

"Of course," Jennifer said, backing toward the door. "Far be it from us to interrupt the...festivities."

Sadie grinned broadly. Daisy truly wanted to set the whole thing right, but her friends understood her well enough to believe she was telling the truth. Still, it didn't look good that she was in bed with a man who was still a stranger.

Sadie recovered first from the shock. "We'll come back when you two are decent."

Robby laughed as he kissed Daisy's cheek and growled. "Don't remember the last time I was described as...decent."

Sadie chuckled as Jennifer elbowed her. "Right. Why don't you call us later? No telling how long this might last." Sadie set the coffee cup on Daisy's dresser. "Hey, Robby. She's a sucker for a man in cologne." She cleared her throat and leaned toward him conspiratorially. "Of course, she claims she's saving herself for marriage, so you don't stand a chance anyway."

"Sadie!" Daisy squawked in horror. Sadie and Robby grinned at one another and he nodded, seeming to appreciate the information. Daisy promised to give Sadie a piece of her mind later. Why did it matter that she was still a virgin at nearly thirty years old? Robby might be the last person who needed that information. She feared he'd taunt her for being a child.

Jennifer grabbed Sadie's arm and pulled her toward the door. "If you two aren't busy tonight, stop by my place for a bonfire around eight," she said. "We'd love it if you'd come!"

She yanked the door closed behind her, but Daisy heard them giggling as they left. She sighed heavily, noticing Robby enjoying the whole thing. She tried to ignore him as she flopped back against the pillows. He lay beside her, touching her hair.

"Saving yourself?" he asked tenderly. "I didn't realize women did that anymore." He studied her face as he spoke as if hoping she'd tell him more. But she didn't want him to mock her choices. She rolled her eyes and sat up.

Robby followed suit "What?" He chuckled. "It's...classy," he said sincerely. Daisy strangely believed him.

"It's not anyone's business." She didn't want to open up to him but in that moment, he regarded her so sincerely that she turned away. "I...wanted it to be something for my husband. I hoped my marriage would be special." She hated that her voice caught on the word. There wouldn't be a husband, and Daisy meant to convince herself she was all right with that.

But with no parents or siblings, she was alone in the world, and the notion that a husband and the family he'd bring with him were no longer possibilities was sometimes a crushing weight. Daisy wondered briefly if she shouldn't throw caution to the wind and make Robby a one-night stand, but her upbringing kept her too reasonable to allow it. She was smarter than that. And that careless behavior had no promise of making her happy in the end. If anything, she'd be emptier than ever. She forced a smile at Robby as she pushed herself to the edge of the bed and struggled to get into her wheelchair. He regarded her quietly.

"So what happened last night?" he asked. "Was it a nightmare?"

Daisy adjusted herself as she looked away from him with a shrug. "Probably. That's all I have."

And with that, she left him in her bed.

11

Robby went back to the guest room and sat on his bed, shocked Daisy had been able to surprise him yet again. She was a...a virgin?

It made Robby terribly ashamed of his past. He had to write a song about her. Trouble was she could write her own—the one she refused to give to him was evidence of that. Maybe he should forget it. Then again, she didn't boast enough money in her account to buy dinner, let alone defend herself in a court case against him. He scoffed. Even if that made sense months ago, he refused to consider it now.

There was too much to this woman that he needed to investigate. She'd even get along with Warren. He smiled, thinking of his mountain of a brother meeting tiny, fragile Daisy. But despite what was obviously a challenging life, she still oozed love to everyone around her. Robby wished she'd talk to him. The minute he thought they were going to really get into a deep conversation she pulled away. Since he only met her a day ago, he didn't blame her for not trusting him just yet.

Robby's suitcase lay open on the floor near the closet. Last night he'd just yanked out what he needed for bed without bothering to unpack. But now he had work to do. He ignored several calls and texts from his agent and bodyguard—both of whom wanted to know where he was. They could wait. He dug out his running clothes and put them on, intent on using exercise rather than alcohol to escape. He wanted to get his head straight before he called anyone.

But he wasn't yet to the door of his room when his cell phone rang.

"I'm fine, Lil," he said.

"Well, you shouldn't be. I am going to come to...to...wherever you are and change that." Lily shouted into his ear. "Where on earth do you get off running out of town and not even telling me how to get hold of you? And without Jazz? You weren't answering your phone. I just contacted a private detective to find you." It sounded like she'd started to hyperventilate, but before Robby defended himself, she finished with, "You can't protect yourself if a lunatic decides to...to..."

Robby smiled. Lily Horton had been his manager for the better part of fifteen years. She'd been with him through really serious stuff and she'd never once wavered, often acting more as his mother than his business manager. Robby respected her because she told the truth—even when he didn't want to listen. More than once he'd fired her and more than once she'd ignored the directive. The longer he was sober, the more he recognized how bad his treatment of her had been.

"I'm fine," he said again. "There wasn't time to call. My uncle fell and broke his leg, and with Warren leaving for Iraq I was the only one to take care of things on such short notice."

Lily snorted. "Don't tell me Mac was telling the truth," she said with a moan, but as usual didn't bother waiting for Robby to respond. "Heavens above, Robby! How are we going to do this when you're in the middle of nowhere?"

Robby sighed and ran his fingers through his hair. He was itching for a cigarette. He had enough to deal with. His problems might have to wait.

"Don't go sending the cavalry out yet," Robby paused. "Can I get some time to myself? To think? And, hey, McAllister has me working on a love song for some movie."

"Yeah—you and about thirty other songwriters." The silence on the other end of the phone stretched for nearly a minute. "You drinking again? Word on the street is the guys dumped you and...I...don't want it to be true, Robby. You worked so hard."

Robby's heart sank. He thought Lily believed in him. He wondered if he'd waited too long to get it together. Perhaps there wasn't a chance for him anymore. Maybe no one would ever believe in him.

"Of course it isn't true. I worked hard to get sober and I'm staying that way." Robby cleared his throat. "Besides...I'm here with Nick's neighbor..."

"Oh...I get it," Lily paused and her tone changed. She sounded like she was smiling now. "That's the girl, is it?"

"But, how did you...?"

"I talked to Mac, remember?"

Robby sat on the bed and leaned back against a stack of fluffy pillows. "Should I even read it?" Mac usually spun stories so they were almost impossible to believe, and they were rarely flattering. It might be enough to destroy Robby this time. He should have been less impulsive. How could he have said Daisy was his girlfriend?

"For once he didn't do too bad, but..." Lily paused to clear her throat and then she chuckled. "You owe him a lot of money for the camera. Anyway, she's a pretty girl. Never thought you'd go for that classy type."

Robby wondered if he should tell Lily everything. Daisy's situation didn't bother him, at least not yet anyway. He wasn't serious so what did it matter? He was surprised to find he was too intrigued by her to care.

"She's crazy-beautiful. And you're right—probably way out of my league," he said. "But, Mac showed up at the right time for a good misunderstanding. I let him believe what he wanted to."

"Got it," Lily said. "Now, why don't you spill it? I don't like surprises."

"OK, but only if you promise not to send Jazz out yet," Robby said. He knew she'd agree to anything he asked. At least if she was clear on the story she might also be able to help him get the song he was after.

~*~

Daisy was in the kitchen cooking something that smelled heavenly when Robby entered twenty minutes later. Her friends were gone and now she was dressed in jeans and an adorable button down blouse. Robby wondered at the effortless way she transitioned from sweet and rumpled morning Daisy to the cute cook working in the kitchen. Maybe if she weren't so attractive, stealing the song would be easier. Of course, he'd wrecked the lives of other beautiful women before.

The difference was they knew what they were in for but she's innocent, Robby reminded himself.

"You want some breakfast?" Daisy asked, her attention on the pancake she flipped easily in the pan. "I made coffee..." Robby sat and began putting on his running shoes.

"I'm going for a quick jog. But it smells great. Save me some..."

Daisy turned toward him and sized up his gear. Her mouth curled upward into an adorable smile. "You're a runner?"

Robby laughed. "I'm slow, but I try. It helps me not smoke as much. When I want a cigarette, I make myself go for a run. I figure I'll eventually be able to kick the habit," he said as he tied his shoes. "And if not at least I'll be in better shape..."

"Hmm...good for you," she said, setting another pancake on a short stack near the stove top. "I'll be in my office getting some work done. I can leave these here for you."

Robby nodded and started for the door. "Is there a good place for me to run? I mean, where I'm not going to cause a commotion?"

Daisy turned to him and pointed toward the main road he'd come in on. "No one comes or goes this way other than Nick, Sadie, Jennifer and her fiancé, Steve. You're pretty safe to run to the crossroads and back. That'd be at least three miles. If you're sure you won't get lost..."

Robby laughed as he stood and surveyed the cabinets. "Glasses?" he asked. Daisy pointed to one near his chest. He nodded and grabbed one as she got a cup of coffee and moved into the next room. Since he hadn't gotten much of a tour, Robby assumed it was her office. She left the door open. It was astounding that she so easily trusted him in her home.

Their conversation about the previous day's events, and what their deal actually meant, would have to wait. At that moment, all he wanted to do was run. So, he got himself a huge glass of water, took a few good drinks and stuffed his ear buds into his ears so he could escape into his workout.

~*~

Several hours later, Daisy was in her office working when Jennifer and Sadie showed up, slamming the door behind them. Both women were carrying boxes full of wedding invitations. It was already nearly three o'clock and they were off for the day. They'd come with a lot of questions Daisy had no answers for.

"Where's Mr. Wonderful?" Sadie asked, not wasting any time as she curiously peered toward the kitchen. She set the heavy box on a nearby work table. Daisy shrugged as if she didn't care when in reality she was wondering the same thing herself.

Nick, too, called to check in, but there was little to report. Once Robby returned from his run dripping with sweat, he drank several large glasses of water, ate the entire stack of pancakes she left for him, and went to take a shower. He played his guitar and sang in his bedroom, but she was working and so was he, which meant there was no conversation between them. His presence in her home was unsettling. Daisy was confused about why she was keeping an eye on him when he didn't seem to do a whole lot of anything.

"My foot, you don't care," Sadie said. "What's he wearing?"

Daisy kept her eyes on her computer screen and

she continued typing. "Last I saw him, he was wearing running clothes—shorts and a T-shirt with shoes that probably cost as much as this house...but now, I don't know what he's got on. I've been working," she said. "He's in his room...I think he's writing a song."

Jennifer and Sadie exchanged glances as they unpacked the boxes and began sorting through the invitations. "You take Steve's side," Jennifer instructed. "Start in alphabetical order and check them off as you go so we don't forget where we stopped." Sadie nodded as she sat down.

"You shouldn't need to babysit a grown man," Jennifer said. "What was Nick thinking?" Daisy shrugged, glancing toward the door to the kitchen, hoping their voices failed to reach back as far as Robby's room. Daisy learned years ago her opinionated friends didn't mind sharing their thoughts and letting the chips fall where they may. Daisy was quieter and more reserved than those two would ever dream of being.

"Hmph," Sadie said with a grin as she stacked invitations and dug through the box nearby. She came up with a calligraphy pen and raised her eyebrows in Daisy's direction. "I'd do it. With that hair and those tattoos, I can't imagine how you're keeping your hands to yourself, Daze..."

"Judging by this morning she isn't." Jennifer started on her stack of invitations.

Daisy glanced toward the door. "Guys, please. He's a few feet away."

Still grinning, Sadie stood and went to close the door. "Has he kissed you yet?" she whispered. "I bet he'd be amazing..."

"Well, that's what he tells me..." Daisy said under

her breath.

"Sadie!" Jennifer exclaimed, shaking her head. "Daisy knows better than to..."

"To what? *Mom*?" Sadie countered. Jennifer stuck her tongue out and both women laughed.

Daisy needed to put an end to their false impressions. Clearly, nothing was going to happen with Robby unless she was anxious to get hurt. The man was reclusive, annoying, and most importantly, leaving very soon.

"That's enough," Daisy snapped. "There isn't anything going on that shouldn't be, and it's going to stay that way. He's not even staying very long. I mean, Nick will be out of the hospital in a few days, right, Jen?"

Jennifer shrugged as she continued writing out an address. "I stopped in, and the doctor said he was still in a lot of pain. She wanted to keep an eye on him until all of the swelling went down. Might be a week. Maybe more."

Daisy's stomach sank. *A week?* She drew a deep breath. She was tough enough for that. Well, maybe. Any more than that and she wasn't sure.

"Anyway, Daisy, I hate to tell you that it's all over the news that Robby is in Pittsburgh with some new girlfriend, and writing a solo record," Jennifer continued. "You wouldn't happen to be that girlfriend would you?"

Sadie squealed. "We'll bring more lip gloss."

Jennifer stopped addressing the envelope in front of her. She looked up. "I don't think a fling with him is a good idea...do you?"

Sadie looked disappointed. "Do you think it's a good idea for her to sit here alone all the time, rehashing what happened?"

The women exchanged a glance, neither willing to state the obvious issue.

"Knock it off," Daisy said. She stopped working and finally turned to her friends.

Jennifer met her eyes sympathetically. While she was often overprotective of Daisy, it wasmeant in good faith. "A man will say he loves you and mean it," she said softly. "But I'm not sure someone like...Robby is that sort of guy."

Daisy reminded herself numerous times that she shouldn't judge Robby based on his face, tattoos, or celebrity since he probably didn't care for that any more than she did. She hoped her friends understood. "He needs a friend...It's fine. I can be his friend."

The women regarded her skeptically. *OK, so he would be a gorgeous, hunk of a friend. But he was never going to be more than that.*

"Besides," Daisy continued with a sigh. "We don't really know much about him. I doubt the media tells you who the real Robby Grant is. I need to give him a chance to be a human being. Honestly, I wonder if he knows how."

Jennifer shook her head. "I still think you need to be careful." The women were quiet for several long moments as they worked. Daisy was finding it increasingly difficult to concentrate. Should she be honest with her friends that she found Robby attractive? And worse, was she crazy for thinking that way?

"How can you be sure a guy is being honest? I mean, when he says he loves you?" Sadie asked, finally breaking the silence. "I'm still waiting on that one myself."

Jennifer sat back in her chair, her eyes far-off, likely dreaming of the man she was soon to marry. Daisy wanted to go back to work, not see her friend's sheer joy. Of course, Daisy didn't begrudge Jennifer her happiness, but the pain it brought her to watch everyone else succeed was sometimes tough to stomach.

"When he looks you in the eye and it's as if a thousand years pass in one second, like you've never not loved him and known he was the one for you," Jennifer said dreamily. "That's how you know he means it."

Sadie sighed.

Right there with you, Daisy thought but said nothing.

"Come on, Daisy…you were in love, weren't you?" Sadie asked as she reached for another stack of invitations. "I mean…before…" She flushed for having brought it up, but Daisy reassured her with a smile.

"I thought I was," she said. "But love isn't something trite you can walk away from. And he did, so…I was wrong."

Sadie grabbed another envelope and yanked the cap from her calligraphy pen. "Well if I can find a man who isn't afraid of me I'm sure I'll be in love," she said. "The pickings sure are slim around here, though."

"So, stop scaring all of the men," Daisy said with a laugh.

Sadie put a box lid on top of her head and twisted her mouth, making a goofy face. "Think I'm doing something wrong?" she asked in a strange voice. The women laughed. The moment reminded Daisy that she wasn't alone and that she'd been blessed to have such good friends.

~*~

Daisy, Sadie, and Jennifer made progress on their work for another half hour, each lost in her thoughts.

As they worked, Robby entered as if he was searching for the stage, his guitar strapped around him. "Ladies..." He grinned widely, his white teeth sparkling.

Daisy tried to avoid his eyes, but somehow, he caught her attention and winked. Warmth rushed to her cheeks. But when the satisfaction of her response to him became clear in his eyes, Daisy was irritated. He realized what he was doing to her, and worse, he liked it.

She wondered why she begrudged him her kindness. Yesterday he'd shown up alone and clearly broken—it was a reflex to take him in and help him. Today he was clean and in control. She didn't want to like him for fear she would fall into a trap and make a fool of herself, get hurt, or maybe both. Her thoughts were wrong. She needed to try and find a little compassion to treat him more honorably than she wanted to.

Out the corner of her eye, Daisy noticed Jennifer and Sadie quietly start to pack their things into the boxes they'd brought. She begged them silently not to leave her with him, though Robby seemed to disregard their presence as he leaned against the desk, easily and almost mindlessly strumming his guitar. The rhythm was slow but intentional. He appeared to be working something out. Daisy tried not to write lyrics in her mind as he played.

Sadie cleared her throat, and Daisy glanced in her

direction in time to catch the lip gloss she tossed her way. Sadie winked, while Daisy glared and set the lip gloss aside, turning her attention back to her work. She wondered if mental telepathy worked and begged her friends to stay. There was safety in numbers. But it was clear they were leaving her alone with him. Some friends.

Daisy was too intent on her work to notice Robby stop strumming. He leaned over to take her hand out of her lap and raised it slowly to his lips where he kissed it open-palm. Daisy groaned inside.

Not Valentino.

The man was good. Too good.

She yanked her hand away and tried her best to scowl at him. "I told you not to touch me."

Robby grinned. "Put on your best dress," he said. "I'm taking you to dinner." Daisy tried to ignore him but he stood firm.

When Daisy failed to acknowledge him, he sighed loudly, punctuating it with a groan. "You do own a dress, don't you?"

"What about the blue one, Daisy? It's amazing on you." Sadie chimed in as she finished filling her box. Daisy glared at her in disbelief while Robby's eyes lit up.

"There you go. The blue one," he said, lowering his voice. "But you'd look amazing in any color, angel." He resumed strumming as if the conversation were over.

He was not getting off that easy.

Daisy went back to work, keeping her mouth in a firm line. "My job is to keep you out of trouble," she said. "I don't have to...to fraternize with you."

Robby acted as if this was hilarious and he openly

howled before going back to strumming his guitar. "She doesn't want to fraternize, doesn't want to fraternize, but all I want is some burgers and fries," he sang in his best country twang.

Daisy fought a smile. He was creative, spontaneous and even sweet. What was her problem? He wasn't the enemy.

No, but pain is, she reminded herself. *And he will only bring pain.*

Robby stopped strumming. "My agent got us reservations, Harpo. I'm bored. I have to go somewhere for crying out loud."

Jennifer shoved another box of invitations at Sadie and dragged her toward the door as Sadie mouthed "Harpo?"

"We, uh, gotta get going," Jennifer said. "We'll catch you guys later, all right? Don't forget about the bonfire at eight."

Robby saluted her and Sadie as they ducked out of the office, yanking the door closed behind them. Daisy went back to work as Robby took his guitar off and set it aside. He tried to move closer to her but she nudged him away to open a drawer in her desk.

Robby picked up a paperweight and tossed it from one hand to the other. As she slammed the drawer, he put the paperweight down and kneeled in front of her, turning her wheelchair so they were facing one another.

"We need to go out in public if our love story is going to work."

A laugh bubbled up inside her and slipped out right into Robby's face. "There is no...love story, Robby...and I'm no actress."

He put a finger under her chin and met her eyes.

"Twenty grand says there is, sweetheart. We need to spend time together—talk about everything so this isn't so...awkward when we're out in the big time."

What did he mean? Daisy wondered, although deep down she understood. And as much as she hated to admit it, he was right. She'd agreed to this, but she was having second, third, and fourth thoughts. She was an idiot.

Daisy pushed her chair back and started typing again. Robby stood and got behind her chair where he began massaging her shoulders. She clung to her strength, but this might be her undoing. His touch was light but purposeful, and it was breaking her will.

"Come on, Harpo, you're the total package," he said. "Blonde, blue eyes...I'm sure I'm not the first man to say you're gorgeous—it's a triple threat. And as long as everything still works, who cares if you're a little short?" Robby paused as if he realized for the first time she wasn't a complete woman.

"Wait. You aren't defective, are you? Your stuff still works...?" For a moment, he stopped rubbing her shoulders and gestured awkwardly over her body.

Repulsed by his animal nature, Daisy shook him off and began typing again. "The doctor says so, but I wouldn't know," she said. Robby leaned beside her again. She inhaled. He was wearing cologne.

Inwardly she groaned again, knowing that even with her best efforts at resistance, the deal was done. She glanced at him, forcing herself to be strong even as she met his sparkling eyes. "This ends when Nick gets home, and don't forget I'm only doing this for my house," she said. "I've got no real interest in helping you."

Robby went back to strumming. "Heaven forbid."

He played a short tune, focusing on his finger placement. "Just remember this has to be convincing." He slowly walked out of the office.

Daisy nodded, wondering if the blue dress from a small town dress shop would work for wherever they were going. "That is what you get when you play pretend with a department store girl," she said to herself with a sigh.

12

Robby returned to his room and threw open his closet doors. He'd hung his nicer clothes and thrown the rest into drawers. Might as well get comfortable since he was going to stay a while. As he started dressing, he noticed he'd missed numerous calls from Jazz, Lily, and McAllister, not to mention three each from Nick and Warren. He set his clothes out on the bed, wondering whether to wear a tie. It might impress Daisy but ties were the work of the devil.

Daisy was intriguing but tough. She wasn't going to give that song to him without a fight, and yet he'd already started to set the lyrics to music, figuring that might make it easier to convince her to hand it over. And yet he was willing to pay handsomely if she would sing it for him. He was sure Daisy had the voice of an angel—and a duet with her would ensure his new career was solid because it would also mean he had his own protégé.

As Robby began to imagine it, his cell phone buzzed again. Though he didn't want to answer he reluctantly pushed the button and pressed the phone to his ear. "Yeah."

"Please tell me the paparazzi are doing what they always do and that this latest bit is the baloney I think it is." Warren's deep and irritated voice hit Robby hard. He gulped, wondering how to stall or change the subject.

"Mm...depends on the story."

"Don't pretend you don't know!" Warren screamed at him. "She is way too good for you, Rob, and if you hurt her I'm telling you I'll be the least of your worries. She's all Nick talks about."

Robby was sure Nick hadn't mentioned Daisy at all, but that wasn't saying a lot. He'd barely listened to his uncle's messages and certainly hadn't read his letters over the last few years. Now he wished he had taken the time to do so. Obviously, Warren was well-versed in his knowledge of Daisy and Uncle Nick's relationship. Now Robby just needed to get that same information. But how?

"You know about Daisy?" Robby asked as he stepped into his dress pants.

Warren laughed wryly. "Forget it. She isn't one of your bimbos."

"Hmm...so maybe you should come back here and..."

"I'm on my way to Iraq, idiot."

"It was a joke, moron," Robby said. "If you're in Iraq, how on earth do you have a clue what's going on in Pennsylvania?"

"I know everything. It's one of the perks of my position."

Robby didn't doubt there was at least some truth in that statement. His brother worked his way up in the military and established contacts all over the world. Finding someone wouldn't be hard for him. It explained how he'd found Robby in the gutter not so long ago.

"I gotta go," Warren said. "So promise me you won't be yourself, OK? Don't hurt this poor girl. Leave her be. The last few years were hard on her."

Robby's ears perked up and he lost focus on his image in the mirror. "What do you mean?"

"If you'd spend more time thinking about someone else there wouldn't be any surprises," Warren said. "I'm not telling you something it isn't possible for you to find out yourself."

"Yeah, whatever, desert storm."

"Rob."

"I'll behave—I promise," Robby said wondering how he could make people trust him. Didn't they all realize he was trying?

Warren released a deep breath and Robby held his as he waited for whatever else was on his brother's mind. He yanked his shirt over his arms and left it hanging open as he sprayed himself with expensive cologne. Daisy's friend said she was a sucker for men in cologne. Robby needed all the help that there was— if it took his best cologne, so be it.

"Everything else OK?" Warren asked. "The guys are all over me, but I keep telling them it's none of their business."

Robby smiled to himself. His brother did care.

"I'm good. Working on a new song." OK, so it wasn't the whole truth but it was close. "Goin' solo. Lil's setting up a band for me and Jazz will be heading this way soon. It's good."

"Nice. Listen, I gotta go. Think about what I said." Robby nodded as he said good-bye and hung up. He tried to imagine Nick's reaction to him taking Daisy out for dinner.

He pushed the question from his mind and continued getting ready for his first completely sober date in a long time.

~*~

A few short hours later, Robby and Daisy were seated in the corner of a high-class restaurant. Daisy informed him, with some awe, that it would have taken the average person months to get a seat in the place. Robby just smiled, unsure how to make her comfortable.

But no one bothered them. No autographs or photos, but Robby was certain—because he made sure of it—that the paparazzi would find them eventually. His fingers itched for the driving he soon would do to escape, hoping it wouldn't scare Daisy.

"How's everything?" he asked softly as Daisy picked at her dinner. She'd pulled her short, blonde hair back in two small sparkly clips on both sides of her face. The delicate hairstyle made her appear younger, but the effort to look her best wasn't lost on Robby. He noted as he sat across from her that she wasn't only stunning, but a woman he could spend a lot of time getting to know. But how did he find out her story without losing her completely? Their situation was precarious already, he didn't want to make it worse.

Daisy kept her eyes trained on her plate. "It's delicious," she said. "Yours?"

"It's good." Robby set his fork down and leaned across the table to capture her hand in his own. Surprised, Daisy raised her eyes. He smiled as he stroked her soft skin with his thumb.

"If we're going to do this it has to be all the way, angel," he said huskily. "Are you sure you're in?"

Daisy nodded, her face flushing with his touch. Robby cleared his throat, remembering his first date back in junior high. He'd taken the girl roller skating and she had the same look on her face that Daisy wore now—a mixture of nerves, hormones, and innocence. Her sweetness still shocked him. He wasn't enough for this girl—a farce of a relationship was all he'd be worth in her world.

"Listen, we got off to a rough start. I'm sorry," he continued stroking her hand, pleased she hadn't pulled away from him. "Nick's a lucky man," he said. "He can eat dinner with you whenever he wants."

Daisy blushed more deeply and took her hand away, placing it in her lap. Robby continued smiling at her and she weakly returned the gesture. He carefully moved his chair to the other side of the table where he placed one arm around the back of her wheelchair, holding her against his side. She inhaled sharply but said nothing as Robby rubbed her arm with his hand.

"You'll have to get close to me eventually," he whispered.

Daisy took a slow sip of water, remaining rigid and cold.

"So, when did you start writing music?" he asked, continuing to gently rub his hand over her bare shoulder. Her friend was right—the blue dress was incredible on her. It only made her more beautiful that she seemed clueless about how stunning she was. Robby dated many women who were fully aware of their appearance, but it was something when a woman lacked that knowledge. Daisy was innocent and a bit naïve, but classic in her beauty. More importantly, her heart was precious, and Robby liked it. He'd spent too much time with women who were filled with street-smarts. With them, relationships were a game—one where honesty would only bring loss.

Daisy shrugged, still refusing to look at him. "I'm not sure," she said softly. "A long time."

"Will you sing for me?" he said. "I'd love to hear you."

She laughed, unsure. "I'm terrible."

Robby laughed, relieved she was no longer pulling away from him. "I find that hard to believe."

Daisy didn't say anything for a moment. Finally, she raised her eyes and met his. "This is silly."

Robby's heart thumped but he tried to regain control. Why was he nervous? "What's silly? Dinner and conversation?"

"Yes...no..." Daisy groaned. "This whole thing. No one is going to believe that you and I...It's ridiculous."

Robby realized she was serious. The wheelchair. She was more hung up on it than he was. He touched her cheek gently with one finger. "No one's going to doubt that I want to date a beautiful woman. I do it all the time. I'm a certified professional boyfriend."

Daisy blushed again, Robby continuing in a low whisper. He turned his head so his lips were near her ear. "But in order to make this believable, we need to talk to one another, spend time together," he reached up and curled a strand of her hair around his finger. "We're going to let the photogs get their way for a bit so I keep myself at the front of my fans' minds until I come out with a new song."

Daisy gulped and nodded. "Can we talk?" she asked, her voice wavering.

Robby shrugged. "Anything—ask away," he said confidently leaning back in his seat.

Daisy thought for a moment and nodded. "OK. Why did you stop drinking and are you sure you're done?"

Robby's breath flew from him in a rush. That was a surprise. And yet there she was, waiting for an answer. "Yeesh," he said softly, sitting up straighter. "All right."

Daisy seemed to be glad she made him uncomfortable. She grinned, batting her long eyelashes.

He laughed, unsure where to begin. "OK—in rehab this last time it was like everyone gave up. The only person who came to visit was Warren...oh, and Jazz, my bodyguard—not my girlfriend or my parents, not even Uncle Nick. The press even gave up on me, and they love a good celebrity implosion—but I was finally old news. I started to wonder why I kept doing this to myself, but I didn't know how to stop—and I saw Warren and the things I admired most about him." Robby paused, thinking. He might not have planned to talk about this, but he trusted Daisy so he forged ahead, even if it did feel like one of his early therapy sessions.

"He was a real man. He cared for me as a brother, showed me what love was. I never had a clue—maybe part of me still doesn't understand it, but I'm trying. I...I want to be like him, strong and secure in myself. I don't want to need that kind of life now. I should just be able to make music and not care what people think..." He paused, meeting Daisy's eyes with a smile.

"So, yes, I'm done. I messed up when the band dumped me, but...as far as I'm concerned it's all behind me."

Robby pressed her closer against him with one arm. "There has to be more to life than women, drinking, and partying, right?" He grinned mischievously as he gazed into her blue eyes. "Well, I don't have to give it *all* up." He wiggled his eyebrows as if they shared a private understanding.

Daisy managed a giggle. Robby glanced around the restaurant but found no one was paying them any mind. Somehow, it didn't bother him.

"Too much information?" he asked. She shrugged as Robby noticed an inquisitive man speaking to the hostess and gesturing in Robby's direction. The hostess vehemently shook her head and tried to nudge the man away, but he continued to persist. Robby grinned, urging Daisy closer against him.

"Score one for team Harpo," he whispered into her ear.

~*~

Daisy's insides were becoming accustomed to Robby's effect on her, though she wasn't sure she liked bouncing between nervous, excited, and sometimes irritated in minutes. He touched her every chance he got through the rest of dessert, even feeding her at one point. And when she resisted, he grew more adamant that she get closer to him. And his persuasion tactics were likely illegal.

But he was kind and she enjoyed talking to him, though after having been alone for so long, Daisy realized it was difficult to keep reminding herself this was all a game. Someone more experienced might have been better equipped for this than she was. She kept forgetting herself and getting lost in his eyes and remembering he saw her as a career boost, not a love interest and then her heart sank once more. Being used simply wasn't any fun.

How did actors do this?

It crossed her mind that she might have fun with Robby instead of overthinking the situation. Sitting at home waiting for the world to come to her was easy, but getting out of the house, seeing new things, and laughing with a self-proclaimed partying ladies' man was more fun than she'd enjoyed in a long time. Even if it was pretend.

And Robby was a musician. It was like a dream come true. Daisy's father taught music and he instilled in her a deep appreciation for all instruments. While the world might dismiss Robby as merely rock and roll, Daisy saw through that easy critique. He wrote good songs, his talent wasn't limited, though he'd—as yet—not stretched himself beyond the standard rock anthems that had garnered acclaim. And now that she had talked to him, she honestly felt that he was too passionate of a person to avoid writing ballads any longer.

"Well, Harpo, you ready to get out of here?" Robby asked with a grin. "We can make your friend's party."

She nodded as he leaned close to her.

"Listen...it's probably going to be nuts when we leave. Just trust me OK? I won't let anything happen to you. Promise." Daisy nodded again and Robby met her eyes. "You sure?"

She smiled with as much confidence as she could muster and Robby smiled back, his perfect teeth gleaming as he reached over and stroked her cheek. "Let's find out what you got." He handed her his jacket to hide under.

Robby pushed her wheelchair out of the restaurant

where several photographers, Mac included, jostled each other near the security the restaurant provided. Each one was yelling and trying to get their attention as Robby ignored them and Daisy hid beneath his jacket. Once they arrived safely at the truck, she lowered the coat and turned her face to him fearfully, but found him grinning as if this were a most common situation. It was overwhelming, and she now appreciated how difficult it was to be normal and a celebrity. In fact, it was probably impossible. Going to the store or out to eat wouldn't be an anonymous experience anymore, and yet he loved it.

Robby opened the truck and leaned over Daisy. "They aren't there," he whispered as he lifted her into his arms. "It's just me and you."

Was the man insane? She met his eyes as he started to turn to put her into the truck.

"I can't see. They're blinding me," she said.

"That's my good looks." Robby set her down and Daisy laughed and handed him the jacket.

"That's my girl." He kissed her cheek softly. "You're getting the hang of it." Daisy's skin burned where his lips touched her. He closed the door and collapsed her wheelchair before placing it into the back of the truck. She heard the reporters yelling at him, but Robby ignored them and hopped in beside her.

"You all right?" he asked. Her emotions were screaming inside her, having finally been awakened, but Daisy couldn't say that. Instead, she smiled weakly, nodding.

"Yeah. You?"

He grinned. "Better than I've been in a long, long time."

13

On the drive to Jennifer's house Daisy seemed happy to have Robby doing all the talking, so he did. He liked talking, especially about himself, but it wasn't making him very confident as to where he stood in relation to getting that song from her. The longer it took, the less likely he'd be able to get hold of it.

"You can park anywhere," Daisy said as Robby slowed his truck and pulled into Jennifer's crowded driveway. He slipped the truck into a space next to a smaller vehicle and yanked the key from the ignition.

"Guess we're a little overdressed." He hoped his smile was playful. Daisy finally seemed to be comfortable with him and he wanted to keep it that way. "Hope everyone understands, considering."

"I'm sure they will. Listen, we don't have to do this if..."

Robby wondered why she never seemed to want anyone to make a fuss over her. More than any person he'd met, Daisy deserved it.

"Now why on earth wouldn't I want to? Making you happy makes me happy." He lifted her hand to his lips and kissed it softly, open-palm as was becoming his trademark. He loved the adorable look on her face when he did that. Shocking her with the attention thrilled him.

Daisy smiled nervously as he continued. "Don't think I missed it that you almost never say a word about yourself, Harpo. I'm hoping your friends can shed some light on the mystery that is Daisy Jane Parker."

"How'd you know my middle name?"

Robby raised an eyebrow. "Just because you don't talk doesn't mean I don't pay attention." He reached over and took Daisy's hand in his, lacing their fingers together. "We can play this however makes you comfortable. You want your friends to think there's something going on, I'm all for it. Practice makes perfect."

Daisy stared at their hands but said nothing as Robby wondered if he'd gone too far. He wasn't trying to mislead her, but he also didn't understand why they shouldn't have a little fun with the game they were playing.

But Daisy was going to keep him at a safe distance, which meant he had work to do. Robby sighed heavily and kissed her hand again.

"All right, Harpo Marx, let's go..."

~*~

The couple made their way to the back yard where a fire pit was burning and people were milling around playing games, eating and talking. Jennifer, Sadie, and Steve were near the food on the back porch, but they spotted Daisy and Robby and immediately rushed over.

"You came!" Sadie shouted. "Oh, my goodness! You're gorgeous! When was the last time we saw you in a dress?"

Daisy beamed. She glanced at Robby and smiled, her face showing the many emotions that seemed to be bubbling up in her. Robby swallowed a lump in his throat and nodded silently at her, relishing the thought that he'd done something good.

Steve coughed awkwardly as he extended a hand to Robby. "Steve Englehart." The men shook hands.

"Robby Grant."

Steve laughed. "Yeah... I...uh, knew that."

Robby got the hint that he should stay put as Sadie and Jennifer dragged Daisy away. Steve eyed the women before he looked at Robby. He was a few inches shorter but was thick with muscle. His dark hair was cut short and there appeared to be a tattoo Robby couldn't quite make out on his left bicep.

He gave Robby a severe once-over before he spoke.

"Before this goes any further, I want to be honest with you. It doesn't matter who you are or how much money you have, or what top ten list thinks you're the sexiest man alive...you hurt that girl and I will make you pay. And jail or whatever doesn't scare me when it comes to protecting my friends."

Robby gulped. "I don't..."

Steve met his eyes. "I give you credit for getting her out of the house," he said. "But..." his voice drifted off as if he wasn't sure he should continue.

Robby dug in his pocket for a cigarette, which he lit.

"She's a nice girl—the kind men fight to marry. Her dad raised her in the church and she lives it out, even with all she's been through. Don't make me regret letting you hang around because if we left it up to Daisy to take care of herself, it wouldn't matter how badly you hurt her. She'd turn the other cheek and let you do it again. And quite honestly, I'm not going to stand by and let that go on anymore."

Robby nodded as he exhaled. He forced a smile in Steve's direction. "I won't hurt her."

Steve regarded him for a moment before he went on. "We, uh, told everyone to be cool about you being here."

"It's fine."

Steve grinned, visibly relaxing. "All right. Now that I've done my brotherly duty and tried to scare the crap out of you, there are drinks in the cooler beside the deck, food on the table, food for the fire on the other table, and the ladies are over there. If I keep you here any longer, my girl is going to have my head..."

Robby followed him over to the fire where a small group sat talking. He liked Steve. He was real, pulling no punches, just like Warren. Robby relished connecting with normal people outside the bubble of Hollywood. There, everyone's top concern was making money and all things superficial. Robby realized his perspective was off the charts by being in that atmosphere for so long.

Most of the group quieted and turned his way as he approached, as if he were going to perform. He tossed his cigarette into the fire, smiling at Daisy as he did. She smiled back as the crowd went completely silent. Steve coughed awkwardly, but then Robby asked, "Anybody got a guitar?" A few people laughed, and after a moment someone appeared with a guitar. It was old and probably out of tune, but at least Robby could give them a little of what they were after. He sat next to Daisy and started to strum, his eyes closing as he melted into one of his favorite songs.

~*~

After a few songs, Robby decided to sing something slow and romantic. He wasn't sure what Daisy wanted her friends to believe but it was easy enough for him to either mislead them into thinking they were in a relationship, or that maybe he was interested in her. And, judging by her face, there was the added possibility that she might actually be interested in him too. At the very least, maybe she'd even start singing along. He needed to try to make that happen, his obsession with hearing her sweet voice making him crazy.

Robby glanced at Daisy as he said, "All right everybody, last one. It's a song you've heard before…and it goes something like this…" Robby played a slow introduction and glanced at Daisy before he started to sing a classic love song. As he predicted, Daisy blushed and turned away.

As he sang, Robby occasionally looked at Daisy and realized that by the middle of the song she closed her eyes and was lost in the music. He figured that was a good sign. It wasn't long before she forgot herself and started to sing along with him. Surprised, Robby kept playing but stopped singing for a moment. Daisy's eyes snapped open, but Robby nodded to encourage her to continue. He sang with her, content that he'd been right. She did sing like an angel.

The song ended to the applause of everyone around the fire. Steve stood as Robby handed the guitar to him with a smile.

"OK, give the guy a break—let's eat," Steve said, leading the crowd toward the patio. Jennifer and Sadie followed him, as did most of the rest of the crowd, though a few people stopped to shake Robby's hand or thank him for singing. Although Robby tried to be gracious, he was anxious to talk to Daisy alone.

Finally, he turned to her in the dim light of the fire. "Thought you had a terrible voice," he said. "Daisy, you need to be in a studio. Now. Preferably with me."

Daisy shrugged and Robby guessed she was blushing again. He smiled as he gently touched her hand. "I'd love to hear you sing *Waiting*. I've got some ideas for the music. I think it'd be great if..."

Daisy grimaced, her posture defensive. Robby had jumped too fast. Maybe he should focus on writing his own song no matter how dry his creativity. When she said nothing, he smiled again and gently tapped on her thigh.

"I want a drink. You want anything?"

Daisy shook her head. He walked away, wondering how to break through to her.

Robby strolled around the yard before grabbing a water bottle and stopping short of where Steve and Jennifer were having a private moment. He stood a respectable distance away, listening and watching.

For as many relationships as he'd been in over the years, Robby was certain he never looked at a woman the way Steve was looking at Jennifer. He felt the envy start in the pit of his stomach and work its way into his heart. He wanted that kind of connection with someone. It pained him to know it couldn't happen.

Robby sighed heavily as he opened the bottle of water and took a long drink before turning his attention back to Daisy. She was sitting with Sadie. They were talking conspiratorially—about him no doubt. He observed their interaction until Daisy began to get emotional. He straightened, ready to rush to her side, but then Sadie put an arm around her and he remained rooted to his spot, unsure.

Robby glanced at Jennifer and Steve again. They were laughing together. In an instant, the desire for what they had nearly overwhelmed him. He wanted a woman to look at him as if he'd hung the moon for her, and yet in the next thought his hopes crashed. A woman wouldn't ever feel that way about him. He was too selfish. If Robby was honest, he might admit that his first concern was his career and he was merely bribing Daisy into playing along. The thought made him sick, so he reached for a cigarette.

He walked slowly toward Daisy but stayed out of her line of sight as he tried to think. Maybe Warren was right. Robby still knew nothing of love. He wished he'd paid more attention in church.

Even as he swore to himself he would take care of Daisy because he truly, genuinely liked her, Sadie said, "Two years is a long time. He's not worth it. Never was."

Robby leaned back against the wall of a little shed so that he was hidden in its shadows. He wanted to listen and perhaps figure out what it was about her everyone but he knew.

Daisy's voice was shaking. "But he's in my head. 'Stop wasting your time, Daisy...what about me, Daisy...'"

"Turn him off," Sadie said. Robby smiled. *Good girl*, he thought as she continued. "You should be using your gifts. I really don't think Robby's a bad guy. The chance of a lifetime is right in front of you."

Daisy stared into the fire for a long moment before answering. "All I've got in front of me is a loan I can't pay on a house I may or may not lose, along with a house guest I don't know what to do with," she said.

"It's about all I can handle." Robby's heart constricted to hear her say it like that.

He stepped out of the shadows and approached them, plastering a smile on his face. He'd learned to be a good actor over the years and was glad for the skills. He tossed his cigarette into the fire as he sat beside Daisy, who grinned, but not for him. He was sure Sadie was doing something behind his back that in other circumstances he'd probably laugh at. He turned his attention to Daisy who was shivering but trying not to. He reached out to touch her arm.

"You're freezing!" he exclaimed. She shook her head as he instinctively removed his jacket and placed it around her shoulders.

"Now you're going to be cold," she said.

Robby grinned as he sat beside her and stretched his legs toward the fire. "But I'm hot! All the ladies, ahem, except for maybe you—think so," he said.

Daisy smiled and huddled into his jacket gratefully. "Thanks."

Sadie stood, shaking a finger at Daisy. "Remember what I said."

"Yeah, yeah..." Daisy waved her off, but Sadie wasn't finished.

She smiled at Robby. "She needs to lighten up."

"I'm working on it." Robby liked Sadie. "But so far she only wants to sleep when we're in bed." The thin woman with a bright smile and wild hair laughed as she walked away. Yes, Robby liked her.

"Tonight's been fun," he said. "Thanks." Daisy nodded but said nothing as Robby took her hand and kissed it. She was still nervous.

He leaned closer to whisper in her ear. "Come on now, what will people think if my girlfriend looks at me like that? I don't want anyone saying I beat you or something equally ridiculous."

"I'm not afraid of you," Daisy said defensively.

"What is it then?" he asked. "At my last check-up, the doctor cleared me of cooties. Said I lost them when I was fifteen or so."

Daisy laughed openly, making Robby warm inside. Other women fell all over themselves to make him think his jokes were hilarious, but when Daisy laughed she meant it.

She turned so she looked directly into his eyes. Although she still seemed nervous, for the first time she didn't pull away from him. "It's just been a long time since...since a man has touched me," she whispered. "I mean, on purpose, for no reason...and on his own, not because he's my doctor. Sorry. It sounds pathetic. I mean it is...pathetic."

The old Robby would already have taken advantage of her vulnerability but sobriety was helping him understand her clearly. He simply nodded and kissed her forehead innocently before urging her to rest her head against his shoulder.

"I like touching you," he whispered honestly. "And you're nowhere near pathetic, sweetheart." He stroked her hair lightly, suddenly grateful for reality and sobriety colliding in that perfect moment.

14

By the time they left the party it was late and Daisy was tired. For the second night in a row, sleep would come easily. Robby, work, a date and a party after that left her struggling to keep her eyes open. Maybe with a fight, she'd even admit that she loved it all. Whatever Robby's intentions, he played a gentleman and showed her a lot of fun. She'd been safe, despite the chaos of the evening. While he was only around for a short time, she considered letting him into her world, and even for a moment that she might write a song with him. She decided to stop pushing the idea away and instead let it fester. Why shouldn't she dream?

After they'd gone inside, Daisy headed to her room to put on her pajamas. She told Robby she was probably going to go to bed, even though the day left her with so much to reflect on that falling asleep might take a while.

Still, she dressed in her pajamas with the intention of getting into bed. She heard Robby rustling around in the kitchen. Curious, Daisy followed the noise in case he needed something. She was surprised to find him still in his dress pants, his shirt untucked and unbuttoned, his jacket hanging on the back of a dining room chair. She didn't want to enjoy that he'd made himself comfortable, or that when he turned he was holding a cookie jar and a huge glass of milk. But she loved it.

He wore a guilty smile. "I never thought I'd get caught with my hand in the cookie jar," he said. Daisy wished he were less adorable. She tried not to stare at all of his tattoos, but her eyes seemed incapable of working for her.

"Hungry?" she asked as she entered the room, training her eyes away from him. "Do you want a sandwich? I don't mind…"

"Nah," Robby sat at the table. "You want some?" Daisy shrugged and went to the table while he got her a glass of milk. It wasn't lost on her that he'd quickly gone from being helpless to serving her. Maybe staying with her was doing him some good.

"Thanks," she said.

"I hope I wasn't making too much noise." He took a cookie and dipped it into his milk. "It's not even that I was hungry, really, I just wasn't ready to go to bed yet. I mean, it's only one in the morning. Too early for rock royalty."

Daisy picked apart a cookie but left the crumbs on the table.

"So, I'm not ruining my rep here with the whole milk and cookies thing?" Robby asked, tossing a cookie into the air and catching it in his mouth. She shook her head and waited for him to drink his entire glass of milk before she spoke.

"But maybe that's why you started drinking. Too much rep—you didn't leave room for you," she said. Robby slowly set his glass down. His eyes glimmered, intrigued.

"You sound like my counselor."

"I've seen enough of them myself. Guess it slips out sometimes," she said with a laugh. She caught herself before she looked at Robby. She expected him to ask about her comment, but instead he stood, deep in thought. He went to the back door, peering out the window into the darkness, his hands stuffed into his pockets. Whatever she said turned him into himself, and she was glad. She wasn't ready to bear her soul to him, but it was fine with her if he wanted to share his.

"You ever think maybe people believe what they want, or what they expect, instead of what's really in front of them?" he asked softly. Daisy thought about this as she took her glass to the sink.

"All the time," she said. "But that doesn't mean we don't have a choice. We don't have to please everyone else."

Robby turned to her slowly, still seeming to work it all out in his mind. Amusement played on his lips before he sobered. "I guess not, huh?"

Daisy smiled. "'Night, Vanilla."

Although it looked as if he had more to say, Robby merely nodded and saluted half-heartedly. "'Night, Harpo."

Daisy went to her bedroom and softly closed the door, lost in thought. Robby wasn't at all what she expected. She was as confused as ever.

~*~

Robby stayed in the kitchen a few minutes longer before wandering into the living room, drawn to the piano. While he preferred the guitar, he wanted to try the song on another instrument—and it was the one he suspected had borne the ballad in the first place. He hoped to wait long enough that Daisy would go to sleep and he could write uninterrupted.

He glanced around the living room and was intrigued. There was a shelf full of knickknacks of various sorts, and books and pictures everywhere. He studied the pictures for a moment, especially the ones where Daisy wasn't in a wheelchair. She'd been built like an athlete what seemed like a short time ago, so he guessed she'd played some sport or other. He wondered if that's what put her in the wheelchair. He wasn't sure why he was afraid to ask.

He told himself it wasn't his business, but really, asking meant he cared. And if he cared, well, he'd have to stick around. That would make stealing her song even more difficult. One thing led to another. Daisy needed a man who would be able to make a promise and keep it. Despite Warren's hopes for him, that wasn't Robby. Maybe it never would be.

Robby stopped looking at the pictures and turned to the bookshelf. It was loaded with titles of all subjects, but there seemed to be a focus on religion. Robby lifted one from the shelf and flipped it open randomly. It landed on a page with a Bible verse highlighted.

"Love does no harm to its neighbor—therefore love is the fulfillment of the law," Robby said softly. He fingered the words Daisy herself had, at one time at least, thought were important. He wondered what the same words meant for him. He didn't want to hurt Daisy but it seemed like there was no other outcome.

Robby sighed heavily and returned the book to the shelf, wishing the verse would leave him. He turned to the piano, hoping to figure out a way to make both himself and Daisy happy.

He sat at the piano and gently lifted the fall. He played a quick tune and then reached into his back pocket and pulled out a wrinkled piece of paper bearing the song lyrics.

Robby spread the lyrics open as he placed his cell phone nearby. He realized he'd shut the power off, so he turned it back on to find numerous texts and voice mail messages. With a sigh, he started going through them, figuring Daisy would be in a deeper sleep by the time he started writing. The first message was from Nick and he discovered, not surprisingly, that he wasn't happy.

"Robert River Grant. You dragged Daisy into your circus. I get it—she's a beautiful woman and you can't control yourself if there's one within a hundred-mile radius, but you better listen to me good. She's special. I will beat your bony little rear end all the way out of the state if you think for one second of doing anything that causes her even the most remote discomfort, let alone pain. You hear me, boy? I'm keeping my eyes on you." The phone went dead as Nick hung up without a sign-off.

Robby drew a deep breath, the severity, and seriousness of his uncle's words sinking in. His plans weren't completely sound, but Daisy was a grown woman. Besides, she knew it was just a game. She could handle it. Tonight, they'd made enough break-throughs that Robby was certain he was closer than ever to getting her song. Better still, he realized that he wanted to kiss Daisy several times as the evening wore on, and yet he'd done something on a date that he'd never before seemed capable of doing—he restrained himself. He actually respected her and it scared him. Despite his intentions to convince her he needed to sing and produce her song, he also didn't want to hurt her. The situation wasn't ideal, but he had time to figure it out.

At least, that's what he thought until he played the next message.

"Robby—it's McAllister. Lily said you've got something for me. We're anxious for a listen. Give me a call."

Robby groaned. He'd told Lily that Daisy wrote an amazing song but that she wasn't willing to part with it. He was more than annoyed that the information filtered through to McAllister. Now, what was he going to do? He either needed to come up with something on his own or flat-out steal Daisy's work—a ballad she adamantly refused to share with him.

Neither option was tempting.

Robby turned his phone off before more bad news came his way. His brain was swimming and he feared he might drown if he didn't take a minute to breathe. He regarded his hands, which landed on the piano keys and lightly played a melody he already liked— one that matched Daisy's words perfectly.

He smiled, thinking. Perhaps if she listened to what he'd done with the song, she'd part with the lyrics.

"No!" Daisy's voice startled Robby as she shouted from the next room. Robby's stomach jumped into his throat. It was as if she'd read his thoughts and felt compelled to stop him from hurting her.

But then he realized she'd fallen asleep and her nightmare was back. Gently, he replaced the fall over the keys and stuffed the paper and his cell phone into his pocket.

"No!" she screamed again as he crept toward her bedroom door. He peeked into the room. She was thrashing around in her bed.

Was this how she'd been living?

He tiptoed to the edge of her bed. "Hey," he whispered, softly touching her shoulder. But his gentle prodding did little to settle her. With a sigh, he tossed his shirt aside and climbed into bed with her as he started singing.

"Oh my, Daisy love, running...running...running too fast for me," he sang softly into her ear as he wrapped his arms around her, pulling her close. She quickly stopped struggling and melted against him. Robby smiled to himself at how well she fit him, not physically but emotionally. Both of them were hurting but he was ready to open up about it while she was still hiding. He decided he wasn't going to let her.

With a deep breath, Robby silently prayed for a way to help her.

15

Daisy woke the next morning with a yawn and deep stretch. She'd rested well and because it was after nine-thirty, she'd also slept in again. She'd forgotten she could be so refreshed. But even as she was beginning to relish the feeling of a good night's sleep, another realization struck her. Robby was in bed with her again. Panicked, she glanced around the room. The shirt he'd worn the night before was now tossed haphazardly across her dresser.

"Please be wearing something," she muttered as she slowly lifted the covers, relieved to find he was still in his dress pants from the night before. She covered him and sighed. She'd never slept, figuratively or literally, with a man before and yet in the two days she'd known Robby she'd done just that—and twice. Was she crazy?

She glanced at the man beside her and realized she'd not yet taken advantage of just looking at him. She'd been too afraid she would find him attractive. But now that he was sleeping, it seemed fair to gawk at him as so many women apparently loved doing. His dark blond hair was splayed across his pillow and most of hers too. The bit of stubble on his cheek made him more human than rock star. Without thinking she reached up to gently touch him, careful not to wake him. He sighed contentedly in his sleep. He really was beautiful, if a little rough around the edges. And he was nothing at all like any man she'd found attractive before, least of all Alec.

Alec was polished, silver gleaming in the sunlight. But like any mirage, he wasn't what he seemed. He wanted things "just-so" and Daisy never quite fit the bill. Yet he'd hung onto her. In hindsight, it must have been because she'd thought it was love. Now she understood she'd endured a lot of emotional abuse. He was sometimes so mean she begged Nick not to go after him to teach him some manners.

To get a better view of the tattoos on Robby's right arm and upper back, Daisy lifted the blanket. There were more on the other side of his body and she'd noticed some on his torso too. She was almost afraid to find out where else he was hiding them. But she was mesmerized by those she could see. They overlapped and intertwined so that it was almost impossible to tell where one ended and another began. There were images of snakes, tigers, a group of music notes, a broken fence, an eagle. She'd never dated a man with tattoos before. Her strict father would have discouraged her from getting involved. Tattoos meant trouble. But then again, maybe she was too close to him already. Anyway, her father's theory was moot. Alec's skin was a blank canvas and he'd been more trouble than anyone she'd ever known.

Unfortunately for Daisy, Robby was more beautiful than she'd imagined. It didn't help that after their conversation the previous night, he'd also revealed his humanity. If anything, that was even more attractive than his physical attributes.

Now it was going to be even harder to pretend they were dating.

With a heavy sigh, she lifted herself off the bed

and into her wheelchair and headed for the kitchen, trying to decide what to make him for breakfast.

~*~

"Daisy Jane Parker."

Daisy bit her lip as she faced Sadie and Jennifer, who were sitting at the kitchen table waiting for her like a firing squad.

"Yes?" she asked weakly.

"What *are* you doing?" Jennifer squealed. "He is in your bed right now. Again."

Daisy laughed at the earnestness on her friend's face. It was as if she revealed information Daisy herself didn't already have.

"Really? And…?" she said sarcastically, fighting a smile.

"And...and...?" Jennifer stammered. "And why is he there? I thought you said nothing was going on. You two were all cuddled up like...well, I don't even know. And the way his shirt was thrown off, I wouldn't be surprised if there are buttons all over the place."

Daisy howled, unable to catch her breath. She hoped her best friends knew her better than to think she'd behave like an animal because Robby was handsome and famous. Even when she might have had a more serious chance with him, her personality wouldn't have allowed it.

"Come on, Jenn, it's funny," Sadie said as she began to chuckle too. "Here, Daze, I brought you a cappuccino."

"Mmm…" Daisy accepted it and sipped, glad for the distraction. She sighed when she discovered

Jennifer watching her with expectation.

"Whatever you're thinking is totally...wrong," she said.

Jennifer raised an eyebrow and pulled out her cell phone. Within moments she turned it to Daisy and held it out. "There. Take it in. See how wrong I am," she said. Daisy accepted the phone. She slowly set her coffee down, barely believing what was on the screen. She and Robby were all over the news. If she hadn't known differently herself, she would have believed they were dating. For a brief moment, Daisy relished the idea that she could act, but she remembered she was trying to convince her friends that what they were seeing and hearing was wrong.

"Listen..." she said.

"So much for waiting, Daisy. Really," Jennifer said.

"OK, stop! I'm...not sure what he was doing in my bed...again, but whatever, it's fine by me. Maybe I just feel safe for a change...I just know I'm sleeping—for the first time since I got home. We are only sleeping. I promise." Daisy took a drink of coffee. "I'm not a different person. And I know better than to get too involved—especially like that." She set her coffee on the table near Sadie, who grinned conspiratorially.

"Smells like you bathed in his cologne..." she said. "Is he a good kisser? Bet he is."

Daisy sighed. "I told you. I don't know!"

"You want us to believe that he slept in your bed and you didn't kiss him?" Jennifer asked. "We're trying to watch out for you. I mean, he's...he's..."

"A guy who needs a friend." Daisy was surprised how calm her words sounded. "And I'm not the kind of girl he'd want anyway. It is not at all what you're thinking."

Robby chose that moment to walk into the kitchen wearing no shirt, his hair a mess, and a big grin on his face as he scrolled over images on his cell phone. Sadie's jaw dropped at the sight of him and despite trying to refrain, Jennifer appeared to be equally helpless.

"Morning, ladies," he said coolly, his attention glued to his phone. He suddenly turned his eyes to Daisy. "Morning, love."

Maybe he was accustomed to the googly-eyed attention because he didn't notice the women's response. Then again, it was also possible he didn't care. Regardless, he went straight to Daisy and leaned over her chair to kiss her cheek and whisper in her ear, "Thanks for last night. You really got me thinking and I...appreciate it. I think we make a good team."

While Daisy understood his meaning, it didn't stop her mouth from going dry. She knew what her friends would think. He brushed some hair from her forehead. "Darn, you're cute in the morning."

Daisy did her best to glare at him but it fell flat. He grinned and flopped into a chair as she started making coffee for everyone.

"Are you aware that the two of you are all over the news this morning?" Jennifer asked coldly, her dark eyes flashing at Robby. He smiled, nodding.

"Yep."

"And what do you intend to do about it?" she demanded. Robby shrugged as he set his phone down.

Jennifer drummed her fingers on the table as Sadie fought another grin. She gave Robby a 'thumbs-up' behind Jennifer's back as the woman spat, "Steve will have your head."

Robby cast a look of shock in her direction. "Me? Steve's my man...I'm a good boy. Scout's honor." He clumsily made the Boy Scout sign. "Daisy, tell them."

"I tried," she said wryly, "but you aren't exactly helping walking in here half nude." She gestured toward his lack of clothing.

Robby laughed. "Oh, sensitive! I'll have you know, I was in the living room writing when you started yelling your head off again. It's a wonder the police aren't over here every night for you disturbing the peace..."

Daisy glanced at Robby. He was grinning.

"The benefits of living in the country."

Robby winked at her. "Right. So...I guess I fell asleep singing to you again."

"Hmm..." Daisy stirred cream into Robby's mug. "How did I ever get along without you?"

She handed him the coffee and he raised his eyebrows. "I'm here now, angel. No worries..." he wiggled his eyebrows at her and she blushed as Sadie and Jennifer exchanged a telling glance.

Still, Daisy smiled at him before she moved to the refrigerator.

"I swear, Robby, if you do anything to hurt her, I will rip your arms off and stuff them down your throat," Jennifer said suddenly. "No more singing, no more guitar. Your career will really be over."

The tension in the room was palpable.

Robby put down his coffee and he and Daisy stared at her as the refrigerator door slowly closed on its own.

"Jennifer..." Daisy began. "I appreciate it, but..."

"No," Robby went to her, gently placing a hand on her arm. "She's right. I mean, they're your friends, and they want to protect you. I can respect that." Daisy nodded, aware of his hand still warm on her skin. She was unsure how she was supposed to react. He held her gaze and smiled before he turned to Sadie and Jennifer.

"Actually...my agent texted me—she booked me to play some benefit show with Carli Cross this weekend," he said, dropping the woman's name as if she wasn't even more famous than he was. "I hoped Daisy would come along."

Although Daisy managed to be calm through the entire Robby episode, so far this idea stopped her cold. Her jaw dropped as she stared at him. It was one thing for her to go to dinner with him and have a handful of photographers harass them, but it was a whole other ball game to go to a red-carpet event loaded with celebrities, television cameras, and every form of media imaginable.

"What?" Robby gave a wry laugh. "I promise she'll be safe. I've got a full-time bodyguard, but I can get more security if that will make you feel better. I'm not out to get Daisy hurt."

Jennifer resumed drumming her fingers as she thought about his proposition. Daisy braced herself. This wasn't going to be good. She'd seen that look on her friend's face before when Alec showed up to beg forgiveness for leaving Daisy at a gala event for the hospital. He'd been so drunk he'd gone home with a nurse and left Daisy to call her friends for a ride home.

"I love imaginary bodyguards," Jennifer said, her dark eyes glittering. "Where's he been this whole time?"

"I didn't tell anyone where I was going. But I talked to Jazz, my bodyguard, this morning. He'll meet us at the hotel and we'll be safe. I promise." Robby squatted down in front of Daisy and took both of her hands in his. "It will be fun. I already gave my agent your dress and shoe size and she's got a team of stylists on it. There will be hair and make-up people..."

She tried to ignore that her friends were staring at her so hard she felt their eyes boring into her. This was her decision, not theirs, and she wanted to do the right thing. But this was a whole new and unexpected level. He was asking for everything, and she had no idea if she was prepared to give it.

But the fact that he was stroking the back of her hand with his thumb was only muddling her brain more. If she saw his green eyes or he did that Valentino thing she would be done for.

"Go," Sadie said to everyone's surprise. They all turned to her and she blushed. "What? It will be fun. Besides, Nick isn't going to be out of the hospital for a while, so there's nothing keeping you here."

Daisy released a deep breath. "This is silly. I'm not Hollywood. Maybe you should go, Sadie."

"Huh-uh. You two are already involved...besides, I scare everyone, remember?" Sadie said with a smile. Daisy's heart pounded in her chest as she turned back to Robby.

He smiled, meeting her eyes. "You're too good for Hollywood, Harpo. Go with me anyway."

Although she didn't intend to, Daisy nodded slowly. "OK."

Robby's face broke into a wide grin and he leaned over to hug her tightly. "Thanks," he whispered. "This is going to be amazing. I promise you..."

While Daisy wanted to believe him, she wasn't so sure.

16

Robby sat on the private plane, not at all interested in the beautiful scenery passing below. He'd seen it before. He was more interested in Daisy as she gazed out the window, fascinated. He wondered if it was the plane or the flying that had her intrigued.

She turned to him suddenly, blushing, as if he'd caught her.

"What do you think?" Robby asked.

"It's unbelievable," she said softly. "It's been a few years since I've flown." They were sitting side by side so Robby reached over and easily took her hand in his and kissed it. He ignored that again she was blushing.

"You're easy to like."

"Robby..."

"I mean it. It's good talking to you. You're...so sweet, and spending time with you makes me forget everything else. I didn't think that was possible," he said, suddenly nervous for what he was saying. "I...kind of wanted to ask you something, though."

Robby lifted his eyes slowly and met Daisy's deep blue ones. Fearing he would push her away before he even spoke, he smiled gently, hoping to ease her fears.

"Well, what is it?" she asked, toying with his hand in hers. He was relieved she didn't seem to be trying to get away from him. Maybe cornering her in an airplane was the only way to get her to trust him.

"Two things," he began. "I...uh, wondered if you

might reconsider the song. I've got great ideas for the music and..." Robby sounded like a child begging for a cookie but he was willing to grovel if it meant he got his way.

Daisy's eyes drifted from his face to the sky out the window. Already he guessed her answer before she spoke. "That song was off the table from the beginning," she said softly. "So, if you're wining and dining me thinking it's going to change my mind, you can tell the pilot to turn around."

Robby sighed heavily. It was worth a shot, but not if it pushed her away. He wanted her to give it willingly, but he was not above changing the game if necessary. He needed that song as much as she was trying to protect it. He should have had something by now, but everything kept going back to the old stuff he'd written. He needed something different, and McAllister was pressuring him more each day.

Robby placed one finger under Daisy's chin, nudging her to look at him. "Hey," he said softly. "I'm sorry. I just didn't want to give up too easily if all you needed was a nudge." Daisy tried to pull away from him, but he held her hand firmly. "There's something else..."

Daisy rolled her eyes. "No, I won't sleep with you," she said defiantly and again turned her back to him. "I'm sure about now you're getting pretty desperate, but I'm afraid you'll have to look elsewhere for your...satisfaction."

Although he tried hard to fight it, Robby began laughing so hard tears soon rolled down his face. Daisy slowly turned toward him, yanking her hand back and crossing her arms over her chest. She appeared to be both relieved and offended all at once. "I'm so glad you find me amusing," she snapped.

Robby gasped for breath and wiped at his face as he shook his head. "Baby, I'd sleep with you in a heartbeat, but that is not the mark of a gentleman as far as I know," he said. "Believe it or not I actually respect you too much." Robby grew serious and exhaled slowly before he spoke. "I've treated too many women that way. That isn't me anymore. I'm just laughing at the way you put it, that's all."

"Humph." Daisy turned away once more.

Robby waited, looking at the back of her head. "Come on, Harpo. I really am working hard, I swear. I've got to stop letting everyone down all the time. Believe in me, please."

But she refused to turn to him.

Robby got out of his seat and grabbed his guitar before standing in front of her and strumming. "Oh, Daisy..." he sang. "When you look at me, I want to hold you close...till the pain goes away..." he waited for some sign but she focused on the clouds outside her window. Finally, he strummed one last time, set the guitar aside, and knelt in front of her. She was crying.

"Hey..." he said softly, taking her hands into his. "What's going on?" She sniffed but refused to speak. Robby reached up and wiped a tear away, which only made her cry harder. He stood silently and lifted her from the seat, placing her in his lap as he sat down. Although she half-heartedly resisted him, Robby was stronger and his will was firm. Slowly, she turned and sobbed into his shoulder.

Robby's heart constricted and his arms tightened around her, wishing away her pain. He closed his eyes and prayed for guidance. It was clear that the song, his career, and everything else no longer mattered if it was causing her this much pain. The trouble was he was clueless about what to do.

"Hey..." he whispered. "Talk to me."

She said nothing for a long time, her head buried in his shoulder, until suddenly and without warning, she sat up and declared, "If there's one thing my father taught me, it was to help a person in need—I think right now that person is you. We are going to write this song together."

Robby tried to follow, saying the first thing that popped into his mind. "But don't you need anyone?"

Daisy sighed. "Nope. I've got what I need. There's Nick, my friends...and God loves me. He wants me to help you."

Robby nodded, not sure what to make of all this. He cleared his throat, afraid to ask the next question. "And what if He wants me to help you?"

Daisy regarded him for a moment before turning her gaze out the window of the plane. "And what would you do to help *me*?" she whispered.

"I'm...I guess I'm not sure yet," He turned her head back. "But I promise I'm working on it."

Daisy nodded. Robby's eyes twinkled as he forced a smile. "OK, so we're going to write a song together," he said as if to make himself believe it. "But...why were you crying? Did I do something? I don't want to hurt you, Daisy."

Daisy avoided his eyes, and Robby wondered why he'd never noticed the small scar on her neck or the faint one under her hairline above her left ear. She turned back to him before he could ask.

"Put me down," she instructed, pushing against him, struggling for her own seat. Reluctantly, Robby easily placed her beside him, still wishing she'd talk to him. "Get your guitar."

Robby's phone started to vibrate with a text. He sighed as he stood. "One second, bossy," he said, yanking the phone from his pocket. He stared at his Uncle Nick's direct words. "Behave. Or else." Robby smiled as it buzzed again. He reached for his guitar with one hand while checking the new message with the other. It was from McAllister. "Call me as soon as you get to LA," it said. Robby shook his head. The last thing he needed was McAllister all over him for the song. He regretted telling Lily. She was a great agent but since her life revolved around selling, he should have known better than to tell her there might be something she could make money from.

Robby flopped next to Daisy, his guitar on his lap. "Now what, drill sergeant?" he asked.

"No more personal questions. We're friends, Robby. I can pretend to date you if we get a few things straight. One, do not touch me unless we are in public. Two, stop asking for the song. If I change my mind, my people will call your people. Got it? And three..." Daisy's confidence was waning as fast as the air from a balloon. But Robby relished the glimpse of it that he'd gotten and he wanted more.

He stretched forward, so their noses were nearly touching. "Three?" he asked.

Daisy cleared her throat and leaned back in her seat. "And three...keep this honest, all right? I won't lie to you, and I'll let you in on what you should know when you have to know it. I've been through enough."

"Such as...?"

"Rule one—no personal questions."

Robby nodded and strummed his guitar. He averted his eyes. "Seems to me that wasn't going to be rule three..."

Daisy drew a deep breath. "It wasn't. Listen...thanks for what you've done for me. This is as personal as it's going to get—but I used to be a whole lot more fun. You've shown me I still am that person. I hope I don't get on your nerves now that I'm coming around."

Robby strummed his hand over the guitar, his head down so she'd miss his smile. "Harpo, you couldn't get on my nerves," he said honestly. "I'll find something for you to write on and you can mess with the lyrics while I sing...but..." he stood and retrieved some paper he tossed to her followed by a pencil.

"But what?" she asked with a soft grin.

"Well, I've got rules too."

"Such as?"

Robby wondered if he should hold back. He could say anything, but he squelched the desire to force Daisy into giving him more. Her trust was too important. He needed to be worthy.

Robby strummed as he spoke. "Rule one— touching will be all the time, everywhere, not just publicly because it will feel forced—the media will latch onto it. Besides," he paused, giving her a wicked grin. "You're so soft and you smell amazing. I have to touch you. It's essential."

Daisy opened her mouth to protest, but he silenced her with his hand. "Twenty grand says my rule trumps yours." Daisy pouted, which made his smile broader as he went back to strumming. There seemed no point in making the rules all serious.

"Rule number two," he continued. "We will write more than one song together—as many as possible, in fact, because we are going to be a great team. I want a duet with you."

Daisy relented. "I can live with that."

Robby's head bobbed as he strummed, still smiling. "And my last rule..." his hand flashed over the strings with an extra flare before he stood. "My last rule is that you, my gorgeous lady, will have all that fun you thanked me for and stop holding back. You're the only one who cares that you're in a wheelchair." Robby paused as he noticed Daisy getting tears in her eyes. Despite the risk, he continued. "Your friends, Nick, and I all want you to be yourself...and quite frankly, that bossy woman who was in my plane a few minutes ago was pretty adorable. I'd like to see her more often, got it?"

He squatted in front of her and found she'd started crying again. He wiped her tears away and moved to hug her. "All right. Knock it off," he said softly. He kissed her cheek innocently. "We've got songs to write."

When he leaned back he found Daisy was smiling, pencil poised above the notebook he'd handed her.

"OK, boss. Let's do it," she said.

17

By the time they arrived at the hotel later that day, Daisy admitted to herself that Robby was right. He treated her like he did everyone else and didn't seem to be put out in the least that sometimes he carried her or helped her with her wheelchair. In fact, it might be wishful thinking, but he seemed to enjoy it, commenting on how she smelled, the softness of her hair, or—her favorite—that she should eat a burger once in a while because she could stand to gain a few pounds. Millions of women would surely be jealous of the way he spoke to her. But instead of resisting, she began to embrace the role. She was Robby's girlfriend.

Well, she was his friend.

And she was a girl.

"Here we are!" Robby exclaimed as he threw open the door to an elaborate penthouse suite on the top floor of a posh hotel that boasted more security than Fort Knox. Daisy entered slowly, drinking it in. She didn't even care that he was enamored of her astonishment in the same way a parent adores a child's wonder on Christmas morning. There were surprises at every turn, from the secret entrances and elevators to the staff that handed Robby his favorite health drink as he entered the building, and the gold handles on everything.

There were flowers adorning the dresser and table, and there was a guitar already waiting for Robby near the bed. The room was equipped with anything Daisy would need too. Tears sprang to her eyes. No luxurious detail had been forgotten. Her favorite candy was in a dish on an end table.

It was overwhelming.

As a child, she and her father took vacations in the summer, staying at decent hotels along the way, but she'd never dreamed she'd be in a place like this. The best hotel she'd ever stayed in had a bidet and left mints on her pillow in the morning. Other than that, her travel experience was limited.

"This seems OK." Daisy tried to sound unimpressed. "But where are you staying?" She turned to Robby. He'd made himself comfortable in the next room on the bed.

"Robby...?" she asked. "You are not..."

He laughed loudly and winked. "You'd miss me if I was too far away, sweetheart."

Exasperated, she peered out the window, trying to ignore him as he returned to the room. She hoped he didn't catch her smile.

"I'll behave, Harpo," he promised, but his tone said otherwise.

She turned to him. "Yeah? Well, maybe I won't. You may want your bodyguard."

Robby smirked. "Sounds good to me. All the sleeping we're doing doesn't satisfy like..."

Daisy looked at him with concern, unsure if he was teasing. She had boyfriends in high school and even college, and perhaps took them too lightly for her strict father's taste, but she meant to be careful with her feelings, and the love she wanted to share with her future husband. While she enjoyed the physical closeness of Robby holding her when her nightmares came each night, she didn't intend for anything to happen between them. Her heart was still too fragile and her mind continued to mull the mistakes of her recent past.

Robby's life was so different than her own, and that was never far from Daisy's mind. Sadness settled over her. He might not know the feeling of being truly loved for himself, or for what he could give or do for someone.

"I want more than that, and you should too," she said softly. "Relationships aren't just sex."

He shrugged, embarrassed for a brief moment. "All mine were, and they weren't so bad." He raised his eyebrows. "Sometimes not behaving is fun...and I am an excellent kisser, if I do say so myself."

Daisy rolled her eyes at him yet again. He took it all so lightly that it was no wonder he'd never been in love. "You sound like your uncle," she said as someone banged on the door, making her jump. She turned toward the noise, not realizing Robby stood in front of her. When she felt his presence and turned toward him, it was too late. He slowly leaned over her chair so they were nose to nose.

Daisy gulped.

"Except, unlike my uncle, my kisses are not lame threats," he said softly. His nearness was enough to make her skin tingle, but she never expected he would lean forward and press his lips to hers, lingering much longer than necessary. As surprised as she was, Daisy didn't resist but found herself melting instead as he deepened the kiss before gently pulling back.

Daisy was in trouble. Robby was telling the truth. Accurately.

"Nick kiss you like that? Huh, Harpo?" he asked

before strolling away to the door.

Daisy stared after him, her mouth hanging open. Had she ever been kissed before? And how on earth would she describe this to Sadie? Before she considered her options, a man who was as large as Mount Olympus shoved Robby into the room so hard he bounced off a wall and nearly fell to the floor. The man lifted him by his shirt while handily kicking the door closed at the same time.

"I'll bet you think this is funny, don't you little man?" he asked in a deep voice. Robby's face turned red as he gasped for air, his eyes desperately trained on Daisy.

With only a second's reflex, Daisy reached behind her and grabbed her gun as Robby shook his head and squeaked, "No!"

The man dropped him to the floor and went to Daisy, skillfully disarming.

"Jasper Kenton, Robby's bodyguard," he said, carefully turning the gun back over to a stunned Daisy. Robby rubbed his neck as Daisy tried desperately to make sense of the turn in the situation.

Robby gasped, pointing at Daisy. "You're lucky she isn't trigger happy."

Jazz shook his head in annoyance. "Why do you pay me, fool? I'm always aware of the situation," the man said, turning back to Robby. "But as for you...you will pay for what you pulled. How can I protect you if you're traipsing all over the country alone?"

Robby slowly stood, his face returning to its normal hue. "I was in Pennsylvania," he muttered. "Nothing important happens there." He glanced at Daisy. "This is Daisy Parker."

Jazz offered his hand to her, and Daisy reluctantly

shook it. What kind of bodyguard tried to kill the man he was charged with protecting? She wasn't going to be quick to trust him.

When he smiled at her and winked, Daisy was pretty sure the struggle at the door was a game. Although that did little to explain what happened between herself and Robby. She pushed this thought and her still-tingling lips aside to focus on the moment, because Jazz was waiting for her to respond.

"Um, nice to meet you," she squeaked.

Robby flopped onto the couch and rolled his eyes. He seemed completely unaffected by their kiss. Was he that good an actor?

"No problems with him, baby. He's all bark no bite," he said confidently. In an instant, Jazz spun and flattened Robby from the couch to the floor. Daisy gasped as Robby lifted himself slowly and went back at Jazz full-on, only to be thrown down again.

Jazz turned his back on Robby and grinned at Daisy while shaking his head. "He's a glutton," he said as Robby dove onto his back, reminding Daisy of a child intent on a piggyback ride. Jazz merely shook his head and walked calmly to a chair where he sat on top of Robby.

"Get off me, you horse!" he bellowed.

Jazz laughed and obeyed. "Stick to music and let me do my job, all right?" he said. "Now...Ms. Daisy...what are you doing with this clown and how much convincing will it require for you to dump him and let me show you a good time?"

Daisy felt her cheeks burn. "I think Robby...um..."

"Mmm...your loss little lady," he said, glancing at the time. "All right, Rob, go get yourself together. Rehearsal's in less than two hours. I want to spend some time with Daisy here before we go."

Robby met Daisy's eyes and smiled as he stood and stretched. "Don't worry—I trust him as much as Nick," he said. Daisy managed to smile as he went into the other room and closed the door.

"He been all right?" Jazz asked quietly. "He hasn't been drinking?"

Daisy shook her head.

Jazz sighed with relief as he sat heavily on the couch.

"Good. Listen, I hate to tell you this, but you got yourself a bodyguard too. The media are already camped outside waiting for a peek at you."

Daisy followed his gaze to the window and slowly made her way over to see for herself.

"Comes with the territory. I can get someone over here now if you want to go out shopping, or whatever, while we're gone."

The thought of leaving that room without Robby was almost too much. Daisy was sure she wore an expression of terror. "No. I don't think I should go out."

Jazz smiled. "Don't be scared, mama," he said. "Your life just changed, that's all...he's never looked at a woman like he did you just now. And here I thought this was all some kind of game..." Jazz yanked his phone from his pocket. "Excuse me." He stood and went to the window as he talked on the phone.

And Daisy was left wondering what she'd gotten herself into.

18

Less than an hour later, Robby climbed into the waiting limo with Jazz. He hated leaving Daisy alone...but he couldn't think about that. She promised she'd stay put while he was gone, and he hoped she stuck to that. If his girlfriend got caught in a media frenzy, he'd never forgive himself.

But she wasn't actually his girlfriend.

"She'll be fine," Jazz assured him as the driver zoomed off. Robby nodded, tapping the glass with one finger. Something bad was coming. He felt it in the pit of his stomach. Or maybe he was nervous because this was a turning point. All he needed was the right song.

Robby's cell phone buzzed in his pocket and he grabbed it, hoping there wasn't anything wrong. "Daisy?" he asked, not bothering to look at his phone first.

"You're a hard man to get hold of." It was McAllister. Robby deliberately hadn't called him back. If he told him there was no song, the deal would be off. The man's power in the industry was formidable and though Robby hated to admit it, McAllister could be the key to his solo career.

"Yeah. Been kinda busy," Robby said, trying to sound cool.

McAllister laughed. "Yeah. I heard. Listen. Is there any way you can get over to the studio? The director really wants you—thinks it will be good to piggyback your involvement with the release of the film in a few months." Robby's heart leapt. Someone actually wanted him?

"I'm on my way to rehearsal now," Robby said. "Not sure there's time…"

"Don't mess around. This is it."

Robby hated how pushy he was and yet he got it. The man didn't get paid if Robby didn't produce and so far, he hadn't given him any reason to believe he would. Considering Robby's history, the promise of a hit wasn't enough.

Robby nodded, trying to ignore Jazz's curious stare. "All right. I'll be over around, uh, four or so," he said. "I'm thinking acoustic, simple."

"Sure. See you over there. Oh, and Robby?"

"Mmm…?"

"Nice work with that girl."

"Yeah," Robby said. He hung up before he said something that sent the deal into question. He hated himself, yet he was sure it was nothing compared to how Daisy would feel when she found out what he was up to.

~*~

The entire day was a whirlwind. Robby checked in with Daisy once while on his way to the studio. It was enough for her that he said he had business to deal with. She didn't press him with questions. His other girlfriends…he was quick to stop that thought, reminding himself the relationship with Daisy was not so intimate that she had any claim to him or his time.

Daisy said she was catching up on some work, then she was going to get something to eat. He smiled when she innocently asked if it was OK to order room service and avoid the photographers. But he already took care of her dinner. He'd talked the chef into sending up a five-course meal complete with cookies and milk for dessert, as well as gourmet coffee. He'd never gone to such trouble for another woman, and it wasn't because of the trick he was playing on the media either. He wanted to do everything he could to ensure Daisy enjoyed herself.

And that was exactly why he didn't bother to tell her that he also lined up hair and make-up people to pamper her the next day before they went to the show. Taking care of Daisy gave him unbelievable satisfaction.

And all of this wasn't related to the fact that Robby spent the rest of the day recording a song she forbade him from taking. At least, that's what he told himself when he listened to the final cut at nearly midnight. It was sure to be a number one song the world over.

~*~

Daisy was awake when Robby slipped into the hotel room sometime after one o'clock. While she was in her pajamas and working on her computer, she was clearly waiting for him. The sight of her, so innocent, made his heart ache with guilt.

He was a horrible person.

"Hey," she said. "How'd everything go? Did you get a lot done?"

Inwardly Robby groaned, wishing she weren't so nice. It would be easier if she was still pushing him away. He managed to nod as he kicked off his shoes. "Yeah. It was good. How about you?"

Daisy smiled. "It was a little quiet around here without you to argue with," she said.

Robby chuckled and nodded as he finally met her eyes.

"Thanks for dinner," she said. "It was amazing...especially the coffee."

"You're welcome." Robby's heart swelled. *You showed her love*, a voice inside him urged. *Don't ruin it. She deserves the truth.*

Her praise increased the weight of his guilt. He did his best to push it aside and said, "Tomorrow's going to be quite a day."

"Oh, yeah?" Daisy's eyes sparkled.

Robby winked as he went to sit beside her on the bed. "Spa treatments—hair, nails...it's a lot of work to be red-carpet ready," he said. "Well, if you're me, that is..." He met her eyes and smiled when she blushed. He pressed his hand to her cheek. "I doubt they'll need to do anything for you."

Daisy laughed. "Stop it—you're the sexiest man alive..."

"According to some goofy magazine." He shook his head. "How stupid that whole thing is, huh?" He didn't wait for her answer before he continued. "Anyway...I think they're bringing something like ten dresses for you to pick from."

Daisy's eyes went wide. "What? Who needs that many?" She gave a weak laugh. "Maybe I best get to sleep."

"Yeah—me too," Robby said, glad for a reprieve from talking. He needed to think. He stood and lifted Daisy from her chair and set her on the bed.

"I've got it," she said.

He shrugged and took her hand to kiss the

softness of her palm. She smelled clean, fresh from the shower. "Yeah. I wanted to make it easier for you. I like spoiling you."

She blushed as she snuggled under the covers, not catching his real meaning. "You have. Thanks. I'm really excited about tomorrow."

Robby smiled and brushed the hair from her forehead, his heart sinking. "Me too," he said. "I'm going to get a shower." Daisy nodded and yawned as Robby left the room, wondering what might stop the impending doom.

~*~

The next day was spent in chaos. Robby was swept away by his own stylist team while Daisy was taken on by three of the kindest women she'd ever met. They brought her dress after dress until she settled on a simple red one they all agreed Robby would love. Next, they gave her a facial and worked on her nails. It was fun, and although cliché she texted Sadie and Jennifer that she felt like a princess.

As the stylists fussed over her hair, Daisy was relieved they weren't making her into something she wasn't. She was herself, only better. Robby must really care to go to so much trouble. Whether he thought of her as a friend or more didn't matter. He was growing as a person and thinking of someone other than himself. She promised to tell him how much his thoughtfulness meant to her.

By the time Daisy was helped into the limo a few hours later, she was anxious to reconnect with Robby. *What on earth could they do to make him more handsome?* But as soon as she was settled in the limo, Robby hopped in and Daisy swooned. He grinned at her, his teeth brighter than usual, his hair a mess of controlled chaos. He wore a dark blue suit that was almost black, and a shocking red tie that matched her dress perfectly. His signature tennis shoes completed the look, which made Daisy laugh. Her own shoes were platform stilettos she would never be able to walk in if the situation was different. But they were amazing with her outfit.

"Wow," she managed to say as she toyed awkwardly with the hem of her dress. "Thank you for today...I mean, taking the time to make this so special. I...thank you..." Her words felt forced and false, but she hoped he understood.

Robby reached over and took her hand and kissed it. He lifted her face to his. "You amaze me, Daisy. I didn't think it was possible for you to be even more beautiful. I was already struggling when I'm with you, but this..."

Robby didn't seem to mind that Jazz was so close by, so Daisy tried to ignore his presence.

Robby whispered softly into her ear, "I'm not even sure I'm pretending anymore. You're stunning."

He sat back. His eyes suggested he was serious. To Daisy's surprise, he kissed her lightly on the neck before settling into the seat and holding her close against his side. She raised her eyes to meet his and he winked at her and took her hand in his.

A short time later they arrived at the line of limos where they sat and waited. Daisy stared in amazement as celebrities she'd never thought of as real people emerged from the limos ahead of theirs. To see them up close was surreal. Daisy didn't even care that she was staring. One by one they gracefully stepped out of their fancy cars and walked slowly into the building, waving and stopping for brief interviews and pictures along the way—all fairy tales unfolding before her eyes. Daisy's anxiety grew as she realized she would soon be in the same position they were, only she wasn't anyone's dream come true.

Maybe no one would notice her. She could hide behind Robby or...

As their limo drew closer to the red carpet, Jazz hopped out and ran to get into a line of security personnel. Robby took Daisy's hand and kissed it, yanking her abruptly from her nightmare.

"You're shaking," he whispered, kissing her hand again. He was calm, though his eyes sparkled.

He was becoming the rock star she'd expected him to be, the one on television and in magazines— confident, sexual, dangerous—the man she'd thought him to be when they first met, but in reality, it was a role he played for his career. The real Robby Grant was so much more.

She shrugged, wishing she could escape. *Why did she agree to this?*

"I'm not sure I can thank you," he said. He peered out his window for a moment before turning back to her. "They're going to be yelling at you, but just ignore it—no matter what they say. Just smile and wave like you don't hear any of it. It doesn't really take that long to get inside if you keep moving." Daisy nodded, her mouth dry, her heart beating wildly in her chest.

Her face must have given her away because Robby squeezed her hand with a sincere smile. "Jazz is going to get your wheelchair," he continued. "I'll get out first and wave, then we'll set you up. 'K?"

She nodded dumbly, wondering what her name was.

Robby smiled and drew closer to kiss her gently. "You're amazing." He paused, searching her face. "And beyond beautiful. You deserve the best, Daisy." He kissed her again, lingering this time. "You ready?"

Daisy wasn't able to hide how frightened she was. She wanted to stay in that limousine forever. But that wasn't an option. She had to go out there and be the best girlfriend she'd ever been. If only she knew how.

Robby held her chin in one hand and smiled. "It's all right, Harpo. I'm not going to let anything happen."

Before she was able to answer, Robby's door flew open and he stepped out. Cameras flashed and people cheered, but Daisy only saw the bottom of his coat and part of Jazz's pant leg. After a second, Robby leaned down and into the car, reaching for her.

"You ready?" he asked. Daisy froze.

"Your public's waiting." He lifted her gently from the car and set her in her chair, kissing her quickly as he did. The crowd cheered, but it was difficult to focus on anything because the action was overwhelming.

The fans were cheering and waving, security was monitoring everything, cameras were flashing and reporters were yelling. The noise was deafening.

Daisy hated feeling like she was part of a zoo exhibit. She forced herself to smile and wave at the people just like Robby was doing.

He pressed a confident and firm hand on her shoulder, and it gave her the courage she needed to keep going. She glanced at Jazz, who smiled reassuringly.

Robby maintained constant contact with her, touching a shoulder, her hair, and even kissing her for a picture. Although Daisy knew it was a game, Robby's words about struggling to pretend, rang in her mind the entire evening.

~*~

Robby led Daisy backstage so she could watch his performance. He said that when he was done, they'd go out and join the audience for the rest of the show. Daisy merely nodded.

She hadn't said a word since she escaped the limo and red carpet line. She didn't need to speak. There was so much to enjoy between the celebrities and their outrageous clothes, let alone what they were doing and saying both to and around Daisy. There was no time for talking.

Robby watched her, but he too said little. He'd left her long enough to change into his usual jeans and T-shirt, promising he'd be back in his suit after the performance. But Daisy didn't care what he wore. She only hoped he didn't regret his decision to bring her. She reached nervously for her lip gloss which she applied robotically, hoping she hadn't embarrassed him.

"Hey." Robby strapped his guitar around himself as he addressed her. Daisy closed the lip gloss and waited expectantly. He squatted in front of her. "You need anything you say the word and Jazz or I will—"

"I'm fine," she said, taking his hand in hers. "Now go out there and do what you do best. I'm dying to see what all this fuss is about."

He grinned. "Thanks. Hope you're not disappointed."

"Me too."

Robby laughed as Carli Cross approached them. She smiled as she fussed with her short, red hair. "You must be Daisy," she said, extending her hand. "I'm Carli. Lots of buzz about you...and this one lately."

Daisy immediately felt at ease with the international singer whose demeanor reminded her of Sadie. She was quirky, fun, and couldn't care less what anyone thought of her.

Carli burst onto the scene a little over five years before with a television show aimed at teenagers, but her musical talent quickly became the focus of everyone's attention. Now she was in every magazine, and her music was played on nearly every radio station all day long.

That she asked Robby to be part of her set meant she believed he deserved a chance. And what the singer said became gospel once the media picked it up. Daisy was sure the event would help Robby's career immensely.

"Nice to meet you." It was hard to believe that Carli was only three years younger than Daisy. In another world, they might even have been friends.

"You too. Do me a favor, would you? Is my hair sticking up on this side?" Carli turned and leaned over so her hair was close to Daisy's face.

Daisy tried not to laugh. Days ago she'd been stuck in her home with no hope of escape, and today she was in Los Angeles at a red carpet charity event. She was touching Carli Cross's hair. It was insane.

Daisy did her best to take care of the troubled spot, though she wasn't sure it was possible for the woman to look anything but flawless.

"It looks great," Daisy said sincerely.

Carli rose to her full height and smiled. "Thanks, hon. I think my hairdresser took a mental holiday," she muttered. "She's usually so good." Before Daisy could respond, Carli nudged Robby. "I'm giving you a real chance here, Grant. Don't blow it."

"Don't think I don't know it," he muttered. "No worries."

Carli gave him a thumbs-up. "Oh, there's none here. But we are on soon," Carli said. "Nice to meet you, Daisy..." And with that, she was gone.

"You're doing fine," Robby said as he turned back to Daisy. "They sometimes forget, but they're just people too."

She nodded and placed her hand on his cheek.

He drew a deep breath as if he were going to say something but stopped, seeming to think better of it. Instead, he drew closer so he could kiss her cheek. He whispered in her ear, "I couldn't have done any of this without you. I can't wait to finish our song." He stepped back and met her eyes. For the first time, she didn't blush. He kissed her again before hustling off to the stage.

Daisy didn't even hate it that she grew warm when he said "our song" as if they were in this together, because perhaps it was true. Before she was able to follow the thought, her cell phone buzzed in her purse. She opened it and read the text from Sadie.

You're gorgeous! They're calling you Cinderella. Call us when you can. Tell Robby to behave, or Nick says he'll kill him ;-)

Daisy smiled as she put down the phone. She loved her friends. And she was—sort of—in a relationship with a man who loved music as much as she did.

As Robby took the stage, Daisy decided she was going to let herself dream again—even if it meant she got hurt in the end.

19

Hours later, the couple was in the back of the limo—exhausted but happy. Robby's performance went well, and Daisy was still smiling. It was nearly two in the morning, but she didn't seem to care as she continued drinking in everything around them. Robby succumbed to the urge to pull her close against him as if it were completely natural. She smiled and gave a contented sigh.

"Thanks, Vanilla...this was so much fun," she said, dreamily.

Robby laughed. "Glad you liked it. I'm sure we can find a few more events if you want...they're always asking me to be at some place or other."

Daisy watched the people still lining the street near the red carpet as she spoke. "It doesn't seem to excite you."

Robby shrugged. "It gets old."

"I can't imagine that doing what you love every day and getting paid for it would ever get old," she said. "Most people don't get that chance."

Her words struck a strange chord with Robby, who swallowed hard against the lump in his throat. He was silent for several moments as he considered what she'd said.

"What is it?" Daisy asked, squeezing Robby's arm.

He met her eyes, unable to mask his emotions. "You're right," he said softly. "I've spent so much time being selfish about the whole thing that I almost missed it." He paused for a long moment. "I'm unbelievably blessed...and instead of gratitude, I've been angry because it wasn't enough." He exhaled as he ran his fingers through his hair. "I'm an idiot."

Daisy leaned her head against his shoulder and shook her head. "No, you aren't. You're just figuring out your life now...we're all working on that." Daisy yawned loudly. "Sorry...I'm exhausted."

Robby helped Daisy get comfortable against him. "Might as well take a nap, Harpo. Traffic's going to be horrible."

Daisy yawned. "OK." The words weren't past her lips before she closed her eyes.

"Lil wants to talk to you," Jazz said, holding his cell phone out.

Robby shook his head. "I'll call her later." He gestured to Daisy who had fallen asleep. He didn't have the energy for Lily. All he wanted to do was relish the peace and love that washed over him with Daisy cuddled close against his side.

"What are you doing?" Jazz demanded as Robby toyed with Daisy's hair. "There are reporters digging into her life right now. They'll take anything they can find to bring her down off that pedestal you put her on," he whispered, gesturing at Daisy angrily. "Do you even know why she's in a wheelchair? 'Cause I'm sure they do."

"It doesn't matter." Or did it? The relationship was fun now. It was easy, but Robby couldn't think far ahead to when it might get tough. Would he resent that she wasn't like everyone else?

Robby met his friend's eyes. "Listen...I wish I could explain what's going on, but she's...fantastic. I like her. I want more of what I'm getting, Jazz, and I don't think I'm wrong." He looked away. "I'm supposed to help her. It's like God told me or something."

Jazz's dark eyes glittered in the dim limo. "You can't make God say things because you want them to be true…" He exhaled in exasperation. "Get out of this now. Before she gets hurt. She's too good for this bull."

Robby felt deflated. The world only seemed able to see the worst in him. Was that all there was? "Why doesn't anyone believe I won't hurt her?" he moaned.

"I'm not stupid," Jazz said. "I'm not saying you want to hurt her—like it's a plan—but this isn't a game. She's a nice girl. She may not bounce back like the others." He sighed. "Not to mention the way the press is digging into her life right now. Guaranteed. She's going to get hurt."

Robby toyed with Daisy's hair a moment longer, and she smiled as she slept. His heart constricted. "Are we going home in the morning?" he asked.

Jazz nodded, choosing not to push the issue any further.

Robby rested his hand on the soft skin of Daisy's shoulder. "I'll talk to her when we get home. Lay out the truth," he said. "That should cover me. Right?"

Jazz laughed wryly. "It ain't up to me, man. You made your bed, you sleep in the messed-up thing."

That was exactly what Robby feared he'd have to do.

~*~

As they sat together the next day on the plane,

Robby's silence surrounded Daisy as his leg bounced restlessly in time to music only he could hear.

She tried not to stare at the way his jaw clenched and unclenched as he wrestled with his thoughts. Maybe they'd made too much of a mess, even for a professional boyfriend like Robby. Daisy closed her eyes for a moment, wondering if she'd done something stupid, yet nothing came to mind. Robby didn't bother pretending he was going to his own bed the night before. He'd gotten Daisy settled, taken a shower and come to bed like it was routine. When Daisy woke that morning, neither of them mentioned that the relationship was evolving into more than they'd planned. She feared if she said anything Robby would disappear like the dream he seemed to be.

The intensity of Robby's nervous twitch snapped Daisy back to reality, and she grabbed his leg to still him. He smiled, though it was a reflex. Her heart twitched. He'd given her everyone's smile, the one that belonged to the crowds—the press, the fans, the women in his life. The one he saved for Daisy was genuine, from the depths of his soul, radiating to his eyes and straight to Daisy's heart. She fought the shudder.

Maybe he was pulling away.

"Hey," she said. "You all right?"

Robby grunted and turned his attention back to his notebook.

Daisy forged ahead. "Do you want to work on the song? We've got a few hours."

Robby shrugged as he moved to sit closer to her. "Sure." He tossed his notebook into her lap. "Here," he said. "It's what I wrote so far..." He stood and grabbed his guitar, slinging the strap over his head as he paced the wide area in front of Daisy. Jazz went into a back room of the plane, where he lay on the bed and quickly snored.

Daisy glanced over the lyrics, trying not to be visibly disappointed. It was clear he was still resisting his own emotions. As Robby strummed beside her, she wondered how to bring out his deeper thoughts. He wasn't one to shy away from any conversation. Usually, it was she who pulled back. She realized in this case, though, she might have to give something of herself to draw him out.

"You sure are thinking hard." Robby began playing a complex melody.

She might as well tell him. "This is supposed to be a love song."

"It is." Robby nodded as he continued strumming and strolling. Daisy feared she was going to get motion sickness.

"Stop," she commanded. "Lose the guitar—we need to fix these."

His deep green eyes lacked their sparkle. "What? They're good."

Daisy shook her head. "They're not," she said honestly. "They're weak and boring and overdone."

"Hey! They are not...overdone." But the tiny worry lines appearing above his eyes told her he knew the truth.

Daisy leveled him with her stare. "Just because a song says the word *love* twenty times doesn't make it a love song. You can do better than this. Just because you like vanilla, doesn't mean you have to be vanilla, do you?"

Annoyed, Robby removed his guitar and set it aside. He sat beside Daisy, but clearly his mind and heart were elsewhere. Daisy awkwardly took his hand and it seemed to shock him into the moment. He looked at her.

"Tell me what it's like to be in love, Robby," she said softly. "Describe it—without using the word love. Tell me."

Robby's mouth dropped open, and he stared at her so long that she blushed, realizing he'd misunderstood. "Not with me!" She hit him in the arm as hard as she could manage.

"Ow!" Robby rubbed his arm, annoyed.

"Sorry—you seemed horrified," she said. "Come on. Haven't you lost someone you thought you'd be with forever? Someone you imagined marrying?" She hated that her voice betrayed the emotion behind the question.

"No." He was becoming distraught.

Daisy exhaled. Maybe she should try a different angle. "Robby...there's a heart inside you that's hurting because somewhere along the line someone failed to love you. That feeling needs to come out. Put it into this song. Right now, all you've got are words with no emotion. No amount of acting can fake it— your fans will see through it." She tapped his chest. "Get in there and root around until you feel what love is, what it was in your life."

Robby nodded and stroked her hand with his thumb until Daisy wondered if she'd gotten through to him.

Finally, he managed a weak smile of apology. "I wasn't...horrified...just...shocked," he said. "And by the way, it isn't that crazy. Women occasionally find me attractive."

Daisy pulled back. "This is a business

arrangement. Don't get any ideas."

"It's a love song," he protested, trying to take the notebook away from her. "A ballad.".

Daisy grasped it firmly against her chest and shook her head at him. "It's hard, Robby, I get that, but you need to trust that what's in there would relate to your fans. They want you back." She gently applied some of her favorite pink goo to her lips and wondered why she couldn't let it go.

"Right. But...how?" He stood and paced, grabbing his guitar and strumming for all he was worth.

"How?" Daisy yelled so loud Jazz woke and grunted in the next room. His snoring quickly resumed. "Stop being stupid and listen!" she continued loudly. "You are a pig-headed, proud shell of a man masquerading as a rock star. Real rock stars would smash the heck out of that guitar and write a ballad already so they could move on. You, on the other hand, are too afraid."

Robby stopped strumming abruptly and stared at her. Daisy gulped, fearing she'd said too much. It was hardly fair to assume anything about him or his life and yet she'd done just that. The only consolation was that booting her out of the plane wasn't an option, but after they landed all bets were probably off.

Before Daisy found the courage to take any of it back, she peeked at Robby.

He was smiling, and a new sparkle lit his eyes. "Did you call me pig-headed?" he asked. "And accuse me of not being a rock star when clearly..." He gestured to his ripped jeans and black T-shirt. "That is exactly what I am?"

Daisy nodded awkwardly.

He sat next to her and took her hands in his,

kissing each as he looked deeply into her eyes. "I think I know what love is now." Daisy tried to pull away but he held firm. "I'm not kidding. I think it's the most beautiful thing any woman has ever said to me."

Daisy snatched her hands away from him. Had he gone mad?

Robby continued grinning at her as he reached forward and stroked her cheek. "So, tell me, sweet angel, how do I write a love song?"

Daisy pushed his hand away as she set the notebook in her lap and yanked the pen from behind his ear. "There isn't a formula. It's a different creative process for everyone." She began jotting words in the notebook. "You can read the classic romantic things—poetry by Blake, Browning, Marlowe or whatever suits you. Watch some movies in the genre. Talk to people who've been in love...but probably the easiest way is to get out and live your life. That's the way real love happens."

"You've been in love, haven't you?" Robby accused with a wicked grin.

Daisy willed herself not to blush. "We aren't talking about me."

Robby leaned back in his seat and put his feet up. "With me?"

Daisy laughed easily. "No."

Robby grimaced. "Not even before we met? What about when I was on TV? Did you love me then? I'll bet you thought I was hot. Probably told Nick you wanted my autograph."

Daisy ignored him as best she could while she scanned the lyrics in his notebook, finding the word *love* scattered like bullet holes throughout. There little worth saving in what he'd written.

She glanced up at him, still frustrated. "I think Nick wanted me to fall in love with you, but I wasn't interested. Your life isn't—reality. Mine is." She pointed to the notebook. "Now, for the real problem. You don't give yourself enough credit. You're forgetting the man under all those tattoos, the guy with a heart and feelings and…it's common sense that I can't possibly fall in love with someone I didn't know until a few days ago."

When Robby looked at her blankly, she continued. "Love is more than physical attraction. It's understanding someone's heart, it's…" her voice drifted off and she paused. "I'm willing to help you if you want." Daisy gestured to the notebook. "These lyrics are crap. Stop worrying whether or not I was in love with you—which I was not—and worry how to fix these."

Robby slowly sat up straight, placing his feet on the floor as he did. "Yes, ma'am," he muttered. "What now?"

Daisy had broken through. She drew a deep breath. It felt so good to be in control of something again. She promised herself to stay focused and not let go. She drew a line over the entire page and smiled.

"Now we start over."

20

A few hours later, Robby and Daisy were home again, settled on the back porch as they continued working on the song. They made progress on the plane, and Robby encouraged Daisy to take charge of the lyrics while he worked out the tune. She made words mean what Robby still struggled to imagine, and even though he'd already recorded one of her songs, he hoped secretly that writing with her now would buy him time. Then he'd not only have new music but time to figure out a way to explain the truth to her. With each moment that his ruse continued, he grew increasingly distraught. What he'd done was wrong but he had no idea how to make it right except to tell her.

It was the last thing he wanted to do. And where did he begin?

"Nick should be home soon," he said in an effort to break the ice.

She nodded but kept writing. Robby cleared his throat. "So, uh, I guess I'll be heading to his house...he'll need help...I mean, that's why I came, right?"

Daisy looked up, her shiny pink lips reminding him of a bow as they curved into a sweet smile. "I'm sure he'll expect you to be there...but knowing Nick, if we're working on something he'll be fine with you being here too...sometimes."

Robby tried to hide his face by looking down at his hands as he strummed. His cheeks felt warm. Was he blushing? Had he ever done that before? He shook his head, trying to clear the thoughts away as he spoke. "And maybe he wouldn't mind if I came over and...slept here," he continued.

While neither spoke of it openly, Robby had slept in Daisy's bed every night since he'd arrived. And yet, other than a few kisses in the hotel room and limo and some 'brotherly' pecks for the cameras, he acted as a gentleman, keeping his hands and lips to himself. She was driving him crazy, but that was of no consequence...yet.

It pained him that he was more concerned with Daisy's feelings than he'd ever been with any woman's. He didn't want to take her to bed and leave her and it was confusing him. He was curious about her thoughts and what made her tick...and dare he think it? He might even be in love with her.

Lord, he prayed, *what's happening to me? Am I really ready for this? Help me.*

"You don't have to." Daisy's voice seemed reluctant, but she continued. "Nick might need you at night. You can't be over here with me...besides, I can hardly imagine that conversation. Broken leg or no, he'll take you out."

Robby coughed awkwardly. *Don't be an idiot. This has to end.* "Yeah...right," he said softly. "But, um, I...I don't mind..."

Daisy shook her head and went back to writing. Clearly, he'd made her uncomfortable. But they hadn't talked about anything, and it was driving him mad.

"Harpo." Robby set his guitar down and moved to sit closer to her. He had to be careful. "Thanks for...taking me in," he said softly. "And for...reminding me I'm a person...I forgot in the last couple years that I was worth anything."

Daisy smiled. "Seems to me I owe you the thanks," she said. "I'm not sure I would have ever left the house otherwise."

Robby laughed, his eyes holding Daisy's. "I...um...want to talk to talk to you about something," he began, sobering quickly. He was ready to burst.

"Sure..." Daisy said as he wrapped one arm around her shoulders. His heart beat wildly. Why? It shouldn't matter that he might break her heart—he'd done it a million other times and none bothered him enough to even resonate a week after. It was what he did. He let people down. From his parents to his teachers and his girlfriends, Robby was a man no one relied on and yet here he was, ready to have a panic attack because he was about to tell the truth, aware that he would hurt Daisy horribly.

You're different now. Why did he want that responsibility? Still, he was without a choice.

"Hey, you two!" Sadie's cheerful voice shattered the moment as she stepped out onto the porch. Robby's heart sank. He'd been ready to spill it all. He slowly removed his arm from Daisy's shoulders and pushed himself to his feet.

Sadie went to Daisy and handed her a huge cup of coffee. Then she turned to hug Robby. "You guys stole the show yesterday. Was it fun?" She flopped into Robby's seat. Daisy met his eyes and smiled.

Sadie stole glances between the two of them and started to stand. "I'm sorry..." she said. "Was I interrupting?"

"Nah. Just working on a song." Robby leaned over

Daisy and kissed her cheek. "We'll talk later, OK?" She nodded and he went inside.

They were already giggling like little girls before he was inside the house. Robby shook his head and went to his room and closed the door. He needed to be alone.

~*~

After nearly an hour in his room, Robby was more frustrated than ever. He still needed to come clean with Daisy, and the longer it took to do that the less he was certain she could handle the truth. He didn't even want to tell her. Whatever was going on between them was too new—he didn't want it to end. He liked who he was around her and feared what going home alone would do to him. Even if he ran to the busyness of LA he wouldn't have Daisy, and the thought cut to his core.

He finally set his guitar aside and turned down the volume on the television as he dialed his brother. Warren would help him.

"Yeah." His brother's voice made panic rise in Robby's chest. How could he say the words?

"You all right, desert storm?"

Warren chuckled. "What do you want, moron?"

"I'm back at Daisy's. It's quiet so far." Robby stood and paced the room. He paused at the window, noticing that several cars were parked along the main road, near the end of Daisy's and Nick's shared driveway. A few people with cameras milled about. He sighed.

"Never mind," Robby said. "Paparazzi are outside."

"Figures. Is Nick even back yet?"

"No. They had to keep him a few extra days because of the bruising and swelling. Daisy's friend works at the hospital, so she's going to make the arrangements with the doctors to get him settled when they release him."

There was a bit of noise Robby couldn't quite make out on the other end of the phone. Warren cleared his throat. "Kind of busy here, Rob. Is there something you need?"

What was he doing? If he admitted what he'd done, Warren would race across the world and beat him so he forgot his own name.

"Nope. Just checking in. Trying to be responsible."

"I'll call you later," Warren said. "Give Nick my best." The phone went dead and Robby slowly hung up as he continued peeking out the window, annoyed Warren hadn't made more time for him. But the guilt washed over him as he realized his brother was in the middle of a war zone, and he had bigger issues to deal with, all of which took precedence over Robby's lame soap-opera.

His phone rang before he had a chance to set it down. "Yeah," he answered, still interested in the happenings outside the window. The crowd was growing.

"You sitting down?" Lily's voice surprised him. Surely, she was going to say something about the song. It was probably the only way things could get worse.

"What's up, Lillian?" He stepped back from the window and sat on the bed.

"That song is better than anything you've ever done. It's a hit!"

Robby fell back on the bed and closed his eyes,

defeated. "Really? I'm not feeling it. Hold it a while. I'll have something else in a few days. Daisy and I did a duet..." Even to his own ears he didn't sound convincing.

"Are you crazy?!" she exclaimed. "The director loves it, you got the job."

Robby thought he might throw up. He shook his head, muttering an expletive. "Not yet. Hold them off as long as you can," he said. "I, uh, changed my mind."

"What is wrong with you?" Lily demanded. "Isn't this what you wanted?"

Robby ran his fingers through his tousled hair. "No—not anymore." He needed to tell someone, so it might as well be Lily. Surely, she wouldn't be against telling them the deal was off and there was no song.

"I stole it," he said softly, hating himself. "Daisy didn't want me to use it, but the lyrics were good so I wrote the music and now, I...I can't...go through with it."

"You're a little late, Robert. You already did." she screamed in his ear.

Robby knew he deserved this and more. He gulped. "I tried paying her for it, I offered her anything, but she wouldn't deal." He wondered why he couldn't ask what bound her so tightly to the song, but he feared her answer would mean he would be trapped. Already he hated that he felt protective of her, that he cared what she thought of him, that he wanted her to...dare he think it? To trust him.

Robby must have exasperated Lily on every level, but he paid her well for it. Whatever the cost he must put a stop to what was happening.

"Look," Lily said. "You were good yesterday, you know? It's finally your time again. You've been through the wringer and now it's time for you to be back on top."

Robby let her words wash over him.

"You look at her like she means something," she continued. "I haven't seen that from you before." Apparently even Lily had a gentle side. "There's more to this, isn't there?"

"No," Robby said a little too firmly. "She's so...nice. She doesn't deserve to be a doormat."

"Hmm..." Lily said. "Maybe you should stop treating her like one." She sighed heavily. "OK—I'll work on a contract for this song. We'll give her partial songwriting credit and a nice bonus too. She'll be taken care of."

The concession helped but Robby still wrestled with uneasiness. "Yeah. OK. But can I get some time before...?"

"I can't make any promises."

"Knock, knock," Daisy entered with a smile, a load of Robby's laundry on her lap. Was there no end to his ability to use her? She managed to look apologetic when she saw he was on the phone, and quietly set his clothes on the bed.

"Sorry," she whispered.

Robby shook his head and pointed to the phone. "I gotta go," he said. "Call you later." He hung up and smiled at Daisy. "Thanks."

"No problem," she said. "Sadie said the paparazzi are outside. You probably shouldn't go running."

Robby sat in front of her and picked up his guitar. He strummed. "Sorry about that."

She shrugged. "That's success, isn't it?" She forced a smile. "Sadie and Jazz went out for coffee," she said, changing the subject. "You two shouldn't be trusted around women. You're all trouble."

"Jazz is a flirt," he said.

"Hmm...and you're not?" she asked.

"Nope." He started playing the beginning of her song. "I want to play something for you," he said. "It's important you hear me out..."

Daisy smiled happily. "You got something? That's great! Play away."

Robby close his eyes as he sang and let the music speak for itself. Near the middle of the song, curiosity and a small amount of courage won out, and he opened his eyes again. Daisy's horrified face was covered in tears. He stopped playing abruptly.

"Hey..." he began softly.

Daisy's lip trembled. "I said no," she stammered weakly, but then her voice grew stronger as she shouted. "I said no! I was helping you write something else but you...why would you do this? It's mine!" She hiccupped. "But you knew I couldn't fight you, didn't you? So, you just went ahead and…"

She was nearly hysterical. Robby was speechless. Words seemed feeble in a moment like this. "You don't understand this business. That song is going to win a Grammy. It will go on forever," he said.

Daisy's jaw clenched as she stayed firm. "I said no and I meant it. Why wasn't that enough?" She seemed to recede into herself, lost and alone.

Robby hated himself. "I'll...leave. I'm sorry…" he met Daisy's eyes.

They regarded each other for a long moment before Daisy pointed and said, "Under the bed." Robby slowly set his guitar down and got on the floor. There were three boxes stacked to the top with ten notebooks each. He pulled them out and opened one. It was filled with poetry, songs, lyrics, and stories.

Daisy sighed heavily. "Take them—all of them—but not *Waiting*," she said. "That one is mine and I can't hear it on the radio every day. It's not about you. It's the one thing I'm not ready to lose."

Robby flipped through the book and tossed it back into the box. "You'd give me all of these?" he asked in disbelief. It was a lifetime of work, feelings, and thoughts she was tossing aside in an effort to protect one moment, one song. Robby's head swam.

Is this what love really meant?

He sat on the edge of the bed in front of her and took her hands in his. "All right, Harpo. We need to talk about this," he said. "Why? Why not give it up?"

She said nothing. Robby caught her eye and smiled, trying to be as smooth as he used to be. Was he failing miserably? He wanted a drink.

"You notice I'm asking what you want," he said. "Trying out the whole be-a-man thing..."

Daisy shook her head, and finally, as Robby continued stroking her hand with this thumb, she raised her eyes to look at him. "Because they're dreams," she said. "...and I don't need them anymore, but *Waiting*...I can't..."

Her words were like a knife in his heart. To think she'd given up on her dreams was unfathomable. Even after all the storms Robby weathered, he wasn't about to give up on getting back on stage, no matter the cost. There was always a way—could she really be so far gone as to have given up completely?

"What happened?" he whispered. It didn't matter that this might be a moment he'd regret. He had to help heal her. She deserved that much.

Daisy sniffed but said nothing as a tear rolled

down her cheek. He reached up and wiped it away. There was a time in his life when he wouldn't have told anyone his darkest secrets either. He feared the judgment it could bring, but he swore she'd find none of that in him.

"Did you ever meet my Aunt Sue?" he asked. She shook her head and Robby squeezed her hand.

"I've never known a man more in love with a woman than Nick was with Aunt Sue. We used to come out and spend the summers with them when we were younger. Dad was stationed in some God-forsaken country and Mom was off chasing her dreams in Paris or London or wherever. Aunt Sue and Uncle Nick were the only normal people in our lives."

He suddenly needed to show her he was lost, that he had problems, but they weren't insurmountable. Daisy could be happy, and Robby wanted to make it happen.

"Anyway, I used to dream of the kind of love those two had," he said. "He wouldn't even let her pump gas herself. It was a shame they couldn't have their own kids...they'd have made good parents."

Daisy smiled, squeezing Robby's hand. "Nick's..." she sniffed. "...been like a father to me since I moved here."

He was glad she understood his meaning. "Anyway..." he slowly released his breath. "That's a dream I gave up. Women want me for what I can do for them—their career, their bank account, whatever. No one really cares about what's inside me...who I am, the things that matter to me. I gave up thinking it was possible to trust people the way Sue and Nick trusted each other. It's easier to become what everyone expects." Robby tried to catch himself before he went too far.

Daisy's eyes were soft and round.

Robby forced a smile. "But it's all right. I chose this. And...I found you. I trust you, Daisy. Thanks for...wanting me to be me."

Daisy smiled and closed her eyes for a moment before she spoke, considering what he said. "My mom left when I was five. She didn't like being the wife of a music teacher—she wanted money and security, not love." Daisy said the words bitterly as if the taste of them nauseated her. "My dad was a good man and he raised me well, but...after..." She cleared her throat and shook her head, seeming to fight a demon that wouldn't be put down.

"Anyway," she continued. "I thought I wanted love, but it's never done much for me. Now, my friends keep trying to convince me it will happen someday, that there's a chance, but I have to be honest, I've come to terms with the fact that there probably isn't a man out there who'd look at me and see wife material." She gestured to her wheelchair. "Not like this." Her voice caught in her throat and she seemed to struggle with a host of powerful emotions. "Maybe if I'd always been this way...but I know that other side and...sometimes it's too much."

Robby tried to meet her eyes but she was lost in her thoughts.

"I don't feel sorry for myself...most of the time," she finally said. "The wheelchair and...the fact that a man will never say he loves me and mean it." She forced a brave, but false, smile.

"Don't..." Robby held her hand tight as she tried to let go. He kissed it. "Maybe you're playing into what people think you are. You don't have to. There might be someone…" Robby met her eyes and tried to make himself go on, the words sticking in his throat.

"I'm not asking you to say something you don't mean." Daisy slowly took her hand back and placed it in her lap. "I am learning to be content with the way things are—it's enough to have my friends, and Nick…" She met Robby's eyes. "Even you, this…whatever we're doing is good. I'm OK. I mean, it's fun having something else to think about. Like you said, until you got here my life was pretty boring."

Robby sighed. He should have told her everything—the truth about his feelings, the song, all of it. But his mind wasn't ready and his lips refused. He was clueless about love and she, of all people, understood it. Still, he was attracted to her for all the usual reasons and so many more.

"Daisy…" Robby cleared his throat as he met her eyes. He slowly reached up and touched her face. Maybe he could… "I don't know if you really get what I think about you." She regarded him innocently and he hoped his next words wouldn't break her heart. "You're so beautiful…where it matters. You are the most precious person I've ever met." His tone was sincere. "When I got here and you helped me—no questions asked—I finally saw something I'd never seen before." He leaned forward and kissed her softy.

"Robby…" she breathed, seeming to understand. "Thank…you." He cradled her cheek in his hand. He wanted to kiss her again so she would understand he wasn't being kind, but that he'd laid his feelings bare before her. He feared she wouldn't see what she already meant to him.

"I won't ask about the song again." Foolish words.

Daisy looked relieved. "Thank you," she

whispered.

The doorbell rang, causing both of them to jump. Robby met her eyes, but she began to pull away from him. "We aren't done yet," he said, holding onto her arm. "I have a lot more to say."

He leaned over and kissed her again quickly before she left the room.

21

Daisy went to the front door, not caring who was on the other side. Her mind was still in the bedroom, stuck on the conversation between herself and Robby. What was holding her back? Of course, giving Robby a whole library of music could hold him off a while, or at least she hoped it would. And if they finished their duet there would be more for the producers to consider. She wanted to let go, and maybe a part of her understood she had to, but she just couldn't do it. She wasn't ready to forgive Alec, and that was holding her back.

Daisy threw open the door and gasped. The members of Robby's band regarded her expectantly and reporters shouted in the background, taking pictures. She gulped, moving backward out of the line of fire.

"Hi. Um, where's Robby?" Mike asked.

"He's um..."

"Can we see him?" Reggie demanded.

Daisy glanced behind her at the empty living room. She backed up and gestured for them to enter. "Um, sure. Make yourselves at home," she practically whispered as she went to the hallway. "Robby!" she shouted. "Can you come out here?"

Robby came out of the bedroom, smiling, as he held up a notebook. He paid no attention to anything but Daisy. "There's some great stuff in here, Harpo..."

he said as he entered the room.

His face fell when he spotted the band.

"Hey," Dave said awkwardly. Robby stared at them and glanced at Daisy.

"I, uh, need to work," she muttered as she moved toward the door to the kitchen.

Robby stopped her by putting a hand on her shoulder. Still at a loss for words, she patted his hand with her own.

Robby handed her the notebook as she left. "You don't have to…"

"I won't be far," she whispered.

~*~

Daisy sat in the office wishing she was in the living room. Did Robby need her?

He's a grown man. The last thing he needs is you to bail him out. She wished Jazz were home. Quickly, she sent a text to Sadie to tell Jazz what was going on.

Daisy tried to focus on her work, turning her computer on and pulling out some files she was behind in writing. The arguing in the next room escalated. "So, that's the new meal ticket?" one of them asked, a taunt in his voice.

Daisy bristled.

"She is hot, though…I can't wrap my head around making it with a cripple…" Then there were sounds of a scuffle.

She could only assume Robby was going after the man who'd made the comment. Strangely, she felt vindicated that he'd tried to protect her reputation, but at the same time, she was beginning to understand how much pain he was in. These men had been his friends for years, yet they'd so quickly turned their backs on him—and why? Because he'd struggled to find himself outside of the partying, womanizing, alcoholic everyone pegged him for? It was terribly unfair.

"Knock it off!" one of the men yelled. "This isn't why we came, Reggie."

The man she assumed to be Reggie chuckled loudly as a bit more scuffling went on. She was relieved when the door to the office opened and Jazz entered.

"Sadie said the boys showed up," he said, gesturing toward the living room. "They in there?"

She nodded and without another word he was off to handle it. Daisy wheeled her chair over to the door.

"Oh, man..." one of the men said.

"You guys done?" Jazz demanded.

"Hey, we aren't here to cause trouble," another one said. "We came to get Robby back. Chase is...we don't fit."

"Really?" Robby sounded bored. "Now you need me?" Daisy was surprised he didn't jump at the chance they offered him, but he'd also been treated so badly, maybe he realized he had a career on his own terms, not theirs.

"Knock it off, Rob. We aren't going to beg," another man said. "Now, go get your stuff and let's go. We can still do the tour if we move a few dates back. Besides, even if you think you still have a career without us, don't act like you can get on the road that fast on your own."

"You guys really make a tempting offer," Robby said.

"What do you think you're going to do yourself—

stuck out here in the middle of nowhere? Huh?" one of the men persisted. "And with a crippled girlfriend? Man. Robby. You've sunk to a new low..."

There was silence for a few moments and Daisy wasn't sure what was happening. Another man spoke. "Unless..." he said thoughtfully, "This whole thing is a sham. Get the public to pity poor Robby, see you as a martyr and bam—you're back in it again? That's twisted!"

"Don't drag Daisy into this."

"It's not going to help you," the man said. "The whole world knows you're one slip up away from rehab."

There was another scuffle, and Jazz's voice boomed. "Maybe you idiots better go."

"This isn't what we came for," a different voice said. "Don't you want to get out on that stage again? The screaming fans singing your songs back to you? You have to miss that. We're willing to do whatever...we can go when you're ready. I mean, if there are things you need to handle here first."

"Yeah, man, it's your call."

Robby laughed wryly. "My call, huh?" he asked.

Daisy slowly wheeled to her desk and started to work, her focus settled on the conversation she'd overheard. Her time with Robby was nearly at its end, a notion that left emptiness in the pit of her stomach. Despite his annoying habits and desperation to steal her music, she liked him—he was fun. But he had to take his band up on their offer—and her world would return to being as small as it had been when he arrived.

~*~

Daisy worked in the office for several hours after Robby went into his bedroom and closed the door. Jazz stopped in to tell her he was heading over to Sadie's café for a dinner date, but he said nothing else. She didn't ask. She was certain Robby was packing. As she began to wrap up her work for the day, Daisy decided to call Nick and find out when he was coming home. She had to clean his house and put new sheets on the beds, but she intended to spend the next day getting ready for his return. And for Robby's departure.

"Yep." Nick's raspy but pleasant voice made Daisy smile.

"Nick."

"Well if it isn't Ms. Hollywood herself," he said. "I was beginning to think you'd forgotten all about me."

Daisy chuckled. "You told me to take care of your nephew, and that's a full-time job."

"Touché. Now, is the boy behaving himself or do I need to get some target practice in before they let me out of here?"

Daisy laughed. Leave it to Nick to be concerned about her honor. "We've had a few moments, but overall he's been fine, I promise. He's actually a pretty good guy."

"Better be or I'll have something to say."

"Heaven knows," she said. "So, when do you come home?"

"The doctors are underestimating me by saying I have to wait until Thursday. I tried to tell them I'm ready now but they won't listen."

"Imagine that," Daisy said. "Listen, Robby really wants my song but...I'm scared. Letting it go is...well, harder than I thought it would be. I've told him 'no' a bunch of times already but..."

Nick chuckled. "He's pretty convincing. He always did get his way with his mom too. It's probably the reason he's gotten into so much trouble over the years—he never did understand being denied anything." Nick released a heavy sigh. "Daisy, you know I love you, honey, but it's your song. I'm not going to tell you what to do. The boy may have a lot of problems but he knows his business. I don't think he'd lead you astray."

Daisy nodded, glancing toward the door. She and Robby needed more time. With the house finally empty, they should finish the conversation they started before the day's chaos.

"Right," she said softly. "Thanks, Nick. I'll, uh, think about that."

"Good girl. I gotta go. Dinner's here. It's meatloaf."

Daisy gagged. "Hospital meatloaf? I'll be sure to make you some real food when you get home."

"Bless you. Bye, Daisy."

Daisy hung up and slowly went into the kitchen to prepare dinner.

~*~

Robby sat in his room for nearly three hours thinking about his band and what kicking them from the house meant. Mike tried to leave the door open with a sympathetic smile while telling Robby to give it a few days before saying he was definitely out. But Robby's gut said it was over. He needed out, and the moment was now.

Where was Daisy? He needed her.

When he smelled the most heavenly aroma

coming from the kitchen, he slowly emerged from his bedroom, looking and feeling awful. He found Daisy peering into the oven. Finally, she closed the door and turned toward the refrigerator when she spotted him.

"Robby!" she squealed. "You nearly gave me a heart attack."

He smiled, realizing with a jolt that he no longer felt any reservations about his decision. Just seeing Daisy confirmed he was where he should be. And he was completely peaceful.

"Are you OK?" she asked softly as she moved to the refrigerator. "You look a little...I don't know...weird."

Robby placed his hand on the door to keep her from opening it. "Where's Jazz?"

"Your flirtatious and useless bodyguard left you in the care of a handicapped woman with a gun to take Sadie out to dinner and a movie," Daisy said, sounding irritated though it was clear she was more amused by the situation than annoyed.

"Mmm..." Robby nodded. "How long till dinner?"

She glanced at the oven, still puzzled. "Probably twenty-five minutes, but if you're hungry there are apples in the fridge—or some cookies in the cabinet over there," she said. Robby knelt in front of her as he took her hand.

"We need to talk," he said.

Daisy simply nodded and allowed him to lead her into the living room where he sat on the couch. Without asking permission, he lifted her from her chair and set her squarely on his lap, glad she didn't bother to resist.

"What are you doing?" she asked.

Robby urged Daisy to rest her head on his

shoulder. He sighed and placed his cheek against her hair. "I realized that I need you," he said softly, still pretending it was about the decision he'd already made. Really, he was more interested in what was going on inside him every time she was around. Did she feel it too? Was he crazy?

"What? Robby..." she struggled against his chest, trying to sit up, but he noticed it was weak. He rubbed her arm gently.

"They want me to go back on tour with them," he said, inhaling the sweet scent of the shampoo in her hair. He kissed her head softly. "Maybe I should..."

Daisy sighed and rested against him. Robby closed his eyes for a moment, enjoying the closeness they shared. "Is...that what you want?" she finally asked, a hint of nervousness in her voice.

His heart constricted, afraid to say what he wanted. "I want to get back on stage," he said softly, toying with her hair. "But I need to stay here for..." he let the sentence drop, the word 'you' on his tongue. He cleared his throat, fearing he'd said too much already. "...for Nick."

Daisy nodded. Robby's fear kept him from turning so he could see her, so he quietly kept stroking her hair instead.

"I promised Warren I wouldn't mess this up. I've let him down too many times already."

"You didn't mess anything up," she said. She reached over to her wheelchair and pulled out a tube of lip gloss that she applied nervously. She slowly put it back as Robby waited.

"Do you want me to stay?" he asked. His heart began to beat faster and his palms started to sweat. Did he really want to know her answer?

Daisy glanced toward the window, thinking. "It's going to be lonely when you're gone," she said. "But, I talked to Nick. He's coming home Thursday, so...you'll need to be over there with him." She turned slightly to smile up at him. "I understand what this was, and it's OK. You weren't unfair to me—you didn't lie. And it's been fun."

He gazed down into her eyes, wanting so much to kiss her. He shouldn't. "Daisy..." he said softly. "You're...so beautiful."

She blushed and turned away. "Don't," she said, shifting. She lifted herself back to her chair, away from him.

Although he wanted to, Robby didn't hold her back. "Why don't you believe me?" he asked, turning so his feet were on the floor directly in front of hers. He leaned forward and took her hands. "Didn't anyone ever tell you?"

Her eyes told him she was remembering something. Tears threatened.

"What is it?" he whispered. "Let me in. Tell me what's holding you back, Daisy."

She shook her head and sighed, forcing a smile. "Dinner's almost ready," she said. "I need to make a salad."

She started to leave the room, but Robby ran after her, jumping in front of her and kneeling on the floor to look into her eyes.

"I'm going to keep saying it until you believe me," he said earnestly. "You are beautiful. Just like you are, Daisy..." He touched her face gently. She was a long way from believing in him or trusting him. But that was OK, for now.

She pressed her cheek against his palm

nonetheless and sighed. "Thank you," she said softly. "But you don't have to save me. I'm OK…and getting even better."

Although he wanted to say more, Robby forced himself to nod. He stood and followed her into the kitchen where he silently helped her make the salad.

~*~

Dinner was a quiet affair. Both Daisy and Robby were lost in their own thoughts about what was happening between them. Daisy was shocked at Robby's insistence on her beauty. None of her boyfriends had ever made such a fuss—even when she still believed she was beautiful. From time to time throughout the meal she glanced at him, unsure what to say. His words and their intent hung between them, an impasse of emotion.

The fact that she wanted him in her life more than she'd wanted anything before didn't help much. Navigating the rocky territory that might lead to a relationship with anyone, let alone Robby, was still too much.

Daisy focused on eating instead.

When Robby was done with his meal he stood and picked up his plate. "I can take yours too if you're done," he said softly. Daisy nodded and he set about cleaning up the kitchen. She sat silently waiting for him to say something. When he didn't, she slowly went into her bedroom, got her laptop, and went to the living room where she moved to the couch and began to work.

As Robby started a pot of coffee, Daisy wondered what was going on. Finally, he entered the living room, his face pensive.

"Thanks for dinner."

"Thanks for cleaning up." She turned her attention back to her computer screen where she got on the internet and typed in Robby's name, something she didn't think she should do, but it seemed wise in light of recent developments in her life.

Pictures, articles, and breaking news all popped up on the screen at the same time. Daisy sighed. She should have known.

"Anything I can help with?" Robby sat beside her, his warm arm brushing hers.

There was no way to hide what she was doing with him that close, so she showed him the screen.

He glanced at it for a fraction of a second before half-heartedly trying to turn it off. "Don't waste your time."

"Aren't you curious?" she asked.

"Nope." He leaned his head back and closed his eyes. "I already know what I'm doing and where I am..."

Daisy frowned. "According to this you and I are planning a family, and you're thinking of building a studio here in Pennsylvania, and..." Robby yanked the computer from her lap and started scrolling through the stories. He nodded and made "humph" noises every so often but otherwise said nothing.

Daisy couldn't imagine what it must be like to have people talking about you all the time, caring who designed your shirt or if you were going to show up at the latest hot spot alone or with a new significant other. Daisy sometimes had trouble deciding which sweater to wear. If the media always commented on everything she did she wouldn't make any decisions at all.

Robby opened a new screen and typed in her name. Daisy's stomach clenched with fear. Would he see it? But instead of her history, pictures of her from the previous week appeared, and Robby scanned through them, making comments.

"Mm...I like that one...You looked great that day," he said at one point, finally pausing on a picture of the two of them on the red carpet.

He whistled. "You are one hot little number, Harpo. Maybe you'll be one of the fifty most beautiful people this year."

"Knock it off..." she said, grabbing for her computer.

"What? Don't like it?" he asked innocently, still scanning the pictures. "Oh...hello, gorgeous!" He held up the computer bearing her picture, laughing when she took it from him.

"What about you?" she asked, returning to her own search.

Robby leaned back again, slumping into the couch, his eyes closed. He tossed his forearm over his face. "I should hope that whatever you find on there is taken with a boulder of salt," he muttered.

Daisy scanned articles quickly, finding he dated more women—mostly celebrities—than she'd imagined. She scrolled through the pictures, names, and stories, herself being the latest addition to his harem. Did she want to be part of this?

"Do you still talk to all of them?" she asked in wonder. The women were all tall and tanned with long hair and legs that never ended. Daisy was convinced she wouldn't be fit to be in the same room with any of them even on her best day.

"All of who?" he asked, and slowly opened his eyes. He regarded the computer screen and sighed. "Some...most of them no. Don't let that give you the wrong idea...I take a woman out for one date and it becomes national news, but that doesn't mean we're in an actual relationship. You get that?"

The idea hadn't crossed Daisy's mind. Those pictures led her to believe he'd slept with all those women. She realized now that this presumption was less than fair. She nodded slowly, understanding. Dating would be different for a celebrity. A serious relationship, or a casual one, under the spotlight of fame would come with its own set of unique issues Daisy had never even considered.

"And..." he continued the thought as he took her computer and set it aside. "Sometimes I need a date for an event...you know, like, for a decoration or something. It's fun, an image...it's not serious." He took Daisy's hand.

She laughed. "You mean like us?"

He kissed her hand gently, his lips lingering longer than necessary. "I've been trying to tell you this is different."

She pulled her hand away, frightened. "Please..." He was getting too close and too serious. And she should go to work before the conversation went any further. Daisy started to get into her wheelchair, but Robby stopped her by putting his hand on her knee.

"You want some coffee?" His voice had taken on a gentle tone that melted a bit of her heart. "Can we do some writing tonight?"

Daisy settled back into the couch with a nod. She swallowed the awkwardness.

"Lots of sugar, lots of cream, right?" he asked as

he headed for the kitchen.

Daisy nodded. It struck her that he knew how she took her coffee.

Robby returned moments later with two cups of coffee. He handed her one and went to the piano where he sat.

"So...are you leaving?" Daisy sipped her coffee. Robby didn't answer, instead toying with the piano for a moment, falling into a beautiful song that made Daisy close her eyes and imagine it was for her. When she opened them, he was smiling.

"You like that?" he asked.

She nodded, embarrassed he'd caught her daydreaming about him.

"Good." He continued playing the tune. "I wrote it for you."

"You're crazy."

Robby laughed. "Maybe...but maybe that depends on you," he said, sighing. "Well, Daisy my dear one, I'm not ready to leave you yet. I like it here. I like you...I want to write more music together. I'm going to convince you I'm right. You're wasting time with what you're doing now."

"I am?" she asked.

"Yep. Get over here. I want to finish that duet." Daisy got into her chair and went to him at the piano. He started into a familiar For Granted song, and she sang along with him. The song ended and Robby's look affirmed what he'd just said.

"Yep. You're getting a new career." He nodded as if he'd confirmed a well-disputed question. "Let's write our song."

~*~

Several hours later Robby and Daisy lay together under a blanket on the couch. He toyed with her hair as she leaned against his chest, sleeping. A classic movie played on television. He only half-watched it. His mind was occupied by the war raging in his heart. Was he in love? Of course that was crazy. He'd never known it, so how could he be sure? He hoped he'd know if it happened to him.

Robby realized he had work to do—and fast. Before he decided where to begin untangling his issues, Jazz entered. He looked at the couple and shook his head. Robby pressed a finger to his lips. Jazz raised an eyebrow and went to his bedroom, closing the door.

Robby smiled. It had been a brilliant evening. He and Daisy were closer than ever, and while he hadn't followed through, he'd badly wanted to kiss her the whole time they'd been working. She liked him, he was certain. And it was more than infatuation. It was real. She laughed at his jokes, and called him out when he was being a fool.

You finally found a real friend. And yet that was probably the last thing he wanted her to be. He held her close against him and enjoyed the warmth of her in his arms as he drifted off to sleep.

22

Two days later, Daisy woke with a stiff neck from sleeping on the couch again. She and Robby had spent several late nights working on their duet and finally finished it—both of them excited for the progress they'd made.

Daisy had completely stopped doing her own work, which meant her balance dropped so low the bank nearly closed her account. Jennifer and Steve stepped in and loaned her two hundred dollars because she had too much pride to tell Robby. Yet another debt.

She was going to have to work twice as hard once he was gone.

The pair settled into a natural, easy camaraderie that came so fast it almost scared Daisy. It had been only a few days since she'd met Robby, yet her life now centered on him. Although he assured her numerous times that he was not leaving anytime soon, she wasn't sure she believed him. Besides, she wanted to enjoy him as long as possible. It fulfilled her to no longer be alone.

Their routine usually consisted of Daisy getting up first and making breakfast, which they ate on her back porch or at the kitchen table. Robby helped her clean up before he left to exercise. When he returned and took a shower, they would go for a walk. While this meant the ever-present media got even more pictures,

Daisy hardly cared. She got the chance to talk to Robby during that time, although he never asked much about her. He knew she was once a dance instructor, and she knew that he could sew, thanks to his mother's influence. As much as she didn't want to admit it, Daisy's feelings for Alec had never come close to this.

More than once, and out the cameras' sight, his gaze told Daisy he thought more of her than he was letting on. His touches lingered, yet he'd been a gentleman for the most part, though they had, to Daisy's pleasure, kissed a few times. Still, she wasn't sure she should take any of it seriously. Perhaps he was practicing for public appearances, playing a role, or maybe even lonely. It was almost impossible to tell since they carefully avoided the conversation Daisy so desperately wanted to have and at the same time spent much effort avoiding.

When their duet was complete, Robby convinced her to record it with him. Today they would go the studio for Daisy to sing her part, as well as play the piano. The thought made her shudder in fear and anticipation. Once she exposed her voice and talent, there would be no more hiding. But maybe she didn't want that anymore. She was going to try for dreams now that she could once again see them. Whether those dreams included Robby was a thought she would not yet entertain.

Daisy relished Robby's arms around her as they cuddled under the blanket on her large couch. She thought she should get up and make breakfast. He sighed peacefully in his sleep and Daisy shifted slightly to see him. The better she knew him, the more she was drawn to him. She discovered his looks were only one aspect of his beauty. She boasted knowledge of the real Robby Grant, a man whose heart was more handsome than his smiling face ever could be. Daisy identified with him more intimately than any of his other numerous girlfriends. It made her superior to any of them and helped her confidence continue to rise.

But at the same time, Daisy dreaded the end of her happiness. Nick was set to come home in two days. Robby would go then.

She worked to disentangle herself from his arms to move into her wheelchair. She'd make him a good breakfast before they departed for the studio to record their song.

~*~

Several hours later, Daisy listened as Robby sang his part of their duet. She was fascinated by him, comfortable not only in his skin but in his work. In his element, he grinned broadly at Daisy, who blushed.

"He likes you," Jazz said as he sat heavily on a couch nearby.

"I like him too…he's a good friend," she said.

Jazz raised an eyebrow. "Is that what you want— or what he wants?" he asked. Daisy squirmed, uncomfortable. She trusted Jazz, but she didn't think it right to say anything to him.

The large man nodded, yanking his baseball hat off and tossing it to the side. "It's none of my business," he continued. He put up a hand when she started to speak. "My job is to protect him—physically. But over the years we got close. We're good friends." He lifted his dark eyes and met Daisy's. "And as his friend—he doesn't know how to do this. I don't think he's ever been in a completely sober relationship before so if he…messes things up…"

Daisy gulped, wondering what he was talking about. "But nothing…like that…is going on…"

"I'm just trying to help."

"There's nothing to help with," Daisy said. She reached over and squeezed his hand. "But I appreciate the thought."

Jazz nodded as Robby came out of the booth. He leaned over her and whispered in her ear. "They're going to play the mix for us in a few minutes." He kissed her cheek.

"Wow…that was fast," she said. Jazz slipped out of the room, leaving them alone.

Robby squatted in front of Daisy. "I've never heard anyone sing a song the first time through so perfectly," he said, placing both hands on her face. He kissed her.

"Robby…" she whispered.

He held her gaze, his face revealing little. "Thank you." His voice was soft. "You gave me back everything I lost and I…"

Daisy swallowed the lump in her throat. One of the guys who'd been mixing the song came out of the booth and nudged Robby. "You two want to listen?" he asked.

Robby nodded and took Daisy's hand. "Let's go…"

~*~

"Hey," Jennifer said as she and Sadie crept in Daisy's back door the next day. Their arms were loaded with boxes they set on the table as soon as they were inside.

"Hey." Daisy began cracking eggs in a bowl as her friends sat.

"We brought the rest of the stuff for the centerpieces. Think you'll be able to get to them?" Jennifer asked.

Daisy poured a bit of milk into the bowl before adding salt and then pepper. "Nick comes home tomorrow, so Robby will be heading over there. After today things should settle down."

Jennifer and Sadie exchanged a glance. "Are you...OK with that?" Jennifer asked.

Daisy tried to focus on cooking to ignore the hurt creeping in. "Writing with him has been fun. But really, it wasn't a secret he wouldn't stay here long. So yeah, of course I'm fine."

"Liar," Sadie said. "You're in love with him."

As much as Daisy wanted to deny the accusation, it was futile. She was pretty sure she was in love with him, but her insides were acting in ways she'd never before known, and she wasn't ready to admit it to herself or anyone else. What if she was wrong? She'd rationalized it so far, thinking she was caught up in the fun. Any woman who spent any time at all with Robby—the man Daisy knew—would fall in love too. She sighed dreamily but said nothing. Sadie and Jennifer exchanged amused glances.

"Never once saw you look at Alec like you do him," Sadie continued.

Jennifer smacked her. "Don't bother saying that man's name."

"I don't love him," Daisy insisted. "At least...I don't think so." She glanced at Sadie. A lot of time had passed since they'd said Alec's name and yet it still wasn't long enough that it was any easier to think of him. "Robby makes me feel...different...than anyone else ever has."

"That's because you lust after his hot, tattooed body," Sadie said with a wicked grin, still teasing.

Daisy groaned. "Don't make him cheap. He's deeper than that."

"Really?" Amused, Jennifer rested her chin on her hand. "Enlighten us..."

Daisy cleared her throat as she focused on preparing cinnamon rolls. "We talk about everything—amazing conversations about music, spirituality, life stuff. He started reading the Bible when he was in rehab—he wants his brother and Nick to be proud of him. He's afraid he let everyone down in his life. And I, personally, think he's doing a good job of turning things around."

"I hope you're right. We don't want you to get hurt in this game you two are playing," Jennifer said.

"So, did you ask him to be your date to the wedding?" Sadie asked.

Daisy placed the rolls in the oven. "That's still almost a month away, and he's going to be long gone by then." Daisy was glad her back was turned, but it was impossible to mask the disappointment in her voice.

"Planes were invented years ago. He can fly in if you ask."

"He's not coming back for the wedding—no offense, Jenn. He'll be back to work and touring by then," Daisy said as she focused on the eggs.

"Jazz is coming...and you don't know if you don't ask," Sadie said. "And don't be stupid. He's so hot."

"Nick told me that the Robby he knows wouldn't

stick around this long for anyone...unless he was trying to get someone into bed." Jennifer blushed as she spoke.

"Daisy took care of that already," Sadie said with a wicked grin.

Daisy stopped working and turned to her friends. "We are only sleeping. He's been a complete gentleman."

Sadie cleared her throat. "Doesn't that prove Jenn's point? If he didn't care about you, wouldn't he do whatever he wanted? Your feelings wouldn't matter."

Daisy went back to work, still trying to convince herself there was nothing going on. "Or he's just using the situation for his career...or he doesn't find me attractive." She wished her friends would drop the subject.

"Oh, boy..." Jennifer muttered as Robby entered the room, running his fingers through his hair. It stuck up in all directions and his shirt and shorts were rumpled from sleep. He grinned at the women and winked before Daisy noticed he was standing there. She blushed, hoping he was still too asleep to have heard what she said.

"Morning, Robby," Sadie said boldly, making kissy faces behind his back to Daisy, who turned away in annoyance. He glanced over his shoulder at the women with a half-smile.

"Ladies..." he said, turning his full attention on Daisy, who awkwardly stirred the eggs to keep them from sticking to the bottom of the pan. He went to her and turned the stove off before kneeling in front of her.

"You still think I'm just using you? That I don't find you attractive?" he asked softly, his eyes searching her face. Daisy gulped, speechless.

"How many times should I tell you that you're beautiful before you believe me? I'll say it a million times every day if I have to. Or maybe I can show you."

Daisy nudged him away, swallowing the lump in her throat. "Don't be stupid. You don't need to prove anything. They know what's going on." Daisy turned the stove back on and stirred the eggs.

"No, we don't," Jennifer said, helping herself to an apple from the bowl on the table. "Explain."

Daisy glanced at Robby, the truth in her eyes. While she was sure her friends realized the relationship was a farce, she never specifically told them so. It was past time she did so, if only so they'd leave her be. "Robby and I are..."

"Falling helplessly in love," he finished. She stared at him incredulously. "I didn't mean to, Harpo...it just sort of...happened," he whispered for her alone.

Daisy stared at him as the eggs burned in the pan. The way he'd spoken the words was so believable that she was having a hard time separating the truth from the lie. But surely he was kidding.

Robby moved the pan to a different burner and again turned off the stove, all while holding her gaze.

"What are you doing?" she whispered.

"I get a say in this too. It's my heart you're stealing," he said.

Daisy had to stop him before he made the whole situation worse. She punched him in the arm as hard as she could manage, glaring all the while.

"Ow!" he squealed, holding his arm and nearly losing his balance. "What was that for?" Daisy's heart continued beating wildly in her chest. What an actor.

She'd almost believed him. And it scared her silly. Why would he play with her? And when her own feelings were already so muddled she wasn't sure she'd ever sort them out. It was cruel.

"Harpo?" He reached for her.

She backed away from him, forgetting her friends were even in the room. "I am a person with feelings," she spat. "You can say things like that when it doesn't matter...but not here in private and not when it isn't true. I can't pretend all the time. You admitted you don't know what love is. Don't act like you figured it out." Daisy had reached her limit. The game was over.

"I can't do this anymore..." she said. "Consider this your break-up. Call your buddies in the press. I'll do a re-enactment later so it's on tape." Daisy moved toward her bedroom. Before going in she glanced at Robby one more time and said, "And stop touching me. I can't handle it anymore."

She slammed the door behind her.

~*~

Robby still kneeled as though Daisy were in front of him and stared down the hallway.

"What was that about?" Jazz groggily came out of his bedroom.

Robby shook his head and went outside, forgetting the paparazzi were at the end of the driveway waiting for a glimpse of him.

"Robby!" they screamed. "Where's Daisy?" He ignored them as he walked around the back of the house and stood staring at the large, green pasture behind Nick's house. What happened? He was trying to tell her he was falling in love with her and she...punched him? She was pushing him away again and it didn't make sense.

Robby's past relationships were easily forgettable. The only one that stood out happened over twenty years ago, when he was in high school. He closed his eyes for a moment and remembered her. Jillian Edwards. She was a cheerleader bent on taming the bad boy of the school. Robby fell for it, and for her. She was gorgeous and every guy in the school was in love with her. While he'd been a bit too cool for most things, Robby still wanted to be accepted and at the time, Jillian was the ticket.

Although there was a short time when he did hang out with the popular crowd because of Jillian, he realized quickly that he didn't like any of them very much. Thankfully, the petite redhead was enough on her own to keep him on his best behavior. It wasn't the long, red hair and her bright green eyes or even her amazing body that held his interest. On top it all, she was also very funny and kind. When she'd finally broken up with him after three months, realizing she wasn't going to tame him, she'd explained that Robby was "too cold," and he "liked being on his own too much to commit to anyone."

While her assessment of him was fair—and accurate—Jillian's words stung and haunted Robby for some time. He didn't want to be cold and yet he was unsure how to warm up to anyone. As for being alone, that wouldn't have been his choice either, but it seemed to be the way things ended up. No matter how much fun he was, how much he had to drink, or what he did to keep the party going, eventually, everyone left him and again he found himself on his own.

Even as he stood in Daisy's backyard he began to

wonder if Jillian was right. Maybe he was still under the spell of all those problems.

So much was different in such a short time. He wasn't a lead singer or a wasted alcoholic anymore, but now he didn't know who or what else he was. He needed to deal with his issues—again—when it seemed he'd spent six months doing that exact thing. Why was it that every time he thought he was OK he discovered he was worse off than the day before? The questions were mounting again and he was even less prepared to deal with them. Was he able to go on as a solo act—without the support of the band? And if he couldn't have Daisy, going on would be nearly impossible.

"You shouldn't be out here." Jazz put a hand on Robby's shoulder.

"Daisy OK?" he asked, wondering if he should go back inside and check on her himself. He cursed his relationship experience. Being a flirt was one thing, it was a different ballgame altogether to be sensitive and considerate.

"The girls are trying to get her to open the door," Jazz said. He was serious, his eyes meeting Robby's. "Lil texted about writing Daisy a check for over twenty-five thousand. That's a lot of money."

Robby didn't even flinch. He kicked at the edge of the grass.

"Gave her a bonus...but it should be more."

"More? What is going on with you?"

"Daisy is the first real woman I've ever met...and I'm the worst thing to happen to her."

"And you think money makes this better? I don't get it, man, but she wants you...not your money...you!" Jazz grabbed him and shook him.

"When are you going to understand? You're enough! Just you! No money, no fame…"

Robby pulled away, his head hanging low as the words stung him deep. "I want to run," he said. Jazz sighed heavily as he followed Robby back into the house.

23

A few hours later, Daisy went to Nick's house alone. Sadie and Jennifer pleaded with her to talk to them but she didn't have anything to say. Robby wanted her for his career, end of story. She didn't care if her friends believed her. She'd nearly lost herself in the dreams she'd been chasing, but it was all happening so fast, and she needed to stop herself before she got hurt. As it was, she was bothered at Robby's flippant attitude toward the whole thing, but she also realized she shouldn't have expected more from a man who admitted to knowing nothing about love.

After her blow up that morning, Robby disappeared. It was for the best. Daisy wasn't sure what to say when he returned. Maybe she'd apologize for blowing up, even if speaking her mind had brought relief. Now, at least he was clear where she reluctantly stood.

Reminders of Robby crowded Daisy's house, making her unable to think. His shirt was tossed in the living room, his notebook on a table, his guitar on the couch. But she had work to do. She needed to get Nick's house ready for his arrival home the next day. Staying busy would keep her mind off everything.

Slowly, she made her way down the path between her home and Nick's, trying to ignore the shouting of the paparazzi. They'd be gone soon, and Daisy would forget the whole thing happened.

Yeah, right.

As soon as she entered Nick's house, Daisy wiped down the kitchen counters and started a list of groceries. Sadie was always good about doing Daisy's errands and shopping. Surely, she wouldn't mind adding Nick to the list.

Next, she headed into the bedroom. Nick might hate it but there was little choice. For a time at least, he would sleep on the first floor in one of the guest rooms since getting upstairs now presented a problem. With his leg broken so badly, it was going to be some time before he was going to be up to walking.

Thankfully, the hall was wide enough in the old farmhouse for Daisy to maneuver herself back to the first bedroom where she began taking the sheets off the bed. As she worked, guitar chords woven together into a melody filled her ears. Startled, she wondered if Nick left a radio or television on somewhere in the house. She cursed herself for not coming over sooner to check. But the voice sounded familiar. She listened harder.

Robby?

Daisy went to the window and opened it to find him standing slightly below her with his guitar, singing for all he was worth. His shaggy hair blew softly back and she noticed that his eyes were closed. He was immersed in the words he sang. Irritated, she lifted her arms to close the window, but then he reached the lyrics, "No questions asked…taking care of everyone leaving nothing for yourself. I'm here for you now. I'll see you through. Angel, I just have to know if you're feeling this too…" As he continued, Daisy leaned forward, overcome with emotion. She braced her forearms against the window sill, letting his words wash over her. Robby held her eyes as he sang. He'd written a love song, one meant for her alone.

Could she have been so blind? She'd convinced herself that while he was winking at her, kissing her cheek or her hand, or even when he woke up beside her each morning, that he was pretending. But it was impossible for him to fake what was happening in that moment.

As he finished playing, he looked up into her eyes and smiled. "You were right. When I got here I didn't have a clue about love, but Daisy…" he paused, seeming to struggle with his emotions. "You've shown me that love is selfless, kind…it's choosing to care for another person who…" Robby gulped. "…who may not even deserve it." He drew a deep, shaky breath. "Can we talk?"

Daisy glanced behind him at the paparazzi using powerful zoom lenses for a better view. The pictures would bring a good price, she knew. She cleared her throat and blinked back the tears in her eyes and waved her hands.

"Get in here and we'll close the blinds," she said. Robby set his guitar aside and braced his hands on the window sill, lifting himself through to stand before her. Shocked, Daisy backed up quickly.

"What are you doing?"

He shrugged. "You said get in here."

"There are doors in the house."

Robby sat on the bed. "I wrote you a love song, Harpo… I poured my heart out, and you want to dicker over my entrance?" He tucked a strand of hair behind her ear. "Surely you have a romantic bone in that little body of yours."

Daisy blushed furiously and wheeled back again,

but Robby grabbed the arms of the chair and stopped her. "Oh no, you don't," he said. "You're not getting away." He held her hand tightly and pulled her closer to him.

"But the window..." Daisy protested feebly. Robby laughed as he lifted her from the chair and into his arms, purposefully staying right where he was. He kissed her deeply, making her weak.

"I don't care..." he whispered. "I want everyone to see what I have."

Daisy desperately clung to reason as she searched his deep green eyes. She wished she didn't have to be in his arms while she was struggling.

What had she been so angry about earlier?

"Obviously, you do care about the window or you feel the need to kiss me in front of it, or serenade me where they can get a good shot," Daisy said. "Now put me down and knock it off. I have to get the house ready."

Robby sat on the half-made bed still cradling her in his arms. "We need to talk," he said. "Lay with me for a minute. I'm exhausted. All this hard work is getting to me..."

Daisy rolled her eyes but didn't make any moves to get into her wheelchair, despite its proximity. She glanced at Robby who was lying back against the pillows, grinning at her conspiratorially.

"Come on..." he begged.

"What have you accomplished today?" she asked, reluctantly lying with him. His grin widened as he saw his victory.

"Well...I realized that since I'm in it, I figured this whole love thing out, and somehow that made you mad." He yawned and stretched. "I ate breakfast, went for a run, finished writing that love song I serenaded you with, sent Jazz for groceries and to bring you a coffee from Sadie's—which I'm sure will take him forever because he's more interested in Sadie than the rest of it. I've been busy," he said, pausing. "Oh, and most importantly, I got you this..." He reached into his pocket and pulled out a check. He handed it to her.

Her heart lurched. She'd never seen that kind of a number written on a check in her life, and yet he gave it to her like it was a five-dollar bill.

"Why is it so much...?" she asked.

Robby rolled onto his side and pushed the hair from her eyes. "Because, Harpo, my girlfriend isn't going to lose her house. And I thought you deserved a little extra for all you've put up with..." He paused, looking into her eyes. "You're going to get more from the songs you helped me write. Those belong to both of us."

It was hard enough wrapping her mind around lying in bed with Robby in the middle of the day, but Daisy was now lost in his words.

As he explained things, Robby laced his fingers through hers and moved closer for another kiss. She placed a hand on his chest and held him away. "Why did you call me your girlfriend?" she asked.

Robby kissed her gently. "Isn't that what you are? And if not, will you be? Not for them..." he gestured toward the window. "But for me? For us?"

Daisy pushed him back a bit more firmly this time. "Wait...what? Robby, you're going to get a speeding ticket."

He leaned his head against the palm of one hand, the other still toying with Daisy's fingers. "You aren't like anyone I've ever met. I..." his voice drifted off but he only glanced away for a brief second before he returned his eyes to rest on Daisy's face. He smiled.

"I'll be honest," he said, releasing a deep breath. "I'm not sure what's happening...but I've never felt like this. Maybe it's just being sober for the first time. I don't know. Can't we see what's going on?"

He kissed her again but she started laughing. His eyebrows knit together as he waited, studying her face.

Daisy stared at him, her confusion swiftly breaking into giggles.

"OK...what?" he asked, frustrated.

Daisy tried to stop, but she continued chuckling as she shook her head. "Nothing. Boy. You really are lonely. You almost got me," she said as she struggled to sit up. He was too much. That he would even try to fool her, as if she were too stupid to figure out what he was up to was unreal. But, at least he'd made her laugh. What she couldn't ignore however was the seriousness in his eyes.

Maybe...

But then her senses reclaimed her. "Come on," she said, trying to sit up. "We've got a lot to do." She reached out to pull her wheelchair closer.

"No!" Robby exclaimed with such force that she took her hand off her wheelchair. "No..." he said more softly, moving toward her, his eyes meeting hers. "Don't blow me off. Please. This isn't some kind of joke."

"I'm not...blowing you off, but...I also don't want to be pulled along like this. That's why I got so angry this morning. I've been through enough already in my personal life to fill twenty books. I'm not sure I can muster the energy for more," she said.

Robby took her hand in his. "And what about me?

I'm supposed to push all of what I feel aside because it makes you uncomfortable? I can't do that. I won't." Robby put some pillows behind him, leaning against them. He motioned for her to follow. Reluctantly, she moved close to him and laid her head against his chest. He was warm.

And safe.

And deep down Daisy knew what he said was true.

"You can tell me I'm wrong. I think you feel something too, Daisy," he said as he softly kissed her hair. "And maybe you're as confused about all of this as I am."

Daisy closed her eyes for a moment. Robby finally crossed a threshold in his own heart, and he shared it openly, with no pretense, not for the cameras or anyone but her. She swallowed the lump in her throat, wishing it was possible to expose her soul to him, but trust was still so far away.

But he's safe…isn't he?

Daisy tried to squelch the hope that was rising in her.

"Please talk to me," he whispered, his breath tickling her ear. "You don't have to look at me if that makes it easier, but I really need to understand what's going on."

Daisy wanted so badly to tell him everything she'd been through, but the words wouldn't come. How did she trust this man she barely knew with the deepest secrets of her heart—the ones that hurt too much to even remember?

Robby waited for her to answer, stroking the back of her hand with his thumb as he did. He meant well—maybe he even believed he was falling for her—but giving herself fully to anyone after Alec was impossible. Her heart still ached. Her counselor told her to stop giving him so much power in her life, but she wasn't sure how to stop. Her heart continued to burn from a betrayal so intense she feared she'd never be whole again. It wasn't Robby's fault she didn't trust him. It didn't matter that he was the most handsome man she'd ever met, or that he shared her love of music. All that mattered was she was still a shell, and barely that. Daisy was convinced she had nothing to offer.

"I wasn't always like this," she said softly. "And when you showed up I was trying to let God teach me whatever I needed to learn to move on in my life. You...took me on a little detour."

"I guess I did, huh?" Robby asked. "But can you say God didn't lead me here for a reason? I would be drinking again—maybe even dead—if I wasn't here, Daisy. If God works through you in my life, couldn't He be working through me in yours?"

Daisy closed her eyes for a moment. For a man who wasn't interested in his faith, Robby certainly was insightful. The fear rose inside her as she tried to force the words out. She could tell him all of it, and he'd see why it was so hard.

"Tell me about your tattoos," she said instead, tracing a finger up his arm.

Coward...

What she wouldn't give for a little lip gloss.

Robby sighed heavily. He wasn't impressed by the turn in the conversation, but he didn't force her to stay on the subject at hand. Instead, he squeezed her tightly against him. "What do you want to know?" he asked. "I'm stupid—I think that speaks for itself."

"You're not stupid," she said quickly. "Are they all about you or do they symbolize something? Someone?"

"They were mostly my idea," he said. "Relationships are temporary, tattoos are forever. I try to be careful what I put on my body—even when I was drunk out of my mind." He allowed her to pull his arm out and she pointed.

"What's this one?"

"That's a fence that used to be near Uncle Nick's barn. I helped fix it a million times, but it eventually fell down," he said. "The one next to it is for my brother."

Something in his voice caught her attention. She shifted her position. His eyes seemed to cloud over and he was suddenly somewhere else.

"What happened?" she asked.

He forced a smile. "We thought he was dead," he said quietly as he squeezed her closer. He cleared his throat as if to give himself clarity before continuing. "But not desert storm. You can't ever count him out. Anyway, I got that tattoo right after they brought him home. He was banged up, but he was all right. I think that was the last time we were all together as a family..." Robby's voice trailed off. "It was about ten years ago."

"You haven't seen your parents in ten years?" she asked, shocked. What she wouldn't give for even a few seconds with her father. She bit her lip and shook her head. "Sorry. It's not my business."

Robby held her tight against him. "It's your business if I'm telling you."

Daisy nodded. It wasn't lost on her that he so easily opened up, yet she remained distant and aloof.

She turned. Although she was nervous, she smiled and touched his face.

"I don't know what you were like before rehab, but I think you've gotten your life back together. Even if you haven't seen them, your family must be proud," she said.

Robby shrugged. "My parents don't care anymore. The bridge between us burned and fell down years ago. It was mostly my fault. I was a horrible kid. A worse adult," Robby said. "Warren and Nick are the only family that matter now, which is why I can't disappoint them."

Daisy nodded. Robby smiled at her and squeezed her hand.

"I'm glad you stopped complaining when I touch you. It's a lot more fun this way."

Daisy blushed, still wrestling with the way the conversation was going.

Robby placed his palm against her cheek. "Please let me in," he said softly. His voice was gentle, a question, not a demand.

Daisy closed her eyes. He told her tattoos were more permanent than people. And yet, part of her didn't care. Taking a chance on a relationship with Robby was the first thought to bring her peace in some time. Maybe she was supposed to do this.

Daisy cleared her throat. She'd never been this nervous. "No man's ever kissed me like you did that day in the hotel room," she said softly. "I'd be lying if I said I haven't thought about it."

Robby gave a soft laugh and Daisy wondered if she'd been a fool. "You're the sweetest woman I've ever met," he whispered. "I really can't believe you'd give a jerk like me the time of day."

Daisy held his gaze. "I think it's a little after twelve-thirty," she said.

Robby laughed but became serious quickly when she continued searching his face. Although it was strange touching him when no one was around, Daisy was certain she'd held back long enough. She reached out with one hand and touched his hair. Maybe she could do this.

He sighed deeply, his eyes closing.

"Robby..." she whispered. "I...like you. I'm just terrified."

He opened his eyes and nodded. "Me too." He leaned forward and kissed her like he did days before, showing her his words were true.

When he pulled away for a moment, Daisy took the chance to say what was on her mind. "Please don't lie to me." Her voice was weak and yet it was only half the emotion she felt. "I've been lied to before and I don't think I can handle it again."

Robby lay back on the bed and gently urged Daisy to lay with him. He rolled onto his side and looked into her eyes. "If I do anything to hurt you, Nick will want a piece of me, and then your friends will take what's left of that, and then Warren...before you know it, there will be little Robby-bits all over that field outside and I'll just be a memory." He paused, studying her face. "I will not hurt you. I promise." Daisy nodded slowly and he smiled, brushing the hair from her face. He kissed her again deeply and then pulled away to look at her.

She hoped she never got used to this, however long it lasted.

The moment hung between them, full of promise and change. Daisy searched his face, knowing that whatever was said next might define them. She feared the future, yet she wanted to know what it would bring, how they might be more together than they were apart. And she finally admitted to herself deep down inside the smallest, most remote place in her heart that she was in love with Robby Grant. The thought took her breath away.

"We really better get up," Robby said. "There's a lot to do." So much for the next words defining them.

Daisy tried to hold him close. "No," she whined. "I thought we were just getting somewhere."

Robby smiled and kissed her again. "Thank heavens. It took us long enough…" He rose slowly and pulled her with him. "But, I'm pretty sure it will be awkward if Nick comes home and finds us like this…But then again…one more can't hurt." Robby rolled his body so he held himself over Daisy. He did a quick push up to kiss her and lifted himself from the bed.

"Good point."

He pulled her to sit up. "We have a lot of time for that later," he said with a wicked grin. "I am not leaving you anytime soon."

"I'm counting on it." She noticed the check was still lying on the bed where she'd dropped it. Reality was already back. She picked it up and held it out to him. He shook his head as he took it, folded it, and stuffed it into the pocket of her wheelchair.

"I don't want to hear any more about it."

Daisy saluted him. "Yes, sir," she said.

He laughed and kissed her again. "All right. Let's get this bed made so we can go home and mess up yours."

"Robert."

He sighed heavily. "It was a joke. I am a gentleman," he said innocently. "Well for now at least." He wiggled his eyebrows at Daisy until she laughed. "Besides..." he drew closer to her as he spoke. "I said I'm not leaving you...even if that means taking you home with me, we're going to be together. I don't want to do this without you anymore."

He lifted her into his arms, but before setting her in her chair he kissed her deeply, taking her breath away. And Daisy knew he was completely serious.

24

Now that the air was clear between them, Robby didn't hold back. He kissed Daisy every chance he got—and when there wasn't a chance, he simply made one. For the first time in years, he felt good, sure of himself, and certain Daisy would be part of his life for a long time. Maybe forever.

If she didn't try to kill him when she found out what he'd done.

He shoved the thought aside. There would be plenty of time to tell her everything—it seemed unfair to make him deal with it now. Giving her part of the truth should tide her over.

Instead, Robby focused on helping her do a few things around Nick's place to get ready for his return. Then he told her he needed to take care of some business, so they could spend the rest of the day together. Really, his thoughts refused to be ignored. Yes, he'd meant what he said about his feelings, but now telling Daisy the whole truth took on a priority he didn't want to consider. He had to figure this out. Now.

Outside of his allegiance to his bandmates, Robby had never made a commitment. Women weren't anything to him, and he hadn't told any of them otherwise. He only had fun. Telling Daisy he could be in love was about the bravest thing he'd ever done— besides go to rehab. He'd certainly never written a song for a woman before. Well, except that one time.

Robby smiled to himself. Wendy still wouldn't talk to him. The fact that the song was number one for several weeks sent her over the edge. But that incident was a blip on the radar. Back then, when he'd cheated on her, he'd told her about it without remorse. Wendy was one of the most beautiful women in Hollywood. There were endless lines of men waiting for a chance with her.

To say he was feeling something special for the first time in his life was an understatement. Robby was already sure he was in love. But Daisy wasn't at all like Wendy—strong and confident. She was as delicate as her name, which meant that not only was he on the verge of destroying his career, her life also hung in the balance.

As Robby walked back to the house, he ignored the paparazzi and dialed Lily's number. As usual, she answered on the third ring.

"What's going on?"

"Lil," he said. "You gotta stop the song. I mean now. I've got more material than I can handle—ten albums' worth. There's no reason..."

"None except the director loves it and showed me the movie. It's perfect. There's no way we can go back now." Lily sighed. "You didn't tell her, did you?"

"Not exactly...I need you to help me. I'm in love with her, and this is the worst screw-up in the history of screw-ups." Robby reached the back porch and sank onto the swing.

"You don't pay me enough. What exactly makes you think relationship counselor is part of my job?"

Robby smiled broadly. "You are a gem among gems, Lil."

"Maybe it's infatuation. She's good to you right now because you're so far removed from the rest of the world," Lily said. Robby flinched. The thought crossed his mind too that he was jumping in too fast, yet he prayed, and with clarity arrived at the same conclusions.

He'd never prayed about a relationship.

"I'm sure she's a nice girl, and we'll take care of her, but you can't stay there. We need you to move on and get back out there, doing press, shows, if you're taking your career seriously. She's only going to hold you back."

Like a weight on his chest, Lily's words settled in. He didn't want her to be right. "You're lucky I don't fire you," he said bitterly.

"I'm coming out there tomorrow. We'll get you straightened out." The phone went dead in Robby's hand. He put it in his pocket and wandered into the house. He wouldn't be able to talk to her out of it. And at this point, what did it matter? It couldn't get worse.

~*~

Several hours later, Robby was in his room getting ready to go for another run. Daisy was still working at Nick's so far as he knew. It was just as well. He needed time to sort out the mess for himself, preferably before Lily arrived to try and do it for him.

A good run should help clear his mind.

Jazz looked concerned as he entered the bedroom. Robby laced his shoes, trying to find the motivation to exercise.

"Lil's worried," he said, flopping onto the bed.

"And?"

"This is different," Jazz said.

Robby smiled as he started stretching.

"Man, don't tell me this..." Jazz picked up a notebook Robby left lying on the bed. The lyrics to Daisy's song were on the first page. He shook his head. "You can't be in love with her."

"Why not?"

Jazz stared at him, his large dark eyes showing his disbelief in Robby's stupidity.

"Do you even know why she's in that wheelchair? You still haven't bothered to ask her, have you? You aren't blind—look around this house and there are pictures of her dancing. There's trouble here, and you can't seem to think of anything but your own lousy career."

"I'm not!" Robby's voice cracked. "Besides, we talked and...we're on the same page. It's OK." Even as he spoke, Robby wanted to see Daisy. If she was close he'd feel better. He smiled, still assured of his plan. "I have time. I don't really care what happened in her past—it can't be worse than mine."

Jazz tossed the notebook aside and shook his head. "She's handicapped, but you're blind. She is in love with you—and not the 'oh he's so handsome' kind either."

Robby raised an eyebrow. There were plenty of women in his life who claimed they were in love with him. Some even made convincing arguments he fell into believing. But it always came down to the same thing. No one actually asked for the Robby that was inside. All those women expected the Robby they'd created or the one the media showed off every day. And if he let them in, they would eventually run once they found out what the real Robby was like.

Daisy wasn't like any of them.

"You think she's in love with me?" he asked, glad for the assurance from his friend. "What's the problem?"

Jazz laughed wryly as he stood and went to the door. "Two words—entertainment news. They'll crush a girl like Daisy. You want that? And are you sure you can choose her over your career?"

Frustrated, Robby paced the room, running his fingers through his hair. "I want both," he said. "She can come wherever I go. I'll hire another bodyguard for her...I'll hire someone to protect her image too..."

"Never imagined it was possible..." Jazz muttered. He shook his head and opened the door. "Dude, sometimes money and fame can't fix the problem because they are the problem. Think about it. She's a nice girl. I'd hate for her get mixed up in all this."

"So, I'm supposed to walk away?" Robby's heart lodged in his throat. "I really think I'm in love with her..."

"I didn't say you had to walk away."

Robby grabbed him by the arm. "Then what?" he demanded. "Sadie told you something."

Jazz easily escaped Robby's grasp and stepped away.

"She wouldn't say anything. Said it isn't her story to tell, and if and when Daisy wants you to know, she'll tell you. This one, I can't protect you from." Jazz left the room.

Robby sighed from deep within his soul. This whole love thing took a lot more work and was more complicated than he'd been prepared for. He truly needed to run.

~*~

Daisy was sitting on the back porch working on her computer when she spotted Robby jogging out of the woods, Jazz following closely behind. At the same time, Robby saw her in the distance and he smiled, glad his mind was clearer after his body was spent from running. He'd taken a cross country run through the woods behind Daisy and Nick's homes so that the paparazzi would be more easily kept away. Now that Daisy was in his line of sight, he ran hard to get to her.

Her smile drew him in.

"Good run?" she asked as he jumped onto the porch and grabbed for the towel she held out to him. He wiped his face as he nodded breathlessly. Jazz stepped onto the porch a moment later. Both men were covered in sweat, but Jazz was even more spent than Robby. A man his size was meant for lifting weights in the gym, not running cross country.

"You need a workout partner," Jazz panted. "You're killing me." He patted Robby on the shoulder and went inside, nodding at Daisy as he passed. Robby flopped onto the swing, still panting. She handed him a bottle of water. He accepted it gratefully and drank deep.

"Thanks," he said finally. "What are you working on?"

Daisy saved her file. "A press release for some guy who won an award for his work with music therapy," she said. "I'm almost done. But I have to get to work on the table decorations for Jennifer and Steve's wedding. Any chance you can tie a good bow?"

Robby laughed. "I'll have you know that thanks to

my mother I am an amazing bow-tier."

He kissed Daisy's nose. "I'd love to help."

Daisy kissed him back. "Good. It will go faster that way."

"Can I take you to dinner first?" he asked.

Daisy stopped working and set her computer aside. "That sounds wonderful."

"Come sit with me, Harpo," he said. He waited as Daisy came to him, moving to sit close on the swing. He took her hand and kissed it open-palm as he had done so many times before. It still made her blush.

"Missed you." Robby leaned forward, not caring that he was still dripping with sweat and probably smelled like death. He kissed her gently. "You're doing something to me..." he said. "I don't know what it is but I'm so...so...happy...and I love..." He kissed her again and whispered, "...figuring this out."

Although she tried to mask it, Daisy sighed dreamily. "Me too...but you really smell..." Her whispered words made Robby chuckle.

"Sorry." He kissed her again. She shrugged as she met Robby's eyes. He held his breath.

"My life's a mess, Vanilla," she said softly. She gestured toward the wheelchair. "And I don't only mean the chair. I was in counseling for a while, but...it's stuff I still have to work through. I don't want it to make this..." she gestured between them. "Harder."

Robby touched her face gently. "You're talking to a recovering alcoholic who's never made a commitment." He tried to laugh and was glad she did the same. "It might not be more difficult than that." He kissed her, hoping to ease her anxiety.

She smiled and touched his face. "I'm so scared,

Robby. There's so much you don't know...so much I don't know..."

"Shh...we'll work stuff out. There's time..." Robby laced their fingers.

"But..."

Robby shook his head and kissed her. "Do you want to be with me? Do we have a lot in common?" he kissed her again. "Do you want more of that?"

Daisy laughed. "Yes."

"Then everything else will come together. You'll see." He kissed her. "I've been praying...it all keeps coming back to us, Daisy."

Daisy blushed and they kissed again as a sleek red sports car pulled into the driveway, the top down. At the sound of tires against gravel, Robby broke the kiss, and he felt all the progress he'd made with Daisy melt away in the seconds it took for the man inside the car to step out and slam the door.

Her face registered shock and her body trembled.

"Daisy...?" Robby began. But she was staring at the man and didn't seem to know Robby was there.

The driver was an average height and build and boasted a shock of wavy black hair that fell a bit below the collar of his shirt. His dark brown eyes glittered when he took in the house, his hands stuffed into his pockets. He emanated an air of superiority that reminded Robby of his father and all the times he told his youngest son who brought him into the world and who ought to control him. It turned Robby's stomach.

He glanced at Daisy as she pushed away from him and struggled to get back into her wheelchair.

"Hey..." he began, but she moved to the edge of the porch in a trance, as if she wasn't aware of anything but this stranger's presence. Robby jumped to his feet and went to her side, his stomach doing gymnastics the entire time.

"Maybe I should have called," the man said.

Daisy said nothing. Robby touched her shoulder, but she continued staring.

"I guess I didn't think it would be necessary to call ahead to visit my own fiancée." He nodded toward the road where the paparazzi scrambled to get a shot.

Fiancée? *What the heck was going on?*

"Enjoying your fifteen minutes?" the man asked bitterly. Still, Daisy stared. He moved forward and leaned over in an attempt to kiss her cheek, but she backed away, leaving him to stand foolishly, glaring. Robby's head was swimming. Did this guy say he was Daisy's fiancé?

"Robby Grant." He pushed the words out, wanting this man to go away as quickly as possible. The stranger glanced at his hand but didn't shake it.

"Dr. Alec O'Dell," the man said arrogantly. "I'm sure you've heard all about me..."

Robby stared at the man. He was her fiancé?

Alec dismissed Robby and turned his attention back to Daisy, who looked as though she might burst into tears. "I came to see this for myself," he said. "I need to talk to you." He glanced at Robby. "Alone."

Alec stepped onto the porch and brushed past Robby, who was easily three or four inches taller. He opened the door and went inside, the screen banging closed behind him. Robby stared in horror as Daisy slowly turned her wheelchair around and followed.

"Daisy..." Robby said, finally finding his voice. "What is this? What's happening? Who is that?"

She stopped at the door but didn't turn. "My nightmare," she said and went inside.

25

Alec leaned against the piano, his face bearing its usual mask of self-righteousness. Daisy entered, her stomach flopping as she stole short glances at him, unable to look for very long, fearing she'd throw up. The judgment was coming, followed by harsher words—ones she'd managed to forget while Robby was in her life. And now he was about to slip away.

It hadn't been long enough.

Despite the time that passed since the accident, seeing Alec was the same as it had always been. Dangerous. Painful. Damning.

They'd met when Daisy was scarcely out of college and starting to teach a dance class at the community college. She'd majored in dance and music and was ready to take on the world when she met the handsome, older, confident emergency room doctor who swept her off her feet with perfect words at just the right moment in her life. She quickly became his captive. It wasn't until later that she noticed the cracks in his perfect façade.

"I'd hoped the media blew this out of proportion, but apparently they were spot on," he said, crossing his arms over his chest. "Did you even think? And what of my career?" His dark eyes pierced her.

There'd been a time when she'd loved his eyes, but that quickly faded and they'd become her undoing.

Daisy moved silently into the room, hoping Robby

was angry enough that he wouldn't hear what she was about to say. He was going to leave her too, and then she'd be completely alone, even as peace was within reach. The swirling, looming emptiness weighed heavily on her.

Alec looked around the room. "I'm getting married. I thought you'd need that information since we...I mean, as a courtesy of course. I wouldn't leave it to the media to tell you...as you've done to me."

He pushed away from the piano and went to her. She said nothing as he squatted in front of her, awkwardly placing one hand on her knee.

Despite his medical background, he was clueless how to handle her now that she was crippled. She feared for his patients.

"Are you on drugs?" he asked softly. "Because he..."

Daisy wrestled with the urge to slap him. But her hands remained frozen in fists, clenched in her lap. He stood, showing he didn't care what her answer was. It didn't surprise Daisy.

"I sometimes wondered what this was like for you..." Alec paced the floor of the small living room and stopped at the window where he briefly glanced outside at the few photographers stationed at the end of the driveway.

Anger oozed from him. His fingers shook.

"Why him?" he demanded. "Why now...?" He paced for another moment before visibly working to calm himself. He looked at Daisy. "Aren't you going to say anything?" he asked. "I'd think after how long it's been you'd at least speak to me."

Daisy slowly raised her eyes, which, like the rest of her body, felt dead inside her. "Congratulations on your wedding," she said softly. "Now that you've gotten a view of your handiwork, please go."

Alec stared at her for so long she began to wonder if he was having a heart attack. Never in their relationship did she snap at him. At one time, she'd wanted so badly to be married that she'd been willing to endure unbearable verbal abuse.

Daisy's stomach rolled as she watched him, wondering how he would accept her defiance. And yet she didn't care. She was going to lose Robby. There wasn't a way for Alec to make it worse.

His presence ruined what she thought was her chance to move on. There was no hope left to cling to. Robby would be hurt she hadn't trusted him—but he'd never asked either. Did he care? Maybe she'd been right holding him off.

Daisy moved toward the door to go back outside as Alec glanced at his watch when his pager went off. He regarded her as if she were little more than a bug to squash.

"Don't mention me in the press," he said simply. "There's no reason whatsoever I should be mixed up in all this..."

Daisy opened the door and started outside, Alec following behind. Something in his words caused her to stop and turn, the door nearly slamming in his face. "I'd like to pretend this didn't happen either, but I can't. And I can't control the press," she said. She went outside, Alec close behind. Robby was sitting on the edge of the porch railing puffing away on a cigarette. Daisy looked away. It hurt too much to acknowledge what she was doing to him—and on purpose. He didn't deserve all the bad things that happened. But neither should he have to endure it. Robby was a man now, and he'd be better off on his own, without her problems dragging him down.

"You'd ruin me?" Alec whined loudly as he trailed after her. Daisy wanted to scream. Instead, she pushed herself down the ramp to the edge of the grass where she stared out at the field in an effort to avoid both men.

Alec followed her, kneeling in the grass so she had to look at him. It shocked her, knowing he might willingly end up with grass stains. He was the type to send her the dry cleaning bill. "I'm not good with words. This isn't how I planned it..."

Daisy wasn't falling for it—though he'd been slick in the past and every time she'd convinced herself he loved her, she was suddenly aware of what she'd done. She wasn't the naïve girl she'd been only two years ago when Alec ruled her life. And now that he was completely gone from her and engaged to someone else, the hurt was still strong but her resolve was stronger.

"This isn't either..." she muttered.

"I was scared," he whispered, his brown eyes almost sincere. Almost. Daisy was away from him long enough that his false sincerity fell flat.

Daisy remembered waking up in the hospital after the accident and asking for Alec so many times that her friends and the staff alike ran out of excuses. Nick, Sadie, and Jennifer lied for as long as possible, but the short answer was Alec left as soon as he'd been released from the hospital with barely a scratch on him. Daisy had fought for her life. He'd gone so far as to move to Arizona, change his cell phone number and never contact her again. Her friends tried to spare her the pain of his desertion. They wanted her to get well.

She found out later that Nick followed Alec to Arizona and bawled him out, nearly getting himself thrown into jail for harassment in the process, but none of it moved Alec enough to make him return.

"And who were you scared for?" Daisy demanded. "It certainly wasn't me. You'll never understand what it was like. And I know you don't care what every day is like when I'm like this..."

"Well I'd say I have some idea, medically speaking...and if I didn't care, I wouldn't be here," he began.

She glared. "That makes it worse. You should be ashamed." She drew a deep breath. "I was never going to be good enough for you even before the wheelchair. I only fooled myself into believing you'd change..."

Robby tossed his cigarette and went down to stand next to Daisy. "I think she wants you to leave," he said. Alec stood to his full height and regarded Robby. It was difficult for him to look down on a man who was several inches taller, but Alec still managed to maintain a condescending tone.

"I believe she can speak for herself and this is no concern of yours."

Steve's truck pulled into the driveway, and he and Jennifer hopped out. They stood back from the action in shock, powerless to stop it unfolding.

Alec returned his attention to Daisy. "I never meant for this to happen," he said without a hint of sincerity in his voice. He was losing his control of the situation. He always preferred privacy to get his way with Daisy. He did his best to dismiss Daisy's friends.

"This has nothing to do with any of you."

Robby drew in a sharp breath, and Daisy realized he understood all she'd been keeping from him since he'd shown up at her door.

"You did this to her?" Robby shouted, his face quickly turning red.

Before Daisy was able to stop him, he shoved Alec, sending the man backward, though he didn't fall down.

Alec stared. "You didn't know?" He turned to Daisy. "Is that what it's like? He's too famous to care...or even ask you what happened? You really do like any attention you can get, don't you, Daisy? I always hated that about you."

Daisy opened her mouth to speak, but a whispered squeak was all that escaped. As she searched for words that would send him away, fix what she'd done to Robby, and control the downward spiral of her life, a light shone in Alec's eyes.

He knew.

He smiled again with a slow, exaggerated nod. "Mmm...I get it. This is all some kind of weird farce. You didn't tell him anything because you two aren't really dating at all, are you? Probably barely know each other, save what it takes to perform for the cameras." Alec patted Robby on the back as if they were friends. "Get out now and you dodged a bullet."

There seemed to be no more inside Robby to restrain him. He lunged at Alec, giving him a solid right hook to the cheek. Jazz came outside and pulled Robby back before he managed another hit. Steve slowly went to Alec and helped him to his feet.

"You're crazy! It was an accident," Alec muttered, blood dribbling down his chin. Steve nudged him forcefully toward his car as Jennifer looked on, distraught, tears spilling down her cheeks.

"You were drunk. As usual. That was no

accident!" she screamed.

Steve dragged Alec to his car and shoved him inside.

"Get out of here," he said. "Or I call the police."

Alec glared at them all one more time and slowly drove off.

Daisy stared after the car for a long moment before she went back into the house, the door slamming behind her.

26

Robby had rocketed from high to low in a matter of minutes. He stood staring after Alec's car until Jennifer went to him and touched his arm.

"With how close you two are, we...assumed Daisy told you...or that you figured it out," she said.

He shook his head. The thoughts were muddled and distorted. They might be that way for a while. "He did that and left? How could he do that?" he asked. He slowly went to the porch and sank down into a chair. The shock was overwhelming.

"From the minute she met him we tried to tell her, but Daisy believes the best in people..." Jennifer said. "The worst was when he left her in the hospital and she was still in a coma. We weren't even sure if she was going to make it, and he just left."

She paused and Steve put a reassuring hand on her back as she continued. "Your uncle tracked him down in Arizona, but it wasn't any use...he was gone, stuck her with all the bills for it too. We've all tried to help..."

Robby struggled to take it all in. How could he do that to her? His heart sank further as he realized this was why she'd been so adamant about the song. And he'd stolen that from her too. He left her nothing—he forced her hand with the relationship, the song, even her privacy.

"Are you leaving too?" Jennifer said.

Robby stood slowly, shaking his head. "No. I'm here for Daisy. You can count on that," he said. "We'll need some time if you guys don't mind. I guess we...have a lot to deal with."

He went inside. He was intent on getting to the bottom of everything as soon as possible. One thing was for sure. Daisy wasn't kidding when she said her life was a mess.

~*~

Daisy was staring at a picture when Robby entered the living room, distraught and unsure. She'd done that to him. Her stomach hurt.

He ran his fingers through his hair—a familiar gesture that meant he was feeling overwhelmed. Daisy recognized the way the sweat from his workout dried in odd-shaped patterns on his T-shirt—and wondered if any amount of running would help him now.

In a few moments' time, she'd resigned herself to Robby walking away. Just like Alec.

It was the loneliness she deserved.

Daisy stared at the picture of herself and Alec after he'd proposed. It was spring, and as was his usual way Alec bought a ring he loved, never giving a thought to what she'd want. And of course, he'd already started planning the wedding without her. Daisy let it go on, losing herself for the sake of having someone care for her. She'd been lonely since her mother left and her father died. She was willing to settle for any attention, even the little Alec felt she was worth. It shamed her to think she'd given up her dignity for him.

She'd let herself dissolve into nothing in his shadow. Disgusted, Daisy hurled the picture across the room.

Robby ducked. It barely missed his head by inches. The glass shattered and flew in all directions, raining down on the floor in crystal teardrops.

Robby stared at her, shocked. He clearly had no idea she was capable of such anger. He slowly crossed the room and sat, reaching out to take her hand.

"You could have told me. I...want to help."

Daisy stared at the broken picture frame. "This isn't about you," she said. She needed to be alone. Forever. It didn't matter that Robby was trying to be there for her or that her friends were probably outside waiting for her, wanting to help.

What could anyone do?

She wanted to crawl into a hole alone. She had no words left to discuss it and nothing would make it go away. Alec might be a horrible person and a dark spot in her past, but Daisy loved him once and didn't understand what was wrong with her that he didn't love her in return. That she no longer felt anything for him was irrelevant. How could she make Robby see?

"I didn't think I could handle it," she said. "I haven't even said his name for nearly a year...but I've sat here like an idiot just waiting for him to come back and..."

"Tell me what happened," Robby said softly. Daisy shook her head. "Come on..." he urged. "You should talk about it. We can get through this, Daisy."

"No," she said firmly. "This isn't your problem."

Robby recoiled. "You made me promise to tell you the truth, remember? Doesn't that go both ways?"

He reached to help Daisy from her chair but she pushed him away. "Don't," she said. "Don't touch me. I...can't do this." She sniffed, still fighting tears. "I was so lonely I...couldn't help myself anymore. But I...I was so stupid…waiting for him…"

Robby let her cry as he held fast to her hand. "I wanted to kill him," he confessed. "But I… how could he do that to you?" Robby struggled with what to say next. "God brought me here so you'd start living again. Let me help."

He leaned over, and when she refused to meet his eyes, he practically laid in her lap. "I get why you were holding onto the song," he said. "But you've got to move on, and to do it you need to forgive—or try to. I went through so much learning to forgive and and figuring out how to move on when I was in rehab. I understand better than you might think, Harpo. Don't let him keep this power over you."

"Don't…I don't want to talk about the song," Daisy said weakly. "And you can't possibly know what's best for me."

The last thing Daisy needed was for Robby to try to convince her to give him the song. She pushed him away and moved across the room to the piano where she sat, quietly thinking. Her life was a disaster and little of it was her fault. But she was still lost. Robby was going to hate her, which was fine. It was now clear he'd be leaving. In the end, no matter the scenario she tried, she would be alone.

But at least this way she could do it on her own terms instead of his.

Robby followed her and knelt down, turning her face to his. Hope rose in her but quickly fell away as she realized that for both of their sakes she had to make him go. It wouldn't be fair to expect him stay while she wrestled through another episode with Alec.

"I don't play games," he said. "Not anymore…and not with you. I meant everything I said in your song."

He gulped as he spoke, as if the words were almost too much for him to get out. She pulled back, too overcome with emotion for thought.

"No!" Robby stopped her from escaping him. "Listen to me! I'm not him. I love you."

Daisy shook her head, closing her eyes to all of it—Alec, Robby, her friends, Nick, her useless legs. There was nothing in her to fight with. Robby didn't love her. How could he or anyone else? She'd spent so much time avoiding her true thoughts that only now as they crashed around her did she understand that pretending her losses didn't hurt had accomplished immeasurable emotional harm.

"This is not about you anymore," she said, trembling. "And you're more like him than you realize—doing things for yourself with hardly any regard for me or what I want…I feel like I've been screaming at the men in my life for years, Robby, and not one of them has heard me yet."

Daisy knew by the hurt in Robby's eyes that he was nearly ready to go. So why was she so unhappy? Wasn't this what she needed?

It was for his own good—and before he found out who she really was. She'd eventually drive him away even if she did everything right. She'd been perfect for Alec and it still wasn't enough.

He cleared his throat and raised himself to his full height. Slowly, he walked to the door. "So, I was wrong about everything? I can't change who I am enough for you…and you'll never trust anyone and let them in. You really don't want to move on or be happy, do you? All that talk about trust and relying on God was a lot of bull, Daisy. You don't trust anyone and you never will. Or maybe it's me—you still believe all the hype."

Robby put a hand on the door, waiting for her to respond. Daisy wanted him to fight for her, but she was exhausted. She couldn't do the same for him. The end surrounded them.

She couldn't breathe.

"You are not a rock star to me. I never played that card."

"You made up your mind as soon as you met me," Robby snapped. "I'm all looks, attitude, and money. Nothing inside."

Daisy swallowed the lump that was forming in her throat as tears threatened to fall. He meant so much to her—she didn't want him to believe he was empty.

"I might as well live up to your expectations..." Robby whispered as he opened the door. "I'll mail you a check for your troubles."

The door slammed and Jazz called out something but she refused to look, knowing Robby was running away. She didn't blame him. If he was going to stay sober, he wouldn't be able to do it with her around.

~*~

Hours later it was getting dark and Robby still wasn't home. Daisy tried not to be worried, reminding herself that Jazz was with him. While Sadie and Jennifer both called her several times, she only answered each of them once. She needed time alone. Even though they tried again later, as good friends do, Daisy still ignored them. She sent Robby a text that might have been the start of an apology, but he didn't respond and she wondered if that was her answer.

Daisy didn't bother to eat dinner and she wasn't

able to focus on playing the piano either. She pathetically organized her numerous tubes of lip gloss and dug into the table decorations for Jennifer's wedding. She promised to make thirty-five baskets filled with flowers and bows made of green and purple ribbons. Each basket was sure to take her more than an hour to finish.

As she worked, Daisy worried over what she'd done. This wasn't Robby's fault—he was just an easy target. But what could she do? He didn't need her. But then, he'd cajoled and persuaded her that he cared yet still walked away when reality struck. She'd known all along that he was only interested in her because there was no one else around, and though she may have tried to convince herself it didn't hurt, it did.

And what hurt more than anything was how right he'd been about her. Daisy knew she was supposed to trust God, and that He'd given her support in her friends but she'd never really allowed herself to invest in any of it, believing she didn't deserve it. Vulnerability was too much for her and now she could see it was unavoidable.

She was going to have a lot of apologizing to do.

With a yawn, Daisy finished the third centerpiece and pushed it aside to start on another one. It was after midnight. The thought of going to bed in the empty house pained her. So, she resisted, telling herself she wanted to be sure Robby was all right, when in reality she was scared.

The accident made going to bed the most stressful part of her day because her mind turned automatically to the night that changed her life. And then there was no rest for her. She'd gone on and off sleeping pills several times. The nightmares were sometimes unbearable. Every night was a replay of the accident, and no amount of medication or counseling helped.

On that night, Daisy had been at a formal hospital fundraising function with Alec. She did something to set him off, though even now she wasn't sure what it was. From the time they'd met it seemed Alec was embarrassed by her even if it wasn't always clear why.

For Alec, Daisy was redeemed by her beauty and because everyone loved her. It helped too that no matter what Alec did, she excused and put up with it. Somehow that was enough to keep them together for the better part of two years.

Alec drank too much that night, again, and she tried to get his keys from him. But he insisted he was fine and, as usual, he was convincing. He'd kissed her before holding her car door open for her, something he stopped doing months before. The unexpected attention filled a void she'd been slow in acknowledging—and again, she pardoned him.

Daisy tried to talk to him about their wedding, a subject he never seemed to have time for unless it was to tell her his plans. Thanks to Nick, she was starting to realize that she needed to stand up for herself if their marriage was going to work. On the drive home, she told Alec she wanted a say in her life, in her future.

She'd cancelled the appointment he'd made to get her hair cut, as well as the wedding gown he'd selected and paid for. She wanted to do those things herself.

He'd gotten angrier than she'd ever seen him and he drove erratically, fast and out of control. She didn't find out until much later that the car flipped three times when it hit the median at over seventy-five miles per hour. Multiple doctors said it was a miracle she was alive at all.

But when she awoke in the hospital nearly a week later, she wanted no one but him. Her friends tried desperately to get her mind on other things but there was no persuading her. That he'd left the hospital with only a few cuts and bruises before she was even out of the coma, never to be seen or heard from until now, was a pain that would hurt for a long time. She'd been left and forgotten by others in her life, but Alec hurt the most because he promised he loved her and would never leave her. Her beauty was enough to hold his attention before the accident, but suddenly with unusable legs and a bleak future, Daisy must have seemed less indispensable. Alec showed his true and garish colors.

Until Robby's arrival, Daisy slept a few fitful hours each night and often spent her days taking rests and breaks to accommodate her ever-present fatigue. She was close to pushing Alec from her mind—or so she thought. She'd almost been able to trust Robby enough to tell him about it. But she was ashamed it ruled her life for so long and it was difficult to find the right words. And how could she ruin a break from the struggles she'd been through? Continuing to avoid it seemed wise given her previous obsession with the subject.

But now she needed to apologize. Would that be enough to get Robby back? Would a man like him really want her if Alec hadn't?

As the hours wore on, Daisy yawned deeply, her head jerking as she tried to stay awake. She glanced at the hallway. She should go to bed. Before she made the commitment, she lay her head on the table and fell asleep in the middle of the craft supplies, her nightmares coming on like wildfire.

27

Robby drove for what seemed like hours, Jazz silently beside him. That he was still in his running clothes, with matted hair, meant little.

Daisy was engaged? And her own fiancé crippled her? Why hadn't she told him?

"Can you tell me what's up?" Jazz asked as Robby slowed and stopped for a traffic light. He reached for a cigarette and lowered his window.

"Some guy showed up and said he was her fiancé." He lit the cigarette and inhaled. "He was the one who put her in the wheelchair and completely fell off the face of the earth—left her at the hospital still in a coma."

Jazz sat silently, taking the story in. The light changed and Robby accelerated. "Why didn't she tell me? Why didn't she trust me? I did everything to prove to her that I…"

"That you…what?" Jazz paused for a moment. "She was probably in shock. A man who put her in a wheelchair shows up after disappearing from her life? What did you expect?"

Robby barely heard him. He swerved to miss a car that was making a turn, laying on the horn as he narrowly missed the other vehicle. Jazz whistled as he double-checked his seat belt. He'd learned years ago that sometimes it was best to let Robby vent—although Jazz should have known enough to take the driver's seat.

"I haven't even told her about the song…I mean, what's she going to do when she finds out?" Robby whined. Jazz stared at him for several moments before speaking, too shocked to say anything.

"I'll pretend you didn't even ask that," he finally said quietly.

"Jazz…"

Jazz shook his head and turned to look out the window as he spoke. "I'm still your man, Rob, but what you just said tells me you aren't there yet. This isn't about you right now."

Robby sighed as he raced up the road. He puffed on his cigarette. Why hadn't she called? He glanced at his cell phone and realized it had no power. He threw it angrily into the backseat and kept driving.

~*~

Robby arrived back at Daisy's at nearly three o'clock in the morning. He found her passed out, her head on the table in the middle of the decorations. His heart constricted.

And he had no clue what to do now that he understood how messed up they both were. His life, not his career, wouldn't be the same without Daisy. But how did he fix this?

He didn't know how to handle a relationship. Besides, she lived too far away, she was handicapped, and she was…everything he didn't need. It was best if he left her alone. She'd already been hurt enough.

But before he left, he was going to record one of the songs she'd helped him write. After that, Robby had no idea what would happen.

Jazz glanced at Robby and shook his head. "We'll need to leave soon," he said. "Six?" Robby nodded. Then he went back to watching Daisy sleep. He gently touched her shoulder.

"Hey…" he whispered. "Go to bed." She didn't stir. With a heavy sigh, he lifted her and put her to bed. Once she was settled, he brought her wheelchair to her bedside.

He loved her.

And he couldn't do anything about it but walk away.

~*~

Daisy woke with the familiar feeling of bone-weary fatigue. She had not slept well and the nightmares were back. She didn't recall how she'd gotten to bed. The last thing she remembered was falling asleep on the kitchen table. With a sigh, she moved into her wheelchair.

Despite being different, the nightmares were still real and painful. The possibility of Alec returning full of apologies and a desire to make things right was gone, and she was left with emptiness. It didn't help that Robby, too, was gone. Now there was nothing left to hope for but that she would pick up on her life again.

She glanced at her nightstand and found the note.

Daisy—I got home late last night, starting early this morning on recording "Burning Love." I'll be back later to get my stuff and then I'll go to Nick's house.
—Robby

It was short and to the point with no emotion to read into. Robby was hurt and it was her fault. The guilt overwhelmed her. The man got her out of the house, he'd paid her handsomely for her help in getting his career back on track, and showed her she could do whatever she wanted—if only she made the effort. What had she given him in return? She was sure Robby had never known more grief than what she'd dished out. Daisy made up her mind that she would finish his laundry and pack his things, and when he returned she would apologize—not to get him back in her life romantically, but because he'd shown her she could live again. She owed him that much.

But he would be better off without her.

~*~

After her morning routine, Daisy went to Robby's room, guilt testing her resolve. But it hardly mattered. He needed to get away from her for his own sake. She'd hate herself if her weakness drove him back to drinking.

Daisy ran a load of laundry from the clothes strewn about the floor of Robby's room, and then she returned to pack the rest of his things. She turned on the television for company and to keep her mind from dwelling too much on her mess. It was almost laughable that at one time she'd believed she would be a songwriter. Now, she'd touched that life and was ready to accept that she would only be a struggling tech writer forever.

"Daisy?" Jennifer's voice called. She entered the room followed closely by Sadie, who carried a cup of coffee. Daisy inhaled gratefully as her friend handed it to her.

"You all right? We didn't see Robby's truck and…"

Daisy carefully folded a shirt and placed it in the suitcase. "He's recording a song. He'll be back later and then he's moving to Nick's." Jennifer and Sadie exchanged a glance but said nothing as Daisy packed.

"We don't have to talk about it," Daisy said. "I'm fine." Jennifer sat on the bed and helped fold a few pieces of clothing.

"Nick's home. He insisted he wants everyone over for dinner at 6:30."

Daisy kept working. "That might be awkward."

"What happened?" Sadie asked gently.

Daisy went to the dresser and grabbed Robby's cologne, fighting the urge to inhale the scent one more time. She dropped it heavily into his bag instead. "I told Robby he was like Alec."

The women gasped in unison.

"You…what?" Sadie demanded.

"It's better this way," Daisy said, suddenly less confident. "I don't need to wait for him to do something to prove what I can see."

Sadie and Jennifer continued staring at her but Sadie spoke first. "I never thought I'd say this…but you are a complete fool, Daisy, if you believe any of that." Daisy ignored her friend and sipped the coffee as the television posted yet more pictures of Robby.

Jennifer pointed. Although Daisy didn't want to care, she did. She turned up the volume and watched in horror as the show host smiled.

"Robby Grant is still in the news. The jilted For Granted singer isn't sitting around waiting for his solo career to get started. Apparently, he's got a new song and we'll be premiering it here at the end of next week. The song, titled *Waiting* is the first solo effort from Robby Grant."

Daisy gasped and dropped Robby's drumsticks. They clattered on the floor and rolled across the room before coming to rest near Sadie's feet.

"Daisy...?" Sadie and Jennifer stared at her.

Daisy covered her mouth with one hand, the betrayal bubbling over into tears that spilled down her cheeks. She'd been worried she hurt him when he already stole her song? She fought hard against the bile that rose in her throat. When did he record it? Her mind raced before it became clear. He acted strangely in New York and all the way home too. The way he'd pampered her must have had little to do with his supposed feelings for her. It was all about his guilt. She was right after all—he never really wanted her. He was merely playing his cards to do what he always did— take care of himself.

"That's my song..." she whispered. "I wrote it for Alec but...I told Robby he couldn't have it..." Jennifer and Sadie exchanged a glance.

"Oh...Daisy..." Jennifer began.

Daisy moved to the dresser. It shouldn't surprise her. He'd been clear when he arrived that he would do anything to get his career back. Even though she denied him the song, nothing she wanted had ever mattered. Not to him or to Alec.

Daisy yanked the dresser open and grabbed a handful of Robby's clothes and threw them on top of the neatly folded clothes she'd already placed in the suitcase. She went to the closet, yanked his dress clothes from hangers, balled them up, and shoved them into his suitcase. Jennifer and Sadie watched quietly as she continued this for several minutes.

Finally, Jennifer cleared her throat. "Um, now may not be the time to say this, but there is one good thing about him."

Both Sadie and Daisy turned to her, shocked. This was the woman who'd been adamantly against Robby, and now she was defending him?

"Traitor," Daisy muttered as she resumed packing Robby's things. She shoved his notebook into the suitcase so hard she managed to bend back the cover.

"Daisy, I want what's best for you...and as terrible as this is, Robby got you living again. I'm actually happy you're so angry for a change, instead of sitting there letting life go by. If it takes a man wronging you to get my Daisy back, then so be it."

"Humph." Daisy turned off the television and threw the remote control on the bed. "I need some time alone."

Sadie stood slowly, yanking Jennifer with her. "Do you want to come over to Nick's?" she asked.

Daisy wanted to say no, but she desperately missed Nick. Reluctantly, she nodded. "I'll go."

"Call us..." Sadie said. "Otherwise we'll be back about six-fifteen and walk over with you, OK?"

Daisy watched them leave. She took a long drink of the strong caffeinated coffee and glanced around the room. His absence, much to her chagrin, was like a dark cloud. And his betrayal hurt in a way Daisy couldn't have imagined. She foolishly believed in him which made this her fault. She should have known better.

The tears fell, silently at first, but finally Daisy's shoulders shook violently with the pain that had been bottled up for so long. This was the release she'd desperately needed but resisted until that moment. Slowly she made her way to her room, where she crawled into her bed and cried until the fatigue caused her to fall into a troubled, helpless sleep.

~*~

Several hours later, Robby was at Nick's house, sitting in the living room strumming his guitar. He'd managed to record a song he and Daisy wrote but when he was finished, he didn't have the courage to face her and bring any closure to their spat. He couldn't get hold of Lily but he'd sent it through to McAllister on the hopes he liked it better than *Waiting*.

A knock on the door brought Robby into the moment, though he didn't move to answer it. There was another knock.

"Get the door!" Nick yelled from the kitchen. Jazz was helping him prepare a large batch of chili while Robby did what he did best—stew over all the wrongs he'd committed in his life and wish he could have a drink. After Nick bawled him out, the men had little to say to one another, and Robby thought it wise he stay out of his uncle's way for as long as possible.

Robby sighed and went to the door. He threw it open and was shocked to find Lily Horton standing before him, her eyes glittering angrily.

"Is that Daisy?" Nick hollered. Robby stared at her, trying to get past the shock of his five-foot, sixty-five-year-old agent coming after him.

"What? No, it's my agent."

"Good thing I made a lot of chili..." Nick muttered. Lily grabbed the front of Robby's shirt and yanked him onto the porch.

"Robert River Grant..." she growled. "I don't think I've ever been angrier with you—and that's saying something, considering I've had to buy stock in antacids since we met..." She smoothed her tailored suit over her tiny frame and glared up at him as the screen door banged shut. He didn't dare test her. Whatever she was angry about was going to be enough for him to handle.

"All right...all right," Robby muttered, allowing himself to be dragged with her. From the porch, he saw the paparazzi had a great opportunity to get as many shots of him as they wanted. He sat on the porch swing and lit a cigarette.

"What did I do now?" he asked coolly, not really caring. His mind was too full of Daisy to try to stuff any other problems inside.

She paced the porch—a tiger wanting to strike. Robby pushed the fear down, wishing he didn't care that he let her down.

"McAllister called me this morning and said you were trying to talk him into using a different song," she said. "Stop being your own agent."

"Mmm..." Robby propped his feet up on the porch railing and blew out a ring of smoke. "Did he like it?"

Lily shrugged, which meant she was going to minimize the truth so her point was emphasized. "He said it's fine but not what they need for the movie. Besides, I told you yesterday they already put *Waiting* in. There's no taking it out now..."

Robby already knew this, but that was a moot point. He always struggled with reality when it failed to suit him.

"You were supposed to buy me some time," he complained, tossing his cigarette at the driveway. Out

273

of the corner of his eye, he spotted Daisy coming down the path toward Nick's. Sadie and Jennifer were following close behind as the paparazzi ramped up their screaming. Lily watched for a moment.

"That's her?" she asked. Robby's eyes never strayed from Daisy. He nodded.

"She'll be taken care of," Lily continued. "Look, she doesn't know this business like I do. Maybe if I explain it to her…"

Robby shook his head. He hated it but he had to come clean without anyone's intervention. It would be ugly.

"No, I have to talk to her," he said.

Like a mother hen, Lily reached out to fix Robby's messy hair. He waved her off as she spoke. "I shouldn't have to tell you that this may be the last chance you get…."

Robby stood and paced the porch, shaking his head. "Warren's the only brother I have, and Daisy…" he said softly. "I screwed all this up for my career and now what? I can't have both, obviously. What I don't understand is why…" He looked at Lily. "Why can't I be happy?"

Lily placed her hands on her hips, still annoyed with him. "You gave her a lot of money, Robby. She's well-taken care of…I'm sure she's a very nice girl, but she doesn't fit your life and she isn't going to make you happy—you hardly know her. Let me talk to her."

Robby grabbed the tiny, silver-haired woman by the shoulders and stared down into her eyes to emphasize his words. "No. For once I'm going to take care of my life myself. I…" He choked back the words he wanted to say but didn't want to admit. He closed his eyes and backed away from Lily, who nodded slowly as Daisy and her friends drew closer. Robby's heart beat faster as he prayed for the right words.

He wondered if God would even listen to him anymore.

His chest clenched at the sight of her. Daisy was as beautiful as ever but something in her eyes clouded over. She'd retreated even deeper into herself to escape him.

Robby swallowed hard. All the progress they'd made was gone.

"Daisy…" he whispered. She pushed herself up the ramp onto the porch and stopped in front of him. Robby leaned down to kiss her cheek and to his surprise she let him. Still, her coolness toward him was apparent.

"We need to talk," he said as the paparazzi shouted below. Lily cleared her throat and Robby glanced at her, annoyed. "Oh…that's my agent, Lily. Lily Horton, Daisy Parker."

Lily stepped forward and shook Daisy's hand. "Glad to finally meet you," Lily said. "Listen, Robby and I were talking and…" Robby stepped between them and looked down at his agent, his eyes communicating words his mouth couldn't.

She nodded, clearing her throat. "Right. I'll go inside for a few minutes and say hello to Nick." Lily stepped away from them and into the house.

Jennifer put herself next to Daisy as she spoke. "Do you want to come in?" Daisy's eyes hadn't yet strayed from Robby's. This was not going to go well. Her gaze was cold.

Without shifting her focus, she shook her head and said, "I'll be there in a minute."

"Want us to stay?" Sadie asked.

"No, thanks."

Reluctantly the women entered the house. The shouting of the reporters intensified as Robby sat in front of Daisy.

"About yesterday," he began.

Daisy moved away from him, to the other side of the porch. The wall she'd built around herself was higher now, stronger. He wouldn't get over or around it without her help.

"OK…" he said. "I won't make you talk, Harpo. You have to know I care about you. It hurt me that you didn't trust me enough to…"

Daisy turned from him, her eyes on the paparazzi at the end of the driveway. "I'm not going to talk about it. Is that all?" she asked. Robby stared at her. She was more welcoming when he was a drunken stranger trying to break into Nick's house. But how could he blame her? He feared her reaction when she discovered his betrayal.

Maybe he should get her gun before he told her.

"The record company isn't going to use 'Burning Love' for the movie," he said.

Daisy nodded, her eyes sincere. "I'm sorry…maybe you can use it somewhere else."

"Yeah…I guess I'll need a plan B now," Robby said, continuing down a line of conversation that brought the burden of his heavy guilt. He'd never had such feelings before, not even when he had to apologize to everyone as part of his rehab. This was different. He had knowingly, while sober, hurt Daisy. This was clearly worse.

Now she moved carefully to the door. "Well, I'm sure *Waiting* will be a hit," she said. "At least that's what they're saying on TV. I haven't heard the final version myself, though, so I don't know."

Like a bomb, the news fell at Robby's feet and exploded. He was unable to speak, see, or hear anything beyond the realization that Daisy knew what he'd done. She opened the door to go inside, but he grabbed it firmly, stopping her.

"I didn't...I wouldn't..." he stammered. "You need to understand...this isn't what I planned."

Daisy laughed wryly. "That sounds familiar..." She pushed him away and entered the house, the door slamming behind her. Robby stared at it and then turned, punching the porch railing as hard as possible, but neither the pain nor the blood registered.

He felt nothing over the disappointment in himself.

28

Daisy was astounded that Robby didn't even apologize for outright stealing her song. Obviously, he got what he wanted and no longer needed her. Her stomach was in knots over the feelings she had for him, and what he must think of her now. She was a fool and now they both knew it. That she even considered apologizing to Robby for their argument was completely forgotten in her anger.

"Daisy!" Nick exclaimed at the sight of her.

Daisy smiled as relief flooded her. It had been too long since she'd seen him. But the joy in Nick's face coupled with the anger at Robby burst forth in a flood of tears she couldn't seem to stop.

"Nick…" she squeaked, trying to get close to him. Their two wheelchairs nearly collided until Jazz helped put them beside one another so she could lean over and hug her friend. For a long moment, she rested her cheek in the safe comfort of his shoulder. She wouldn't ask Nick to choose between her and Robby. It wouldn't be fair. But she was confident he would support her and give sound advice in the face of yet another treacherous man.

"I've missed you, honey," Nick said softly, clutching her hand. "That hospital food nearly put me six-feet-under." She chuckled in spite of the tears running down her face.

Nick reached out to tenderly wipe them away as

he met her eyes. "You all right?" He smiled gently. "Surprised you didn't shoot him when he showed up."

Daisy didn't want Nick to worry—or strangely, to blame Robby. She hated to think he'd be as alone in the world as she was. Nick and Warren were all he had. She squeezed Nick's hand in reassurance. "I'm fine."

He nodded and leaned toward her. "We'll talk later. Don't think I intend to excuse my nephew's behavior."

"I finished filling the glasses with ice," Sadie announced returning to the small kitchen. "Daisy, why don't you come help me with the silverware?"

Daisy hugged Nick again and followed her friend into the dining room.

~*~

A short time later, Daisy was at the table—stuck between Robby and Jazz as the meal was passed around family style. Once everyone was served, Nick cleared his throat.

"In my house, we thank the Lord for His provision. I don't care if you like it or not," he said. All heads bowed and Robby reached for Daisy's hand. She let him touch her, reluctantly, as she felt Jazz take her other hand.

"Dear Lord, we thank you for each and every one that is with us here today. May this food be a blessing to our bodies and we to each other. Amen."

"Amen," Daisy said softly, releasing Robby's hand, the fire of his touch searing into her palm.

"So, it's a problem again that I touch you?" Robby whispered. Daisy shifted in her seat so she faced Jazz.

Robby grunted and began shoveling forkfuls of

chili into his mouth while Jazz smiled in appreciation. "Good chili, Nick," he said. Nick nodded as Sadie poured a glass of lemonade.

"So Nick, you think you'll be up to spinning Daisy around the dance floor at the wedding?" she asked. Nick raised his head and looked at Sadie and then over at Daisy.

"Hmm...I'd think someone else would like that honor," he said, nodding in Robby's direction.

Daisy flinched. So much for Nick having her back.

"I think someone needs to go home," she muttered before taking a drink.

Robby glared. "I think... someone made up her mind as soon as she met a certain someone and never planned to give him a chance no matter who he was or what he did."

Daisy threw down her spoon and turned to him. "Like stealing a song and recording it when I specifically said, multiple times, that it was off-limits?" she demanded. "I gave you everything you wanted— except that stupid song, but you just couldn't take no for an answer, could you? Well...I'm sorry if it pains you to admit you're a total, selfish jerk."

Robby tossed his spoon across the room. "How is that worse than forgetting to tell me you were engaged? And after I went and made a complete fool of myself writing you a...a...love song!"

Jennifer and Sadie exchanged a surprised glance while Nick continued eating as if nothing at all was amiss.

Ashamed, Daisy turned away. She didn't care that her friends had to see this. Now at least they'd know the truth about her and Robby. They both brought seemingly insurmountable problems to the relationship and had made many mistakes. And now they both were paying the price.

The passion in Robby's face showed he did care that she'd lied. But Daisy hadn't meant to hurt him. There was a time when she would have immediately trusted Robby regardless of his background or how long she'd known him, but Alec ruined her, down to her core, and she wasn't sure how to begin healing. She spent the morning praying—trying desperately to give it all to God but clinging to her pain anyway.

"I'm sorry if you feel you were made the fool," she whispered reluctantly. "I know the feeling well and that wasn't my intention."

Robby's eyes softened and for a moment Daisy imagined he might say he was sorry and it would all be over.

But even then, she would have to let him go. There wasn't another way.

"Let's go outside," he pleaded softly.

Daisy wiped her mouth with a napkin and carefully set it on the table. "I packed your things," she said trying to hold her composure as she felt it slowly slipping away. "Maybe Jazz can pick them up for you later."

She backed up her chair and glanced around the table at the shocked faces staring back at her. "Excuse me, everyone. Welcome home, Nick." Before she could move any further, Robby reached out and took her hand. She pulled away, tears threatening.

"It's over. And I told you not to touch me."

Daisy went outside, the door slamming loudly behind her. Her eyes were blurred by tears as she slowly made her way down the ramp from Nick's porch to his driveway. She wiped at her eyes and continued toward home as the paparazzi yelled and cameras flashed.

How could she have been so blind? She'd wanted to give Robby a chance. She thought helping him was a good idea—she'd even given him all of her poetry and lyrics to do it.

"Daisy!" Robby's voice reached her as she paused once again to wipe her eyes. Steeling herself, she waited, ready to open fire as soon as he was within sight.

"Wait," he panted, running to catch up with her. The yelling of the photographers and reporters grew louder when they spotted him. Daisy slowly turned her chair to face him.

"I'm sorry," she whispered. "I forgot all about your grand finale break up. So, tell me what to do. Should I weep and beg or do you want something more dramatic like a good slap across the face? Because I'll do whatever you want, whatever suits your career best."

Robby stared at her, the soft look in his eyes turning to a blaze almost instantly. He pointed toward the sea of reporters watching them. "It's not about them anymore and you know it."

"Do I?" Daisy turned and started toward her house.

Robby threw his hands up in the air. "So, that's it? You're done stringing me along? You're just going to run away, Harpo?"

He said the nickname with so much venom Daisy drew a deep breath to gain control. She'd liked that he called her something so cute and personal, but using it now made her feel cheap and fake, just as their relationship had been.

Daisy turned to him angrily. "Remind me again who was paying who."

Robby growled low in his throat, shaking his head as he paced back and forth. Daisy watched silently as he ran his fingers through his wild hair and leaned over her, bracing one hand on either side of her chair so their faces were inches apart.

"We both understood this was a publicity stunt. It's not my fault it didn't stay that way," he said. "Then again, maybe it is just me. Maybe you still have feelings for him."

Tears stung Daisy's eyes and her lip begin to tremble. She reached with a shaky hand for her lip gloss and slowly applied it. Robby yanked it from her and threw it as far as he could.

"I didn't even know!" he screamed. "Didn't you think for a second that it was something we should talk about? For heaven's sake, Daisy, I thought we had something."

He tried meeting her eyes but she refused him, staring into the distance, a cold feeling of numbness settling in.

"You know what?" Robby continued as he stood to his full height. "Forget it. Forget you, forget us, forget all of it. That's what you want, isn't it? You can go back to hiding from the world if you want, but it's been waiting for me long enough."

Daisy backed up as Robbie pressed on.

"I'm not going to pretend to know what God wants for you—or me for that matter. But I can almost guarantee that hiding in your house for the rest of your life is probably not on the list."

Robby's words hit hard because they were true. And she knew it was the last time she'd see him. It felt like her heart had been torn out and thrown away like her lip gloss. There was nothing left to feel but the loneliness that had been her companion for so long.

As the tears started falling, Daisy made her way home, ignoring the roar of the paparazzi and her dying heart.

~*~

Robby wandered off alone toward Nick's barn, his hands stuffed into his pockets, his mind blank but for Daisy's face. The image of her, tears streaming down her cheeks, had burned itself inside his mind. He would never forget it. His words and his actions caused that pain and those tears.

But he couldn't ignore that he was hurt too. He tried everything he knew to get her to trust him but was denied at every turn. It was no solace that even at his best he still managed to hurt the only woman he ever considered giving his heart.

Robby sat heavily on a hay bale, dead inside. His fingers itched for a cigarette, his stomach burned for a drink, but he knew neither would help. Even as his cell phone rang, Robby reluctantly admitted he was lost and alone—again. But this time was so much worse than ever before.

Dear God, what did I do?

Robby yanked his cell phone from his pocket and glanced at it. The text from McAllister read, *You're going to be on Ellen next week to perform Waiting. I'll send Lily the details.*

Robby turned the message off and sighed. He had everything he wanted and yet nothing at all that he needed. He stood and walked slowly back to Nick's house.

~*~

Late that night, Robby tossed to his side for the millionth time, finally admitting he wasn't going to sleep. It amazed him how quickly he'd come to depend on holding Daisy to find rest.

He sat up and roamed the quiet house, stopping by the window that faced Daisy's house—in the hallway outside his bedroom. Her lights were on, but it hurt to think he was no longer welcome to check on her. He trusted she would be all right on her own. But it was three in the morning and if she wasn't asleep it was because the nightmares were now his fault.

Robby trudged to the kitchen and rooted around until he found an unopened bottle of scotch and a glass. He took them to his room and sat, turning the television to the twenty-four-hour entertainment station. He hated that he so badly wanted to drown himself in the amber-colored liquid, but he felt powerless to stop it. He set the glass and the bottle on the nightstand and drew deep breaths, trying to talk himself into letting it go.

He thought he was OK before he met Daisy, but now he realized he had feelings that were numbed for years in the haze of his inebriation. Sobriety was a painful reminder that he still hadn't learned to trust God. He wondered if he'd ever get there.

Defeated, Robby gave in, lifting the bottle. But it never reached his lips. The bedroom door burst open and like a superhero of sobriety Jazz flew in, leveling Robby with one hard shoulder to the chest. Robby's breath rushed to escape his lungs and the bottle flew across the room, crashing and exploding as it hit the far wall. How his best friend knew what he was up to was a mystery, as it always was. But in that moment, and despite the throbbing in his chest, Robby was grateful. He hadn't taken the drink he so desperately wanted.

And more importantly, he was reminded how much God loved him to give him such a good friend.

Jazz barely rolled off Robby and helped him to his feet before Nick entered, puzzled and half-asleep. His silver hair was sticking up.

"What are you doing?" he asked.

Robby tried to speak but was still painfully breathless as he lowered himself onto the bed.

Jazz waved him silent, pushing him in the tender spot on his ribs. "This idiot found some scotch and thought it would be a good idea to drown himself in it."

The disappointment was apparent on Nick's face. Robby looked away, rubbing his chest in an effort to speak.

"Give us a minute, would you, Jazz?" Nick asked. "And make sure you two didn't scare Lily." Jazz nodded and left the room, casting a glance back at Robby before he did. Robby nodded, ashamed.

"He's a big boy. Hope he knocked some sense into you."

"I didn't want to," Robby said. "I just wish it would stop. Feels like I'll never get free."

"You can't run to it every time something goes wrong," Nick said.

"Yeah. I'm sorry."

Nick nodded. Words were useless.

Robby was ashamed of himself. He couldn't fix this. He said the only thing that seemed right, "I think it's time for me to go home. I'll uh, get Jazz to set up some help for you and we'll all get out of your hair. Maybe tomorrow."

Nick shook his head. "Leaving isn't going to make things right. You should have learned that in rehab. A man can run, but the problems will follow even if they take their time getting there."

Robby closed his eyes, wishing he was tired. He remembered Daisy's face, the hurt a mask she'd wear for a long time. Still, he felt sorry for himself and couldn't help but whine, "Warren's right. I sing about love. Other people's words because I have no idea what it even means." He kicked his toe at the carpet. "I'll never be good, Uncle Nick. I've tried and it...isn't me. I ruin everything."

But Nick wasn't about to accept his nephew's excuses. "Just remember why you started drinking in the first place. It sure wasn't her fault," he said. "All you're doing now is hoping there's an easy way out. There isn't. I speak from experience."

"You act like there was a choice!" Robby cried. "She didn't even tell me she was engaged! And then I pay her to help me and she still won't give me her song. It's like she hates me and I tried to be nice, really I did."

Nick glared at him so fiercely that Robby looked away. The responsibility was his, and yet he sounded like the spoiled, selfish idiot Daisy now thought him to be. He hated himself.

"Don't you dare blame her. There's always a choice."

Nick moved toward the door, muttering. "Nearly forty years old and you still act like an abandoned child. You got what you wanted and now you'll get what you deserve."

Robby grabbed the bags Jazz retrieved from Daisy's and tossed them to the door. "I'm leaving in the morning. I screwed up again. There's nothing I can do about it now."

Nick nodded. "You do what you have to. Just remember the part you played in all of this...actions have consequences," he said. "You'll always be my nephew—and I love you. I'm only asking if your career is worth the look on her face at dinner tonight."

"Uncle Nick..."

The old man raised a hand to silence Robby's protest. "I'll be praying for you both. Change isn't easy," he said. "But it's worth it. I promise."

Robby thought about that for the rest of the night as he stared at the remnants of the bottle of scotch scattered across his bedroom floor.

~*~

The next afternoon Robby was on a plane sitting between Jazz and Lily, his head throbbing with what had happened over the previous days. He wasn't able to bring himself to see Daisy again, knowing that anything he said would only bring her more hurt. Besides, now there were shows scheduled, promotions to do, and most importantly, notebooks full of songs he needed to write music for.

He concocted more excuses to avoid reality, only now he didn't have a bottle of alcohol to see him through. As much as he didn't want to admit it, this meant that the only thing left for him to do was pray he'd find a way to fix things—even if listening had never been a quality Robby had been known to possess.

Robby had been trying to reach Warren for several days. When his brother heard what he'd done, he'd be on the line first thing. It hardly mattered. What could he say that would possibly bring Robby more pain?

"Just heard from the drummer," Lily said, tapping Robby on his knee. "You got a new band, kid."

He didn't bother to glance at her as he nodded. Lily and Jazz exchanged a look and the small woman stood, going to a different seat to give the men privacy.

"She's worried about you. Thinks you might want to talk to that counselor again," Jazz said. "We don't want to lose you this time."

Robby grunted. "She worries about everything."

"I get that…but you haven't eaten, spoken, or even looked at us since…"

With effort, Robby raised his eyes and looked at Jazz. "How do you know I haven't eaten?"

"Because you pay me to know," Jazz said. "Now. The question is, what are you doing?"

"I'm going back to work."

Jazz stared at him for several long moments though Robby tried to pretend he didn't care. "Right…"

Robby didn't acknowledge him. His insides were churning with feelings he didn't recognize and certainly couldn't define. He didn't say anything to Nick before he left, though his uncle did hand him a worn copy of Bible devotions. Robby wasn't sure if or when he would look at it. God was probably as disappointed in him as everyone else.

Robby's cell phone buzzed and he yanked it from his pocket, part of him expecting to see Daisy's number. But it was Warren.

"Not now…" he muttered, pressing the button

and holding the phone to his ear. "Yeah?"

"Where are you?" Warren's voice was gruff, loud in Robby's ear.

"On my plane," he said. "And don't start on me, desert storm. I set up care for Nick—he'll be in his glory. The nurse I left him with was in her fifties and completely enamored of him."

"What did you do?"

Robby cleared his throat but said nothing.

"You're still a child," Warren said. "When are you going to knock it off? Life doesn't revolve around you, moron!"

Robby hung up the phone and tossed it aside. He covered his face with his hands and rubbed them over, as if to wipe away all he'd done and all his brother thought him to be. But he was still there, as if change were a reluctant dream he'd never be able to grasp.

Letting it go was all he could do. Nothing else remained for Robby but his career, his music, and memories of the time he spent falling in love with a woman who would never be able to love him in return.

29

The sun filtered through the blinds and nudged Daisy from the state she was in—stuck somewhere between sleep, daydreaming, and the heaviness of being alone. She rolled onto her side, pulling the blankets over her head in an effort to block out the day. She had been holed up in her house since she left Nick's, refusing to answer the phone or door. Even when Sadie and Jennifer let themselves in to check on her, she told them to go away, thankful when they understood.

Daisy then spent the night wondering how she let herself get into such a mess. There was a time in her life when she swore she'd be able to stand on her own and yet here she was, crushed that a man, once again, let her down. She was ashamed. Since she met Robby she had done things that only weeks ago seemed impossible—not the least of which included getting on an airplane and meeting celebrities, and finding that most of them were receptive to her and barely seemed to notice her wheelchair. She'd spent nearly two years—wasted them really—feeling sorry for herself when she should have been exploring all that she had left and could still do.

Daisy's friends tried to show her these things, but she'd needed Robby to make them real. Somewhere in the early hours of the morning when she finally convinced herself to try and get some sleep, she made the decision to forget Robby, but not what he'd done for her. She was going to live again and do whatever was necessary to be part of the world she'd accused of leaving her behind.

God placed a beautiful man in her life for a purpose—and she wasn't going to let Him down, even if she had to push her feelings for Robby away forever. All she ever needed was God—and wherever she was now, it was part of His plan.

"Hey, Daisy..." Jennifer's soft voice called out gently as she and Sadie pushed the bedroom door open. Daisy groaned, tugging the covers over her face.

"Rise and shine!" Sadie exclaimed, lifting the blinds. "I brought cappuccino." Daisy's answer was muffled by her comforter so it came out as, "mmthhyou..."

Sadie sat on the bed beside her, nudging her arm as she did.

"Nick begged us to get over here. He's really worried."

"Umm... fine." She reluctantly lowered the covers.

"But Robby..." Jennifer said.

Daisy yawned. It was too early for this. "I'm fine. Don't want to talk."

Jennifer and Sadie exchanged a glance and both women nodded reluctantly. Daisy reached for the coffee, which Sadie handed to her with a smile.

Daisy took a sip and handed it back. "Why are you here so early?" she asked, pulling the covers back over her head and lying down. It was one thing to be sure she was going to be all right, it was a whole other issue to actually start the process of moving on.

"I have a crisis, Daisy. I need your help," Jennifer said.

Daisy lowered the blanket and peeked out at her friends. "What?" she grumbled.

"My pianist realized she double-booked my wedding with an anniversary party in Cincinnati..." Jennifer whined. "She's blowing me off. I need you...please..."

A few weeks ago, this would have tortured Daisy, but not now. "OK," she said. She lowered the blanket and reached again for her coffee. Sadie handed it to her as she and Jennifer exchanged a look.

"We're going to yoga, Daze, you want to come?" Jennifer asked.

Daisy raised an eyebrow. "Yoga?"

"I cleared it with our instructor. She...understands..."

Daisy pushed herself to sit up against the pillows. "What are you up to?" she asked suspiciously.

Jennifer looked away, clearing her throat. "Well...um, I also need a soloist and I was hoping that, well, since you're going to play the piano anyway, maybe you'd, well, at least think about singing too..."

Daisy felt a twinge of desire that was quickly squelched by fear. "I...I don't know," she said. "I'd rather do the yoga."

Jennifer smiled brightly. "All right then, let's go..." she said. "You can think about singing while we work out."

"Ugh..." Daisy groaned but slowly got out of bed. She was going to go to yoga.

~*~

A few days after Robby returned to New York, his schedule was so full there wasn't time to think about

Daisy, Nick, or anything else. And yet, they were never far from his mind.

He met his new band, a group of guys who were much more solid than his former group. The drummer, Marc Dixon, was a Christian and patiently answered a million questions for Robby about his faith and God's work in his life.

Robby also began rehearsing new songs, but always found himself returning to the last time he saw Daisy and her tear-stained face. It turned his stomach so badly that he had no choice but to drink or work harder. He continued choosing work over all else, a decision that was empowering, though not entirely healing.

He even went to church with Marc. And for the first time, he didn't hate it—he only wanted more.

Robby hadn't spoken to Warren since their conversation on the plane, but he called Nick to apologize. Strangely, Nick wasn't angry. The men skillfully avoided talking about Daisy, however. The closest either came to broaching the subject was when Robby said, "I just wanted to apologize if I hurt anyone." Nick said everyone was fine and that he would take care of her. Robby hadn't pressed the point, choosing to keep Daisy's name sacred.

Meanwhile, *Waiting* went to the top of the charts with no signs of coming down. Every time Robby played or heard it, however, he was wracked by guilt. Getting everything hadn't been what he'd planned at all. It crossed his mind more than once that he'd trade the success for Daisy's complete forgiveness, even if that didn't include her heart, which he was convinced he did not deserve and never would.

Healing might have been as strange as meeting

someone like Daisy in the first place. Robby had a long way to go but there were many changes in him because of the time he'd spent in Pennsylvania. Losing his band hurt him, losing Daisy pained him, but on his own, relying on his talent, Lily, and Jazz gave Robby the chance to think about what he'd been through.

He opened the book of devotions Nick gave him as well as the Bible Warren brought him months ago while he was in rehab. In both, he found that as much as he wanted to believe God didn't want anything to do with him, the opposite was actually true—God wanted him as he was, fully and without reservation. Robby wanted to behave and do good things, and deep down he was starting to believe he actually could come through.

Maybe he wasn't a total failure.

Clearly, he was going to be all right and his career would survive. In the process he needed to tie up the loose ends he'd left behind with Daisy and Warren if he was ever going to move forward. But the courage to follow through this part of his journey was still elusive.

~*~

Days after they returned home, Jazz entered the back gate of Robby's house. Robby was swimming and didn't even notice his friend until he finished his last lap and came up for air.

"Jazz." Robby lifted himself from the pool and reached for a towel. "What's up?"

Jazz shifted from one foot to the other.

Robby laughed at seeing the big man look so unsettled. "Out with it."

"I got Alex Farena to handle your security when

you do the Ellen show," Jazz said, stuffing his hands in his pockets. "I need a few days off."

Robby stopped rubbing his head with the towel. "You never ask for time off," he said. Jazz shrugged.

Robby tossed the towel aside and grabbed his phone to find fifteen messages. He glanced at Jazz. "Why?"

Jazz visibly gulped. It was laughable that the six-foot-six-inch man was afraid to tell Robby anything. Robby scrolled through missed calls and texts in case anything needed his immediate attention. One thing sobriety brought him in spades was organization. He was much more efficient now.

"Sadie wants me to go with her to Jennifer's wedding, and I…miss her," he said.

Robby looked up from his messages. He tried to mask his emotions as he set his phone down and looked away. They hadn't mentioned anything about Pennsylvania since coming home.

He nodded and forced a smile as he turned back to Jazz. "No problem. Alex is good…" He preferred Jazz but Alex was a close second choice. He'd worked for Robby and For Granted a number of times in the past and it always went well. He was much quieter than Jazz and lacked a sense of humor but that wouldn't be an issue.

"It's fine," Robby assured him. "I can't expect you to stop your life because mine's…" his voice drifted off with all he didn't want to say.

"You want to meet me there after the show?"

"Not yet," Robby said as he went inside the house. Although it had been a few weeks, his bags were still packed and by the back door. Jazz glanced at them as he entered the house.

"You ever going to unpack?" he asked. "Look, maybe you need to call one of your counselors...let them walk you through this." Robby opened the refrigerator and yanked out a bottle of juice. He poured a glass.

"I don't need to talk about every little thing with my counselors. I'm doing OK. I'm back to work, I haven't had a drink in months...I'm fine."

Jazz sat down slowly and shrugged. "You can't say her name. That's weird."

Robby laughed wryly as he took a drink. "It's weird I don't talk about feelings? Where have you been?" He went to Jazz and held up his arm, which bore a new tattoo. Jazz's jaw dropped and he looked up into Robby's eyes.

"No."

Robby playfully punched Jazz's arm. "I'm fine. If and when I talk to her... that could be it. I don't want to take it lightly. I just need time."

Jazz cleared his throat and nodded. "Right." He stood.

Robby put the juice away before returning to the counter. He drank the glass empty. He didn't want to tell Jazz that he wasn't solely filling his time with career work. He'd been doing numerous things in Daisy's name, but he wasn't ready to talk about any of them, even with Jazz. It seemed too private. He'd already done enough to belittle what Daisy was to him—he promised himself he wouldn't do it anymore.

"If you need anything..." Jazz said.

"I know where you are." Robby met his friend's eyes. "You're the best friend a guy could have. Thanks."

Jazz nodded. "Yep. You're lucky to have me."

Robby nodded as Jazz left. He stared at his bags for a moment and slowly went to them. Opening them was too much. It meant the ride was over and he was actually home. Instead of admitting defeat, he dragged his luggage up the long staircase and dumped them just inside his bedroom.

And then he shut the door.

30

The morning of Jennifer and Steve's wedding was warm and clear. Daisy still wasn't sure she was ready for her role in the day but her friends' confidence was enough to get her out of bed and into the living room, where she laid her hands on the keys of her piano and began playing, her spirits lifting with each note. The music soothed her fears.

Thank You, Lord...

She could do this.

Out of necessity she had pushed Robby from her mind and from every conversation where he might be mentioned. She scarcely listened to the radio and television where it seemed he alone was keeping several networks in business—and unfortunately her picture often accompanied his. Although there had been a few stray calls and knocks on her door, for the most part the media was no longer interested in her and ended their driveway vigil when Robby and the rest of the crew left.

Even with the pain that rooted itself deep in her heart, Daisy was relieved to see that Robby wasn't up to his old tricks. In fact, he seemed like a completely new man. She just couldn't understand why he hadn't responded to the letter she'd tucked into his bag. As the days wore on, she felt ridiculous. Maybe he never meant any of what he said, and this was his plan from the beginning.

Well, if that was the case, she wouldn't have to see him again and the letter wouldn't matter anyway.

But as Daisy played on, rehearsing the songs she would perform in a few hours for all of Jennifer and Steve's family and friends, she wondered how Robby managed faking the love song, his kisses, and even the way she'd caught him looking at her. He'd meant all of it, she was sure, but her lack of trust in him must have been enough to push him away forever.

Daisy sighed heavily as the song ended. She had to get dressed and pretend she was fine. This wasn't the day to figure out her life. It was a day to celebrate her friends. She went back to her bedroom, intent on looking and sounding her best and ignoring her problems completely until the day was through.

Or maybe forever.

~*~

Daisy was soon dressed in a beautiful green gown that complimented those worn by the bridesmaids. Sadie and Jazz rented a van so she and Nick could get to the church easily in their wheelchairs. While it was great to see Sadie happy and the new relationship blossoming, Daisy struggled to keep her questions about Robby to herself with Jazz close by. She was relieved that he was too occupied with his own relationship to worry about hers.

"Go on." Nick smiled as they approached the front of the church where the piano awaited.

Daisy smiled back, wondering how she'd let herself so easily be convinced to do this when she wasn't ready. She drew a deep breath and moved forward. Without taking time to think, she began to play, glad to focus on the music and not the emotions that threatened to overtake her.

Nick smiled at her as she played. Relief. He wouldn't leave her.

She only wished the twinkle in his eye didn't remind her so much of the one in Robby's. His absence had left a hole in her heart, but it also brought her opportunities she never imagined. Already she'd received three phone calls from musicians who were interested in hiring her to write them songs. While she hadn't yet made any commitments, it appeared to be the beginning of an important turning point.

She was wanted. People believed in her.

And if things ever did work out between her and Robby, it would be with a clear conscience on her part that she could take care of herself without his money, fame, or connections to sustain her.

Once Jennifer was at the front of the church, she took Steve's arm and the ceremony began. Daisy moved to a place reserved for her beside Nick. He patted her arm reassuringly. Since Robby left, Daisy reminded herself that there was a lot to be thankful for, and she wasn't going to waste another minute feeling like something was missing. Still, the nagging feeling haunted her.

She missed Robby.

"You all right?" Nick whispered as Daisy wiped a tear away. She smiled and nodded, not wanting him to know her thoughts.

Nick took her hand and squeezed it. "I'll bet he's missing you too."

Daisy choked back a cry, covering her mouth as she did. The last thing she needed was to be a blubbering idiot when she hadn't even sung yet. Nick wrapped his arm around her and Daisy turned her head into his shoulder. She might be capable of composing herself if she believed she had no reason to feel guilty for falling so hard for a man as unreachable as Robby. It was too much.

Nick squeezed her tight against him and she sighed heavily, wiping her cheeks as she straightened to watch the service. She didn't want to miss her friends getting married because she was too wrapped up in her own problems. And that's when the realization hit her—she'd been doing that ever since the accident.

While she could make an argument that she deserved to be bitter and angry, at least for a time, when did those emotions take over and become an obsession? It would ruin her. Daisy was at an important moment of decision. Did she waste her life waiting for something that wasn't going to happen, and probably shouldn't happen, or did she move on and focus on everyone else in her life and what she could do for them? As long as she had breath in her, she could be a blessing. That's what God would want.

A few moments later, Daisy moved back to the front of the church, a new resolve in her heart. She hadn't sung in front of a crowd in years and yet it was as if she'd been on stage only days before. She stole a glimpse at her friends. Sadie clung to Jazz's big suit sleeve, crying for all she was worth.

Daisy managed to hang on and finish the song without tears, her strength restored. She smiled— happy for her friends and now for herself and the peace that filled her heart.

As the song ended, Daisy realized she wasn't off the hook yet. She still owed Robby an apology—a real one from her directly. Despite her drive to see things differently, it was clear this might be harder to do than anything else.

~*~

A short time later, Daisy and Nick were seated at a table in the reception hall, watching everyone dance and have a good time while they ate, talked, and laughed together. It seemed there was a lot to catch up on as Nick had half of the nurses calling to check in on him since he'd gotten home—but the one who really intrigued him was the in-home caretaker Robby hired before he left.

Barbara McCreadie had a lot of work to do before Daisy would pronounce her worthy of her dear friend's time, but so far, the woman had been all she'd prayed Nick would find in a relationship. She was funny, kind, hard-working, and best of all didn't take any of Nick's thinly-veiled bullying. Good-natured or not, the man sometimes needed to be put in his place and Barbara was willing to do it.

Now Daisy wondered if she might find solace in Nick's return to her life, as well as the possible entrance of a new friend in Barbara. Because she'd been so occupied with Robby, the hole Nick left while he was in the hospital wasn't noticed. But she'd missed him fiercely. It felt good to have things return to normal, even if "normal" was, for the moment anyway, a fluid concept.

"Having fun?" Nick asked.

Daisy turned her attention from the dancefloor to look at her friend. "Absolutely. And Jenn's just gorgeous."

"She's got nothing on you," Nick said. Daisy met his eyes as Sadie flopped into the chair next to her, Jazz close behind. He removed his jacket and tossed it over the back of his chair before he sat down.

"I haven't danced like that since high school!" Sadie exclaimed.

Daisy chuckled as she looked at Jazz, who wiped his forehead, exhausted. Keeping up with Sadie was often harder than it looked.

"You enjoying this as much as she is?" Nick asked.

Jazz smiled, shrugging. "If she's happy, I'm happy."

"Aww..." Sadie leaned into him.

"Smart man." Nick winked. "Sadie, let's go get something to drink."

Sadie quickly kissed Jazz on the cheek. "What do you want?" she asked.

"A gallon of water."

Sadie nodded and turned to Daisy. "And for you, my dear?"

"I'd love some water too, please. Depending how their coffee is...?"

"Only the hard stuff. Got it," Sadie said as she and Nick left for the bar.

Daisy glanced at Jazz. Could she keep this conversation away from the one topic she wanted to discuss? "She's something else, isn't she?"

"It's why I'm back," he said. "You know, Robby is too...something else, I mean."

That didn't take long.

"Look, you're none of my business, but he is all my business. I've worked for Robby for the last fifteen years and we've been through some serious stuff. He's a good guy, but things haven't always been easy for him, you know. Getting clean was ugly."

Daisy didn't want to, but she hung on Jazz's words. Could he give her insight she didn't already have? Perhaps she never understood Robby at all, maybe he hurt from their separation too.

She nodded to keep Jazz talking, wanting him to continue but not openly admitting it to herself.

"Anyway...Don't think leaving was easy for him. He's kind of mixed up when it comes to relationships and he got scared. He's not talking, but...he's always been a lot of fun—just isn't much for committing to anything outside music."

Jazz's honest words sunk into Daisy's heart. She really shouldn't have expected more though, should she?

Jazz met her eyes. "Don't be too proud to call him out. Sometimes guys need that." He focused on the dance floor where couples had gathered for a slow dance. He didn't speak for a while.

When he did, the words hit Daisy hard. "You know, he hasn't told me as much, but I don't think he's calling you...says you're out of his league."

Before Daisy could respond, Sadie set two water bottles on the table. "I may be an elitist, but the coffee was questionable so I stayed with water."

Daisy looked at her friend. "Huh?" she asked.

Sadie yanked her chair closer to Jazz and shook her finger at Daisy. "He's all mine, honey. Back off." Daisy forced a laugh, still wondering over what Jazz said. If Robby thought she was out of his league, exactly whose league was she in any way? Jazz was just trying to make her feel better.

"How about we show them how it's done?" Nick asked.

Daisy looked at him as if he was crazy. "What...?"

"Come on. I'm not bringing a gorgeous date like you out for the night without at least trying to cop a feel." He said it so seriously that everyone at the table went silent and turned to him. Nick burst into a fit of laughter so intense that tears rolled down his cheeks almost immediately. He grasped his sides in an effort to breathe. Soon everyone was in the same position, until finally Daisy gained control and shook her head at Nick.

"I will not have you trying to take advantage of me, young man," she said.

Nick grabbed her hand. "All right, come on..." he said, yanking her in the direction of the dance floor.

~*~

Daisy and Nick had a fabulous time with Sadie and Jazz. By the time they got home late that night, Daisy was sure she would sleep well when she finally climbed into bed. Sadie helped her inside, while Jazz took Nick home to get him settled.

"I can't believe what happened to my makeup," Sadie complained as she leaned over to look into Daisy's bedroom mirror.

Daisy yanked her earrings off and tossed them onto the dresser. "No wonder—you didn't sit all night."

"No kidding. My feet are killing me," Sadie said, hopping onto the bed. "You think me and Jazz might...get married someday?"

Daisy shrugged. It was bad enough Jennifer was married, and like it or not that meant she wouldn't be around as often. Not that Daisy faulted her for it—it was natural she'd spend more time in her new home, building her life with Steve rather than caring for Daisy. If Sadie got married to Jazz, she might even move away.

She wasn't yet ready to think about it. "Maybe? It was nice of him to come back for the wedding though."

Sadie sighed dreamily. "It was, wasn't it?" she paused. "He goes back in a few days. You know I was thinking…"

Daisy shook her head. "Don't…"

"Not that! I wasn't going to say anything about… him," Sadie said defensively. "I was going to say, that you should do a little mini-show at the café sometime." She looked at Daisy seriously. "You sounded amazing."

Daisy thought. She wanted badly to say yes. She gulped, nodding. "I don't know…but I'll think on it…"

Sadie smiled and threw her arms around Daisy's neck. "Yay!"

Jazz appeared in the doorway. "What's going on?" he asked.

"Daisy said she'd do a show at the café…"

Daisy peeled her friend's arms from her neck. "I said maybe…"

Sadie jumped off the bed, pointing at Daisy with a huge grin. "That just means I have to talk you into it. Piece of cake."

Sadie grabbed Jazz's hand and pulled him to the doorway, Daisy gaping after them "But… but…" she began.

Sadie continued smiling at her. "Yes?"

"I don't like you," Daisy pouted.

"I'll bring you coffee tomorrow."

Daisy folded her arms over her chest. "Fine.

You're not so bad."

"Thanks. You too. Call if you need anything."

Daisy waved to them. "All right. Get out of here."

"See you later, Daisy," Jazz said.

"Bye, sweetie!" Sadie called as they left.

Daisy watched them go, missing Robby more than ever.

She went to the piano to work.

31

A few days later, Robby rolled over in his bed, the blankets wrapped around him like the shell of a soft taco. The notion that the doorbell was ringing struck him and he sighed. He wasn't expecting anyone, and whatever imbecile managed to get through his security gates could come back later. He finally got a much-needed day off and he wasn't getting out of bed until he wanted to.

It was bad enough he'd gotten in from California the day before, shuttled straight to the studio and stayed there until three that morning to record another song. He was exhausted and had started falling back into a deep sleep when the ringing stopped and the banging started.

Robby wondered if he could use his mind to maim the person.

Finally, the banging stopped and his cell phone rang on the nightstand. With another sigh, he shoved his hand out from the safety of the blankets to grab the phone, which he yanked back in and pressed to his ear.

"Mm…is the house on fire?" he asked groggily.

"Let me in. Or I find a way to break in." It wasn't possible that whatever Warren wanted at this hour was more important than sleeping.

"Ugh…" Robby hung up the phone and pushed it out from the blankets where he dropped it next to his lamp. His hand fumbled around the nightstand before he located the remote control for the house. He pressed several wrong buttons before he found the one that unlocked the front door. It opened and slammed quickly, followed by his brother's loud, clumsy footsteps up the stairs.

"Uggh..." Robby groaned again, yanking the covers tighter around his ears. He was not up for listening to an assessment of his screw-ups from his perfect brother. Maybe tomorrow, but certainly not today.

"It's eleven already, loser. Get up," Warren said, nudging his shoulder.

"Go away," Robby muttered. "I was up all night working."

Warren sat heavily on the chair near Robby's bed, his size enough to make the entire room shake. Robby peeked out to find him bearing a huge cast from the top of his shoulder to his fingertips. He lowered the blanket and stared.

"What happened?" he asked, realizing suddenly that Warren was not yet supposed to be home.

"Helicopter went down and I got a little banged up," he said, shrugging. He dismissed the incident as if it were a fender bender.

"What the...it looks bad," Robby muttered, concerned. His brother was nearly killed once already and now this. "You all right?" he asked, full of emotion.

Amused, Warren met his younger brother's eyes. "I'm fine," he said, putting his feet on Robby's bed. "No big deal. I'm just home for a while, so I figured it was time to harass you."

Robby pulled the blanket back over his head. "Glad you're OK," he said, his words muffled. A strange feeling overcame him that, this time, he might have lost his brother. The relief that Warren was still there passed through him. He cleared his throat in an effort to squelch the emotion.

"You all right?" Warren asked.

Robby nodded, though his brother couldn't see him. After several moments of silence, he said, "Just glad you're OK." He peeked out again, and this time, Warren understood.

"Thanks, little brother." He smiled and Robby released a deep breath. "You going somewhere?" Warren changed the subject, nodding toward the luggage still lying by the door.

Robby closed his eyes again. "Never unpacked."

Warren stood, grabbing the bags. He tossed them onto Robby's bed where they landed heavily, half on Robby's stomach and half on the bed itself. Robby groaned under the weight.

"Don't you think it's time?" He opened the bag Daisy packed with his things when she was angry. Robby didn't want to think what was in there. She probably shredded his clothes and stuffed them into the bag like a piñata. He deserved that. Or more.

Warren pulled Robby's journal out of the suitcase, the cover folded back over itself. He inspected it and then yanked an envelope out of the side of the bag. "Here—it has your name on it. Looks like a girl's handwriting. Fan mail?" He tossed the envelope at Robby who slowly reached his hand out and took it. He sat up. Sleep would now be impossible. Warren thought six am was sleeping in, which meant eleven in the morning was practically supper time.

The envelope was from Daisy. His stomach sank. He didn't want to read it, and certainly not under his brother's gaze.

"What is it?" Warren persisted.

Robby dropped the envelope.

"It's from her, isn't it?"

Robby shrugged, irritated that Warren didn't see he was avoiding the conversation.

"Want me to open it for you?"

"No!" Robby practically shouted.

Warren put his good hand up as if in defense. "OK…"

Robby sighed. He needed to know what was in that envelope as much as Warren wanted him to see it. He ripped into it and pulled out a piece of paper that had been folded several times. The check fell out. Robby's stomach rolled. She would rather lose her house than accept his money, that's how low she believed him to be. It didn't matter that she'd earned that money—Robby understood in Daisy's eyes it was tainted simply because it was his.

He hated the tears that filled his eyes. He was ashamed as he scanned the paper, taking in her beautiful handwriting, and the words so full of Daisy he could almost hear her saying them.

Dear Robby-

I can't accept this money—not when I'm so confused about what's happened since you came. I'd never be able to tell you this to your face, but I owe you—not the other way around. Thank you for making me live again. I don't think I ever would have left the house if you hadn't tossed me into your truck that first day.

Robby paused, closing his eyes and smiling at the memory. She'd been adamant with him but, as usual, he'd wanted something and he'd taken it. And here she was thanking him for being himself—an absolute jerk. He sighed heavily and continued reading.

I should have told you about Alec. I'm sorry. At first, it just wasn't important, and I had no idea how to trust you, or if I even should. Since I hadn't seen or heard from him in so long and you weren't staying, it wasn't worth dumping that on you. And I liked being able to escape the way it consumed my life before you came. Because we had fun, Robby—and I hadn't had any fun in so long... I just wanted to enjoy that.

But when he showed up... I'm sure it hurt you and I'm sorry. It doesn't change whatever was happening for us—at least for me. Still, I'm sure you're back to your own life, and things are better. It wouldn't have made sense for you to get any more emotionally involved. We don't work. In almost every way possible, there are just too many miles between us.

Don't beat yourself up over the song. I needed to stop controlling everything anyway. I'm glad you took it, take all of them...I don't need them anymore.

And for what it's worth, I think you might be right about God. He brought you to me, and I'm glad. I hope I was a blessing to you too.

You're so talented. Everything will work out with your career. I'll be cheering for you, Vanilla. I know you'll be on top of the world again.

Love,
Daisy

Robby read the letter several times.

He hated himself. He'd hurt her and yet she was apologizing to him, practically excusing what he did. He didn't deserve her and never would. It wasn't long before the anger inside him boiled into rage. He grabbed the journal and threw it across the room, where it hit the wall with a loud thud.

"I'm such an idiot!" he shouted.

Warren whistled, reminding Robby he was still in the room. "You missed your chance to join up, little brother. The Army lost out," he said as he sat back down.

But Robby barely heard him. When he looked up, Warren was studying him.

"I'm guessing it's not good?" Warren lifted the check from the bed. He whistled again. "Why would you give her this much money?" He raised an eyebrow as if putting it all together. Horrified, he turned to Robby. "You didn't...buy her off, did you?"

Robby rolled his eyes as he tossed the blankets aside and stood, pacing the room. "No. Well, not exactly." He might as well tell Warren everything. A solid fistfight with his brother might help unleash his frustration.

"I found a notebook at Daisy's with a bunch of song lyrics in it. I thought I needed them to save my career. I offered to buy them, but she wasn't going for that. Eventually, the press found me and thought we were dating. So, I...asked Daisy if we could just let them keep thinking that, if you know what I mean...any press is good press."

Warren looked disgusted. "You have to be kidding me."

Robby put his hands up in protest. "Spare me the lecture," he said. "I got my career back, which is exactly what was supposed to happen. She's fine. I'm fine."

Warren grabbed the letter and scanned it. He looked at Robby as he tossed the paper onto the bed. It was clear he wanted to do more.

"She doesn't sound fine to me."

Robby began rooting through his closet until he came up with a T-shirt. He yanked it over his head as he spoke. "You don't know her like I do. She's tough."

Warren leaned back in the chair. "Tell me. Go ahead. Convince me this is what she wanted. You here and her there, miles away."

Robby yanked on a pair of jeans, sure he was going to rip Warren's head off given the chance. How brothers could do this to one another was a mystery to him.

"And what great experience do you have with women?" Robby asked. "I don't see a ring on your finger."

"You'll be at my wedding soon enough. I asked Daphne before I left."

Warren smiled in a way Robby had never before seen, which made him stop dressing, fascinated by this turn in the conversation.

"Since I'm home now for who knows how long we may just do a quick Justice of the Peace thing and then plan a big reception later. Her son needs a man around…"

Robby stared at him. He vaguely remembered something about a girlfriend, but Warren didn't mention it again, so Robby didn't know it was serious. Had Robby even met the woman? And there was a kid? He wondered if he was still asleep.

"Well." Robby cleared his throat. "Congratulations."

Warren smiled broadly. "Thanks." He fussed with his cast for a moment in an effort to get comfortable. "We met when you were in rehab so I didn't say anything. You had your own stuff going on. But she's...well, what I've been waiting for."

Robby met his eyes and nodded, wondering how he managed to have his brother open up to him like this. He wasn't sure the last time they'd spoken this way. If ever.

"She has a kid?" Robby asked, turning to the mirror so Warren couldn't see his face. His brother always put his career before anything else and he put himself in harm's way almost as if he wanted to be hurt or killed. Robby didn't remember him saying he wanted to be married or have a family. Was everyone going mad?

"They married young, he ran off with someone else...the usual story," he said. "Her son's name is Tommy. He's five. Great kid, and for some reason he even likes me."

Robby chuckled. "Give him time..." The look of contentment on Warren's face struck Robby hard in his gut.

Warren laughed but quickly grew serious as he looked at Robby. "I spent a lot of time working on getting ahead, you know? I see you doing the same thing—just like Mom and Dad. We all work so hard and for what? I'm done. It's too lonely. And I don't want to end up like either of them."

Robby sat on the bed, shocked. "What are you going to do?"

"Retire. Come on, Rob, I'm forty-three years old. I don't want to live in a war the rest of my life. I've done my time, no reason I can't move on and do something else. I don't want to get married and have to go back to Iraq or anywhere else and never come home again," he said. "I couldn't do that to them..."

The far-off look on Warren's face told Robby all he needed to know. His brother was in love.

Warren looked up at him. "From what I saw on that paper, Daisy isn't done with you," he said. "You can't tell me you're done with her."

"She's amazing," he said, trying not to smile. He sobered quickly. "But...I would be lying if I didn't say I'm scared."

Warren nodded. "The wheelchair?"

Robby shrugged, ashamed for even thinking it. But he also knew he had to talk to someone so that he might figure out what was going on inside him and if he could get past it.

"We never talked about it—why she was in one. I thought it didn't matter, but I know it does." Robby lay back on the bed and stared at the ceiling for a few moments. "But then I can't stand being without her, you know? It's like I don't even see the wheelchair. All I see is Daisy—her smile, her hair, her stupid lip gloss...besides, sometimes I get to help her. It's like she needs me—even though I know she doesn't." He laughed. "She's tough."

Robby paused, not able to look at his brother as he spoke. "But it's more than that. She gets me. She loves music as much as I do and she...she's nice. I can't explain it. Even when she didn't recognize me when I showed up drunk and beat up, she was an angel—and I could have been anyone. She took me to her house, cleaned me up, got me coffee, held my hair back when I got sick..."

Warren cleared his throat. "She saw you at your worst and still did all that?" He shook his head. "So, when are you going to talk to her?"

Robby looked away. "She doesn't need a jerk like

me to ruin her life. She already went through that...he put her in that wheelchair," he said. "She's been hurt enough. I can't promise I won't do worse."

"You always were a baby." Warren stood as if the conversation were over. "So, I'm going to visit Nick for a few days—see how he's doing. He said some girl is singing at a café...so if you wanted to come along and check it out, you could. Jazz is going."

Robby looked at him, his nerves nearly overtaking him. "Jazz is...? When?"

"Saturday. Call me if you want us to swing by and get you."

Warren left and Robby sat for a long time staring after him. There was a lot to think about and maybe a lot to do before he made any decisions at all.

32

Saturday felt like a promise.

Daisy glanced over her desk and out the window as she tried to work on yet another press release, but she was too distracted. She had just put the final touches on a new song that she intended to sing at Sadie's later that day and she wanted to practice. Sadie advertised the event, but they had no idea if anyone would actually be interested in hearing her perform. She had three or four songs that she'd done before in her set, but she was nervous about the new one. It was personal, and she wasn't sure she was ready to share that much of herself yet.

"Hey, hey, Daisy!" Sadie entered the office carrying a cup of coffee and the mail. Nick was close behind her with a box of doughnuts.

"How's my beautiful girl?" Nick asked with a flirtatious wink. Daisy accepted the coffee and took a sip.

Sadie smiled and tossed the mail onto Daisy's desk.

"Doughnut?" Nick lifted the lid and stole one for himself.

Daisy shook her head, but Sadie took one and Nick set the box down. Daisy took her mail and began sifting through it.

"All ready for tonight?" Sadie asked. "I think we'll get a good crowd. People remember when you used to sing for us…and of course, some are excited by the whole Robby thing."

Daisy raised her eyes. "I hope you were clear that he wouldn't be there."

Sadie shrugged. "It's good for business. I didn't say one way or the other."

Daisy rolled her eyes and went back to her mail. She sighed heavily when she spotted an envelope from her mortgage company. Because she'd been so caught up with Robby, she forgot that she was several months behind on her payments. While she signed a few contracts to work on song writing, she hadn't officially written any lyrics for anyone yet, which meant her bank account remained low. Reluctantly she tore the envelope open.

"Oh my…" she gasped, nearly dropping the paper. Sadie looked at her, cream from her doughnut stuck to her lip.

"What's wrong?" She swiped at her lip, leaving a streak of white in its wake.

Daisy gaped at her. "Did you do this?" she demanded and then looked frantically at Nick. "Did you?"

"Do what?" Sadie asked. Daisy looked at her again, her mouth hanging open.

"This," she said, holding up the statement. "Did you pay off my house?" Even as she said the words, she already knew the answer. Sadie did well for herself, but she didn't have that kind of money. Nick didn't either.

Sadie and Nick exchanged a glance as Daisy crumpled the paper and threw it across the room. "I gave him back that money. Where does he get off inserting himself into my life and paying my bills…?"

She seethed as she moved away from her desk.

"Daisy."

The young woman drew a deep breath before turning to Nick, who continued. "Did you ever think that maybe he did it because he wanted to?" he asked. "He cares about you. We all saw it."

"But…" Daisy wanted him to stop.

Nick held up his hand. She would have to listen whether she wanted to or not. "Just say thank you. For once, I think my nephew may actually be trying to do something good."

Pride rooted deep—Daisy didn't want to listen. Instead of agreeing, she said, "I'll pay him back. Same as I would have the bank."

"For heaven's sake, stop it!" Sadie said. "Listen, I know you don't want to talk about him—OK, fine, but maybe you need to."

Daisy started toward the door, angry that everyone seemed to have turned on her.

Sadie rushed to step in front of her. "Jazz said Robby realized his feelings for you and tried to stop the song, but it was too late. He really wasn't trying to hurt you," she said quickly. "It all happened so fast and he was…scared, confused. I don't know. I wouldn't doubt being sober and figuring out life wasn't easy for him. You could be sympathetic."

Daisy raised her eyes slowly and looked at her friend. Sadie's eyes pleaded for her to understand.

Robby wasn't intentionally mean, that wasn't to be debated. But he was guilty of so many other things, the biggest of which was leading her to believe in the possibility of their love.

"I'll see you guys tonight," Daisy said softly. "Steve said we'll be there by five-thirty so I can warm up."

Sadie nodded but said nothing.

"Daisy," Nick said.

She slowly turned to her rock, her friend, her father. He wouldn't fail her, would he? She met his eyes.

He smiled. "I asked Robby to stay with you because I didn't trust him. But now... He made a mistake, and he even acted like an idiot, but he made it right doing this for you. I think he's just a little behind on maturing. But it seems to me he's working on it, just like you're working on all of your stuff too."

Daisy was shocked. Everyone gave her time to heal but maybe Nick was right. It was time. Thanks to Robby she knew she still had the mettle to live. No one would accept less from her now. It was frightening, but she understood.

Daisy nodded, not sure what to say. "Thanks. I, um, need to do a few things before tonight."

Daisy went into her house. She might focus on the music for a time, but eventually, she'd be forced to deal with the newest situation.

Robby, unfortunately, wasn't going to be a memory yet.

~*~

A few hours later, Daisy entered the café, still trying to push Robby from her mind. She was doing a horrible job of it. It seemed she'd have to accept that he would overshadow everything until she found the strength to call him and put their relationship to an end once and for all. Already she'd spent the day praying and picking up the phone and putting it back down again, courage eluding her.

The finality of such a phone call took her breath away. Better to focus on the intimate concert first. She could call Robby tomorrow.

It had been a long time since Daisy visited the café. The large front window was decorated for summertime with a picnic basket displaying signs for some of the sandwiches one could purchase inside. The counter was the same, but Sadie changed the tables and chairs to make more room for a small piano near the front of the space.

"It's great, huh?" Jennifer entered right after Daisy. She put a comforting hand on her shoulder. "You're going to be amazing."

Daisy quietly went to the front of the café. From behind the counter, Sadie spotted her and raced over.

"Daisy!" she squealed. "I'm so glad you're here! What do you think?"

"Where's the back door?" Daisy joked, trying to ignore the nervous tingle in her stomach.

"Don't even think about it!" Sadie exclaimed.

When Sadie and Nick left earlier that day, Daisy decided it was time for her to try and chase her dreams again. She held back before, when she'd been with Alec, and then once the accident happened she feared everyone's reaction to her limitations. But now that she had accepted everything, and more importantly seen that she could live again, she was ready to go for it.

She would start the small show with a new song about all she'd learned from Robby called "More than I knew." Then, she'd play three more that were familiar, ones she'd written ages ago—before life had gone into a tailspin. And if things went well she might even play a few familiar favorites she sometimes covered from other artists.

"You want to check things out?" Sadie asked, leading her to the piano. "I love your hair."

Daisy self-consciously touched her short hair. She'd put a small sparkly barrette in one side.

Sadie pushed her hand away. "Don't. You'll mess it up. You want to warm up? You have time...I'll get you some coffee. What's your pleasure tonight?"

"I'll need an espresso to get through this... A double..." Daisy said, fighting the nerves that threatened to overtake her.

Sadie hugged her. "If you're half as good as you were at the wedding you don't need to worry," she said with a smile. "I'll be right back."

Sadie ducked behind the counter and Jennifer, Nick, and Steve took a table near the middle of the café. Nick smiled at her and started talking to Steve. Daisy sighed as she placed her hands lightly on the smooth piano keys, relishing their familiar feel. Playing had always brought comfort—when her mother left her, when her father died, when she was useless from the accident—the piano had been her solace.

God had been so good to her.

"Here you go," Sadie said as she set a steaming cup of espresso in front of Daisy as she played.

"When should I start?" she asked.

Sadie glanced at the clock and shrugged. "I'll introduce you in about ten minutes," she said.

As Daisy watched people filter into the café and place their orders, she began to feel more at peace than she had in some time. She'd wasted so much time on Alec, but she swore she wasn't going to make the same mistake with Robby. Was her pride worth the pain and loneliness she would endure without him? Saying "thank you" wasn't a big deal. But why would he still want to take care of her? When he left, they'd both been so angry—there had been no possibility they would even speak to one another again. What had happened to him that he would change his mind?

Daisy stopped playing abruptly in the midst of a light tune. Sadie looked at her and a few customers did too, so she smiled shyly and started playing again, picking up where she left off as if nothing had happened. Suddenly playing in front of the small crowd in the café paled in comparison to the difficult conversation she was going to have with Robby. She prayed he would understand and forgive her. She was ready to forgive him.

Sadie got the microphone and set it up. "OK, everyone!" she shouted. The café quickly quieted and the crowd turned its attention to her. "Welcome! Thanks for coming out with us tonight! My dear friend, Daisy Parker, comes to us all the way from…" she laughed and everyone followed suit. "OK, so this is her home…but if you haven't heard her sing before you're in for a real treat. Take it away, Daisy…"

Daisy drew a deep breath. While it wasn't a huge crowd, there were certainly more people than Daisy expected. She cleared her throat and spoke into the microphone, focusing on the table filled with her friends. "Thank you for coming tonight. This is a new song called 'More than I knew'. I, um, wrote it when some things happened in my life that I didn't expect, but they made me a better person. I…um, hope you like it."

Speaking into the microphone was much harder than singing into it. Daisy drew a deep breath and closed her eyes, which made it easier to focus on the emotional side of the song she'd written for Robby, imagining he was standing before her.

As she sang, there was little left in her to hold back the warring flood of emotions. The song was her release. All she wanted to say to Robby came through her words and in the lovely sound of the piano. The peace that had eluded her was finally found.

33

Robby slowly followed Warren and Jazz into the cafe. Sadie smiled broadly when she spotted them, winking at Jazz who winked back in return, his smile bigger than hers. Nick glanced at them and nodded for them to join his table. Robby stood unsurely at the door, his hands stuffed in his pockets as if he'd made a mistake.

But then Daisy sang and he was rooted to the spot. Her voice was stronger than he remembered. She'd changed. The timid woman who lacked confidence was now ferocious, attacking notes that were higher than he'd ever thought she could go. Robby was dumbstruck.

She's amazing...

Jazz grabbed Robby's arm, yanked him over to the table, and nudged him into a seat. Robby didn't pay attention to the people in the café staring at him, some reaching for cell phones and cameras so they could get a picture. Most were discreet, but a few showed signs of making a scene until Jazz got their attention and merely shook his head.

Daisy was too invested in her performance to notice. Robby watched in fascination as she sang, the emotion in her soul spilling out for all to see and hear. This was *his* song. He swallowed the lump in his throat.

"She's better than you. Watch your job, moron," Warren whispered.

Robby hit his good arm and Warren grinned, flexing his huge muscles. Robby rolled his eyes and focused back on Daisy.

"Even if we stood through the time so tested, it was easy to see you'd never be mine and I...I never would have taken you there. Some things stop and some things wait but some things just come around too late..." she sang.

Robby cleared his throat as Sadie set a cup of steaming black coffee in front of him. He nodded gratefully and took a sip. He wasn't sure what Daisy would do when she noticed him. He spent the whole trip from New York talking about her until Warren and Jazz finally begged him to stop. It was clear that since they separated he was lost, but did that mean he loved her? Looking at her now, as she sang and played the piano, Robby knew the answer.

Everyone clapped and cheered as Daisy smiled at them, glancing at her friends and at the same moment spotting Robby. They stared at one another and the crowd fell deafeningly quiet.

Warren leaned toward him. "Go talk to her, bro," he whispered.

Robby heard him but he was glued to his seat. He really was in love with Daisy. He'd never been in love before, hadn't known what it felt like. He thought he was going to be sick. Or scream.

Both?

"Robby..." Nick whispered.

Finally, Jazz stood and used one big hand to lift Robby to his feet, pushing him toward the front of the café. Daisy waited, her hands still poised over the piano keys as if she'd stopped playing mid-song. Robby found his footing and made it through the crowd to stand in front of her. Together they looked like a couple of thirteen-year-olds who were too shy to speak to one another at the school dance.

Robby shuffled his feet. "Hey, Harpo..." he whispered.

She stared at him, her large blue eyes wide. If this was going to happen in front of a crowd, so be it, but Robby was confident in what he needed to say and do. He walked around the piano and leaned over Daisy, his hands on either side of her.

"I understand if you never want to talk to me again." He paused to gulp. "But I need to know that you heard me say I'm sorry. I owe you that. I stole the song—it might have been one of the worst things I've ever done. I'm so sorry. I was wrong." Robby shifted his weight as he searched for words. "I don't know if it matters, but I realized too late that I had feelings for you and I...guess I just thought what I did didn't matter—that we'd work it out." He sighed. "But it mattered to you and that should have been enough...I really am sorry for putting myself ahead of everything else—and especially you. You didn't deserve that."

Daisy pulled her gaze away from him, staring at her hands as she spoke. "Fine. I forgive you...and I'll pay you back. You shouldn't have done that," she practically whispered.

Robby remained close, aware that the café was silent as everyone tried to hear what they were saying. "You'll get more. *Waiting* went number one."

Daisy started to push away from him but her hand brushed his arm as she did. She hesitated, her gaze fixed on the new tattoo on his forearm. It was a pile of daisies woven together to form her name. Robby smiled and held it out for her inspection. The piece was not only intricate but impossible to miss. He'd done it as a statement and a testimony. Regardless of what Daisy felt for him, he would never be the same for having met her.

Sadie started the café music and motioned for Robby to take Daisy away from the curious crowd. He nodded.

"I'm sorry too," Daisy said. "But you didn't have to come."

Robby stopped her from moving by taking her arm. "Yes, I did. Um, can we go outside? Please?"

He started for the door, but Sadie shook her head and motioned him through the kitchen door instead. He turned to make sure Daisy was behind him. She followed, her face an unreadable mask.

Once in the kitchen, he turned and watched her enter. She looked amazing. He couldn't help but smile, even if she didn't seem as excited to see him. He watched her nervously take out her lip gloss and methodically apply it to her lips.

Finally, he knelt in front of her and slowly took the lip gloss from her hand and set it aside. "You and that lip gloss," he muttered with a smile. "I missed it so much."

"You shouldn't be here," she whispered. Robby took her hands in his and kissed them both open-palm, as he'd done so many times before. When he lifted his eyes, he found Daisy was crying quietly, tears spilling down her cheeks.

Love swelled inside Robby's heart—her beauty took his breath away so he could hardly speak. "I was so wrapped up in my own problems it didn't occur to me you had your own. I'm so sorry I didn't ask...didn't try harder to get close to you." He reached up and slowly wiped her cheeks with his thumb. "I meant what I said, God sent me to you—but it was for both of us, Daisy. You showed me there's more to me than what everyone sees—there's a person deep inside who deserves to be loved for who he is, not for all the superficial stuff."

Daisy closed her eyes and he continued. "I've never been in love before...but I think it's safe to say I'm in love with you...so much I can't think straight. Or sleep."

Robby touched her hair, pushing it from her face. Her eyes were still closed, but she sighed dreamily when he touched her. "I know getting a tattoo doesn't fix things. But...I think I know love now...thanks to you. And no matter what happens between us today, I will always have this to remind me of what we had together, even if it was only for a few days."

Daisy opened her eyes and met Robby's. She reached up slowly and pressed her hand against his cheek. It was Robby's turn to close his eyes. He leaned into her soft, warm skin.

"You really do love me?" she whispered.

Robby smiled and released a deep breath. He gazed into her eyes. "I do. I love you so much it hurts—like my chest is going to explode right now." Robby laughed as he said the words. "I'm sorry. It's silly and powerful at the same time."

Daisy nodded as she started crying again. She kissed his cheek. "I love you too, Vanilla. But..." She drew a deep breath. "I'm sorry too. I should have trusted you enough to tell you about Alec. I was so scared. He said he loved me too—and I believed him. I made so many excuses...I was afraid I was going to do the same things with you. You aren't anything like him. That wasn't fair."

Robby shook his head and pressed his finger to her lips. "I understand. And it's all right. I didn't give you any reason to trust me…and then I made it worse…" He met her eyes. "We're messed up, aren't we?"

Daisy nodded as he leaned over to lift her into his arms. He sat on the counter, holding her close. For a long moment he gazed at her, searching her face despite knowing he didn't need to memorize it—he'd have her for a long time. Maybe forever.

And then he kissed her. The door to the kitchen swung open, but Robby didn't care if he had an audience this time.

Sadie, Jennifer, Nick, Steve, Jazz and Warren noisily filled the remaining space, yet Robby continued kissing his love.

"For crying out loud, moron, it took you long enough. I was about ready to kiss her myself," Warren muttered.

Robby waved him off as Daisy pulled away with a smile.

"We have an audience," she whispered.

Robby held her close. "Get used to it. And I don't care." He kissed her again.

Daisy pushed against his chest. "Robby…" she said. "I only sang one song…the people wanted more than that…"

Robby groaned. "Right. Want to sing a duet?"

Daisy smiled. "I thought you'd never ask."

34

An hour later Daisy and Robby finished singing their last song. The night had gone better than she could have imagined. Still shocked that Robby came for her, she couldn't wait to be alone with him. There was a lot they needed to talk about.

As the song ended, a small woman in a suit entered the café. With the excitement of Robby Grant's presence, no one noticed until she screamed, "Robert River Grant!" The crowd quieted and turned toward the door where Lily stood, her hands on her hips.

"Oh, boy…" Robby muttered, ducking behind Daisy, who laughed and took his hand in hers.

Lily approached and the crowd resumed talking and eating. "You can't run off like that and not answer your phone!" she exclaimed. "I was worried sick. I didn't have any idea where you were." She visibly softened. "But when Jazz told me, well, I just had to come and see for myself." Lily appeared to choke up.

Robby exchanged a glance with Daisy. "You all right, Lil?" he asked, one eyebrow lifted in amusement.

"I'm fine," she barked at him. "It's like you're finally growing up and…" She cleared her throat. The drill sergeant was back. "So, when are you two going to get it together and go on the road? That song was fantastic—you sounded great!"

Again, Robby looked down at Daisy and she smiled. His eyes sparkled in amusement, but he said nothing.

Finally, Daisy couldn't stand it anymore, "Aren't you going to answer her?"

Robby shrugged, stuffing his hands into his pockets. "I can't speak for you," he said. "So, aren't *you* going to answer her?"

Daisy's mouth went dry as Robby grinned mischievously but tried to look innocent at the same time. Daisy pinched his arm.

"Ow!" he squealed.

"I guess we'll have to talk about it," Daisy said.

"Fair enough," Lily said. "And Daisy, we'll need talk about some other things too. I'd be interested in representing you—officially. Now that he finally has it together I can actually take on another client."

Daisy nodded, not sure what to say. It was like a dream even though she was awake.

"Look out, Harpo. She's seeing dollar signs," Robby warned.

Lily rolled her eyes and smiled. "All right then. I'm going to get some coffee."

The café bustled with people, but Robby didn't seem to notice as he sat near Daisy. He took her hands in his and leaned toward her. "Let's get out of here," he said softly, brushing her hair from her cheek.

Her body tingled at his nearness and she couldn't help the tears that spilled down her cheeks.

"I'm sorry," she whispered, swiping at them angrily. "I just can't believe you're here."

Robby appeared to search her face and then he nodded. "I can't believe it took me so long to come to my senses." He leaned forward and kissed her. "I'm not going anywhere, anymore, without you."

She looked up into his deep green eyes and didn't even have to ask if he meant it. She knew he did.

ACKNOWLEDGEMENTS

Jim Hart, thank you for believing in me when I was starting to doubt myself. I wouldn't be published without you.

Susan Baganz your insight in editing made this story stronger when I thought it was already strong enough. Thank you for your help and wisdom.

My dear former student, Sierra Shipton, you've taught me more than you realize. Thank you for helping me with Daisy so she could be real. You are a woman of faith, courage, and intelligence who graciously answered my questions about your experiences. I am in your debt.

Bill Boggs—my mentor and friend. Thank you for your willingness to always answer my questions and encouraging me when I needed it. I am exponentially blessed by your friendship.

BIOGRAPHY

Kimberly Miller enjoys the seasonal weather in Pennsylvania with her husband, two daughters, and one ornery cat. She teaches writing and film courses, and in her spare time loves reading, watching movies, making jewelry, drinking coffee and eating one of God's amazing gifts—chocolate and peanut butter.

Thank you

We appreciate you reading this Prism title. For other Christian fiction and clean-and-wholesome stories, please visit our on-line bookstore at www.prismbookgroup.com.

For questions or more information, contact us at customer@pelicanbookgroup.com.

Prism is an imprint of
Pelican Book Group
www.PelicanBookGroup.com

Connect with Us
www.facebook.com/Pelicanbookgroup
www.twitter.com/pelicanbookgrp

To receive news and specials, subscribe to our bulletin
http://pelink.us/bulletin

May God's glory shine through
this inspirational work of fiction.

AMDG

You Can Help!

At Pelican Book Group it is our mission to entertain readers with fiction that uplifts the Gospel. It is our privilege to spend time with you awhile as you read our stories.

We believe you can help us to bring Christ into the lives of people across the globe. And you don't have to open your wallet or even leave your house!

Here are 3 simple things you can do to help us bring illuminating fiction™ to people everywhere.

1) If you enjoyed this book, write a positive review. Post it at online retailers and websites where readers gather. And share your review with us at reviews@pelicanbookgroup.com (this does give us permission to reprint your review in whole or in part.)

2) If you enjoyed this book, recommend it to a friend in person, at a book club or on social media.

3) If you have suggestions on how we can improve or expand our selection, let us know. We value your opinion. Use the contact form on our web site or e-mail us at customer@pelicanbookgroup.com

God Can Help!

Are you in need? The Almighty can do great things for you. Holy is His Name! He has mercy in every generation. He can lift up the lowly and accomplish all things. Reach out today.

Do not fear: I am with you; do not be anxious: I am your God. I will strengthen you, I will help you, I will uphold you with my victorious right hand.

~Isaiah 41:10 (NAB)

We pray daily, and we especially pray for everyone connected to Pelican Book Group—that includes you! If you have a specific need, we welcome the opportunity to pray for you. Share your needs or praise reports at http://pelink.us/pray4us

Free Book Offer

We're looking for booklovers like you to partner with us! Join our team of influencers today and periodically receive free eBooks.

For more information
Visit http://pelicanbookgroup.com/booklovers